THE PLANET STORIES LIBRARY

STRANGE ADVENTURES ON OTHER WORLDS
AVAILABLE EXCLUSIVELY FROM PLANET STORIES!

FOR AUTHOR BIOS AND SYNOPSES,
VISIT PAIZO.COM/PLANETSTORIES

Publisher's Cataloging-In-Publication Data
(Prepared by The Donohue Group, Inc.)

Moorcock, Michael, 1939-
  Sojan the swordsman / by Michael Moorcock ; cover illustration by
Kieran Yanner ; interior illustrations by James Cawthorn & Claudio
Casini ; introduction by Erik Mona. Under the warrior star / by Joe R.
Lansdale.

  p. : ill. ; cm. -- (Planet stories ; #29)

Planet stories double feature
Sojan the swordsman originally published in 1956.
November 2010.
ISBN: 978-1-60125-288-3

  1. Adventure and adventurers--Fiction. 2. Battles--Fiction. 3.
Monsters--
Fiction. 4. Fantasy fiction. 5. Science fiction. I. Yanner, Kieran.
II. Cawthorn, James. III. Casini, Claudio, 1977- IV. Mona, Erik. V.
Lansdale,
Joe R., 1951- Under the warrior star. VI. Title. VII. Title: Planet stories
double feature

PN6120.S33 M66 2010
808.83

Double Feature

SOJAN THE SWORDSMAN & UNDER THE WARRIOR STAR

BY MICHAEL MOORCOCK & JOE R. LANSDALE

COVER ILLUSTRATION BY KIERAN YANNER ◆ INTERIOR ILLUSTRATIONS BY JAMES CAWTHORN & CLAUDIO CASINI

PLANET STORIES is published bimonthly by Paizo Publishing, LLC with offices at 7120 185th Ave NE, Ste 120, Redmond, Washington, 98052. Erik Mona, Publisher. Pierce Watters, Senior Editor. Christopher Paul Carey and James L. Sutter, Editors. *Sojan the Swordsman* © 1956, 1957 by Michael Moorcock. New version of *Sojan the Swordsman* © 2010 by Michael and Linda Moorcock. Interior illustrations for *Sojan the Swordsman* © 1956, 1957, 1977 by The Estate of James Cawthorn. *Under the Warrior Star* © 2010 by Joe R. Lansdale. Introduction © 2010 by Erik Mona. Planet Stories and the Planet Stories planet logo are registered trademarks of Paizo Publishing, LLC. Planet Stories #29, *Sojan the Swordsman & Under the Warrior Star*, by Michael Moorcock and Joe R. Lansdale. November 2010. PRINTED IN THE UNITED STATES OF AMERICA.

Double Feature: Notes from the Projector Room

by Erik Mona

Four years ago, when I began sketching out the broad overview of the project that would become Planet Stories, the idea of the book you hold in your hands would have been preposterous. For starters, our shoestring budget dictated a focus on affordable reprints rather than new material. Fantasizing about one day releasing original science fiction and fantasy adventures from modern grand masters to stand alongside our reprinted classics by giants of the past seemed like an extravagant dream—something that might happen one day, if we worked hard and were extremely lucky, but in the end highly unlikely. And yet here we are with a brand new Planet Stories book featuring exactly that unlikely development, and it turns out our grand masters have been with us since the very start.

Back in 2007, Joe R. Lansdale wrote the introduction to our edition of Robert E. Howard's *Almuric*, a tale that transports a barbaric character very much like Conan the Cimmerian to a brutal planet filled with ugly monsters and beautiful princesses. "A few pages in and I was as hooked as bass on a handmade fly, right through the gills," he wrote. I hoped that meant Joe would be interested in writing his own take on a sword and planet adventure in the tradition of Edgar Rice Burroughs's John Carter of Mars. After all, his *Almuric* introduction claimed that it had been Burroughs's planetary adventures that shifted him from wanting to be a writer to *needing* to be a writer.

"When I was a kid I read Edgar Rice Burroughs for the first time, and his stories blew the top of my head off and sent it into orbit." One imagines Joe's reading chair, spattered with blood from all of the times sword and planet has exploded his brain, slashed through his gills, or done him grievous harm while leaving an excited smile on his face. I thought he'd be a shoo-in for a new original story, so I asked if he'd be interested in writing one for us. "Erik," he said kindly, "you can't afford me." And that was that.

Michael Moorcock was also one of our most enthusiastic early readers, and his introduction to Leigh Brackett's planetary adventure *The Secret of Sinharat* was an early coup for our fledgling pulp reprint line. Like Lansdale, Moorcock's discovery of Burroughs at a young age forever changed him. "For half my youth I yearned to be riding some strange, complaining reptilian steed across the dead sea bottoms of Mars, while for the other half I longed to be wearing a trench coat and a snap-brim fedora, walking the rain-sodden streets of the big city."

Leigh Brackett's noir-influenced style merged these influences perfectly for Mike. "If my very earliest teenage stories were influenced by Burroughs, there was no doubt that my first published adult fantasy stories were influenced by Brackett." Mike agreed to let us publish three of those early adult fantasies in the form of his Kane of Old Mars trilogy (*City of the Beast*, *Lord of the Spiders*, and *Masters of the Pit*), but I was even more intrigued by those "earliest teen-age stories" about Sojan the Swordsman, written as extended serials in the *Tarzan Adventures* magazine he edited early in his career. They'd appeared once in a rare British collection, but never in the United States. It seemed the perfect opportunity for a new Planet Stories edition. "Those stories were an act of nostalgia, not taste!" Mike wrote back rapidly. "Believe me, you don't want them!" And that, once again, was that.

What was it about the sword and planet works of Edgar Rice Burroughs that so intrigued not only Joe Lansdale and Mike Moorcock, but also Robert E. Howard, Leigh Brackett, Edmond Hamilton, Manly Wade Wellman, and nearly every other professional science fiction writer born in the last century? Why did so many of these writers not only cite the John Carter stories as influencing them to become writers themselves, but also to follow along in the tradition of John Carter with their own adventures of Earthmen transported to savage planets?

Nearly 100 years ago, Edgar Rice Burroughs published *Under the Moons of Mars*, a multi-part serial in the pulp pages of *All-Story Weekly*. The tale concerned the adventures of a Confederate Civil War veteran named John Carter who mysteriously found himself transported to a Red Planet peopled by decadent societies of honor-bound swordsmen, roving tribes of bestial noble savages, armadas of airships and a veritable parade (as the series continued) of incomparable princesses in constant need of rescue from the machinations of nefarious evil-doers. *Under the Moons of Mars* quickly graduated to books, where it gained a new title, *A Princess of Mars*, and swiftly became one of the most important and influential science fiction books in the history of the genre.

With little concrete science to speak of and swordplay and barbarism running as major themes in almost every chapter, *A Princess of Mars* and its sequels were precursors of the sword and sorcery movement that would emerge from the pulp work of writers like C. L. Moore, Clark Ashton Smith, and Robert E.

Howard. Howard's *Almuric*, viewed through a characteristically brutal lens, is the crossroads where sword and planet meets its younger, more fantastical cousin. Like almost all the authors who came to the tradition, Howard brought his own vision and unique elements to the sword and planet tale, but the fingerprints of Edgar Rice Burroughs are everywhere.

By the time Howard got to the trough it had been fairly well picked over by other writers, folks like Ralph Milne Farley, Ray Cummings, and Otis Adelbert Kline. These authors used many of Burroughs's conceits to chart adventures of their own (usually on other planets such as Venus and Mercury) featuring swordplay and revolution on distant worlds. But, really, it all comes back to the pattern established in the outset of *A Princess of Mars*.

Roughly stated, the pattern is this:

1) Hero with sword-fighting skill is mysteriously transported from Earth to a savage planet.

2) Hero is surprised at his ability to leap great distances and his relative strength thanks to the lower gravity of his new planet.

3) Hero encounters a dangerous monster.

4) Hero encounters a seemingly evil outsider culture, but then becomes adopted by that culture for his prowess at arms.

5) Hero meets incomparably beautiful Princess. He falls instantly in love.

6) Princess gets kidnapped.

7) Hero rescues Princess.

8) On the eve of Hero and Princess' wedding, the Hero is mysteriously whisked back to Earth, where he shakes his fist at the sky and swears to get back to the savage planet.

9) The end.

In the pulp era, the best-regarded sword and planet author other than Burroughs was Otis Adelbert Kline, a member of the editorial staff of *Weird Tales* and a frequent contributor to *Argosy*, *Amazing Stories*, *Thrilling Wonder Stories*, and similar magazines. His pioneering trilogy of Earthman Robert Grandon's adventures on Venus actually beat Burroughs himself to the Green Planet, and paperback reissues brought his tales to the readers of the 1960s (albeit in badly edited, highly abridged versions). We targeted Kline as one of the key authors for our Planet Stories line, and in 2008 we released Kline's two Mars adventures, *The Swordsman of Mars* and *The Outlaws of Mars*, in handsome trade paperback editions. As with all Planet Stories editions (except for this one), we wanted to get famous writers from today to comment on and contextualize the classic stories in new introductions.

Undaunted and still eager to publish some new sword and planet in the 21st century, we turned once again to our grand masters, Joe Lansdale and Michael Moorcock. Mike's introduction to *Swordsman* contained an alluring reference to those old Sojan stories ("none of them, I must say, as good as Kline's"), as well as additional admiration for Edgar Rice Burroughs and the escapist nature of the sword and planet tradition. Joe Lansdale concentrated on the visual appeal of the worlds painted by the planetary adventure authors. "There is plenty of color and beauty and a sweeping approach to story that reminds me of the cinema," he said. "In fact, with the popularity of such films as *Star Wars* and Indiana Jones, I would have thought by now, considering special effects have improved to the point of being almost as incredible as our most astounding dreams, that Burroughs and possibly Kline's characters would have been updated and filmed. Certainly, it's this color and sweep and majesty of background that makes these stories so damned appealing: they are like movies in the head."

And soon, they will be very much like movies in the movie theater. As I write this introduction, Disney's Pixar studios is hard at work on a big-budget version of *A Princess of Mars*, set for release some time around the 100th anniversary of the tale's original publication back in *All-Story*. Over the last four years, our own Planet Stories has reprinted many of the seminal tales in the sword and planet tradition, from Leigh Brackett's adventures of the swordsman Eric John Stark to Otis Adelbert Kline's tales of romance and danger on Mars. Sword and planet reprints are chugging along, and the genre seems more energized now than it has in decades.

But still, you can't have a renaissance without something new, and after all these reprints we still never got our original sword and planet Planet Stories adventure. Until now. After plying these guys with ratty paperback and pulp copies of some of their favorite sword and planet tales from their youth, they've both come around. Mike agreed to let us present all the Sojan stories (slightly updated and corrected here and there) for the first time in an American edition, and Joe finally decided that we could afford him after all. This Planet Stories Double Feature is a two-fisted punch of pulp planetary adventure by two grand masters, one experimenting with the Burroughs tradition in some of his earliest fiction exploits and one drawing his blade anew at the height of his writing career. I trust you will enjoy the tales of Sojan the Swordsman and Braxton Booker. Sword and planet may be nearing its century mark in these early days of the new millennium, but as long as writers look to the stars and think "I'd love to write a story like that!" the skies will always be full of adventure.

So let's all go to the lobby and pick up our favorite refreshments. At long last, the Double Feature is about to begin!

Erik Mona
Publisher
August 2010

ERIK MONA *is the publisher of Paizo Publishing, LLC, creators of the Pathfinder Roleplaying Game and the Planet Stories line of pulp fantasy novels. Mona has won more than a dozen major game industry awards and his writing has been published by Paizo, Wizards of the Coast, Green Ronin Publishing, and The MIT Press.*

Sojan the Swordsman

Michael Moorcock

With special thanks to Graeme Talboys for his incredible feat, worthy of Sojan himself, in restoring this text to electronic form; and also for John Davey, as always an outstanding editor and astonishing friend, who resurrected the texts from their original appearances together with Jim Cawthorn's illustrations.

Parts of this book originally appeared in Burroughsania *(1954),* Tarzan Adventures *1957–8, Savoy Books 1976, publishers Britton and Butterworth, who were the first to discover the stories, reprint a version of them and commission fresh illustrations from Jim Cawthorn. This is the first time the Introduction has been published.*

AUTHOR'S NOTE:

Sojan the Swordsman was the first fantasy character I created, around 1954 or '55 when I was fourteen or fifteen. He appeared in the first issue of my Edgar Rice Burroughs fanzine *Burroughsania*, which I sold at school for a penny. Later, when I was asked by the editor of the juvenile story paper *Tarzan Adventures* for something in the manner of Edgar Rice Burroughs's fantasy stories, I remembered Sojan. These are the stories as originally conceived, warts and all, roughly as they appeared as serials in the magazine from 1957. They would all be published by my good friend Jim Cawthorn, who would work with me all my writing life until he died in November 2008. Jim's illustrations are taken both from the magazine and the reprinted but unrestored stories commissioned by Savoy Books in 1977. This book is dedicated to Jim Cawthorn, who remained a mentor and an inspiration.

Michael Moorcock

ZYLOR

The World Of
SOJAN SHIELDBEARER

J. CAWTHORN &
R. LUMLEY

Introduction

There is a story told across the many inhabited worlds of the universe about the fate of brave men and women where the pursuit of money and power is prized less than the pursuit of honour and self-respect.

They die noble deaths and are destined to be reborn over and over again on distant planets, often taking the place of another heroic person who has died in action . . . This is a form of reincarnation, the universe's way of ensuring that some kind of balance is struck between those who are motivated by greed and those who work for the general good.

One such fighter was Sir John de Courcy, of an ancient line going back to the days of the Conquest on his father's side and to a race of Irish warrior-statesmen on the other. The de Courcy family had served their country as soldiers since before Agincourt. They had given their blood, lives and treasure in selfless defence of all that was best in British history. Until the First World War they had commanded cavalry but now served in tank regiments. The current holder of the family title had commanded light, fast-moving vehicles in the North African desert against the cunning of Rommel, the infamous Desert Fox and later served with Montgomery in the European campaigns which had gradually pushed the Nazis back to Berlin. Now, once again side by side with his American allies, he was fighting in Korea against an enemy quite as single-minded as Hitler's forces and quite as ready to crush individuals in the name of a "greater cause," though this time they did not call themselves National Socialists but Communists.

The conflict had been going on interminably for many months, with the North Koreans and their Chinese allies neither giving nor expecting quarter, just as the Anglo-American forces remained implacably determined to win. On more than one occasion Sir John had been able to strike deep into the enemy's territory and return with his entire squadron intact but, as the war continued and the fighting grew fiercer and fiercer, things grew increasingly desperate.

The conflict had taken de Courcy and his squadron into a part of the battlefield seeded with land mines, an area of narrow gullies and low mountains, full of ruined buildings, torn up barbed wire, filthy mud and burned-out war machines. It had come on to rain and the mud had become so deep it was increasingly difficult to steer the Centurion tanks. Fearing for the safety of his crews and their machines, Sir John had decided that it was time to return to home base and broke radio silence to give a coded message to that effect. The driving rain had increased. What was worse, the mines were everywhere and his charts did not allow him to pinpoint their likely positions.

The narrow canyon in which they found themselves was a natural trap. In spite of all intelligence reports, including those from the air, Sir John's tanks found themselves under attack from a large number of enemy war machines and infantry armed with anti-tank weapons.

Bombed from the air and bombarded from the ground the British tanks fought valiantly to extricate themselves from their position. Eventually, however, they ran out of ammunition and were reduced to just three Centurions as night came down. Sir John ordered his remaining vehicles to leave the field and return to base but they had lost radio contact with their headquarters and for the most part with each other and the last message he received from the nearest tank was that it was on fire and that the crew was having to abandon their machine. He ordered his own tank to go to the aid of the crew, his searchlights moving back and forth over the vast, desolate plain as they cautiously sought the stranded soldiers without wanting to pick them out for the enemy.

At last Sir John caught sight of the guttering wreckage of the tank and nearby a few men sheltering in a shallow foxhole, their uniforms badly singed and one of them, the driver, evidently wounded. He ordered all lights and radio to be extinguished and, while the enemy sought them out, left the relative security of his Centurion to try to help the stranded crew to safety. Reaching their foxhole, he ordered them to board his own tank, helping the wounded man through the mud and filth of the battlefield. He had almost reached his vehicle when a squadron of MiG jets flew low overhead and from ground level enemy searchlights flooded the field with light, making him and the wounded man an easy target.

"Come on, man," murmured Sir John to the driver, "not much further to go!"

"I'm sorry, sir," the driver gritted, "but I'm all in! Nothing left, sir. Better go on without me, sir. I'll just have to let the blighters capture me."

"Nonsense, man!" No de Courcy had ever abandoned one of his men and Sir John was determined to get the driver back to his own tank which had already turned, with its companion, and was waiting to pick them up. The problem was that his tank was overcrowded and moving very slowly through the rain-swept darkness. He and the soldier he had rescued were forced to climb onto the turret and hope for the best as they rumbled very slowly back towards base.

Suddenly the ground became a thousand columns of spurting mud as the MiGs opened fire with rockets and machine guns. By some miracle nothing hit them and it seemed they would soon reach the relative safety of a low overhang, half-a-mile from where they were likely to pick up some covering fire from nearby American allies.

Then, suddenly, just as they seemed to reach relative safety, Sir John's tank hit a mine which sent it swerving to one side, rocking and lurching, knocking him clear of the turret, its wheels screaming as it reared into the muddy air, covering him with filth. He made a grab for the tank's gun and missed it, and then he was rolling down towards the ground as a searchlight beam caught him in its glare, picking him out so that a low-flying MiG could get him in its sights and aim a stream of tracers at him. His body was on fire. He gritted his teeth against the pain and he was suddenly blind.

Then the waves of agony faded slowly. He had the impression of sailing upwards, away from the battlefield, away from the filth and the horror, up, up into the dark velvet of the sky, through the white blaze of stars which merged one by one into a mingling of a thousand colours and he was sinking down again to a brilliant softness which embraced him like the body of a lover . . .

Even as these sensations took him to themselves his mind became vague until he had almost forgotten his own name and had ceased to wonder at the strangeness of the smells and sights around him. What was his name? Sir John? Sar Jan? No! Now he remembered—it was So-jan. Sojan. The pain was fading. He wished he could remember where he had been. What was the nature of the conflict? Where was he now? Where were his men? What had he been doing? He screwed his eyes against the light which no longer flashed, no longer hurt him. He clambered slowly to his feet, wiping sweat from his face with his free hand. In his other hand there was an object both familiar and unfamiliar. He recognized it at last.

A long, slender piece of slightly curved metal with a complicated guard around his hand.

It was a sword

A sword such as his ancestors had borne into battle for over a thousand years! A saber? No, a *vilthor*.

With a shrug, Sojan sheathed his sword and caught hold of the trailing rein of his mount which, happily, the men who had attacked him had not harmed. He was safe and so was his riding *myat*. It came back to him now. He was heading for a city to offer his services to its warlord. He had been attacked by a group of thieves who had given a reasonable account of themselves before he had killed them. Now he drew the beast to him and swung up into the saddle . . .

Chapter One

Sojan the Swordsman

A myat trotted peacefully across the broad, seemingly never-ending plain which made up the landscape as far as it was possible to see. No sound issued from the cloven hoofs, muffled by the moss-like substance which clothed the ground in a mantle of vivid colour—purple, green and yellow, with a trace of crimson or violet here and there. Nothing else grew upon that plain. It was a wilderness, barren and empty—the greatest desert on the planet of Zylor.

A wandering warrior sat aside the myat's broad back. At his steed's side hung a shield, a virtually unknown accoutrement on Zylor, but the clan to which the rider belonged had perfected it as a valuable asset. The man's name was Sojan and the beast upon which he rode was a big, sturdy animal. From both sides of its huge, tapering head grew long, sharp horns, curving outward. More like a reptile than a mammal, the myat's head resembled a snake's. Its tail was thick and it, too, tapered.

Sojan was dressed in a bright blue jerkin reaching to his knees. His legs were bare. Tough boots of myat hide were upon his feet, reaching to about two inches from his knees. Over the jerkin was a leather harness of simple design. Two straps crossed his shoulders, coming to his waist. Attached to a broad belt were his weapons—a sword, a long, sharp dirk, and a holster containing his big, round-butted air-pistol. As he rode he recharged the pistol and fitted the ammunition into its chamber. The myat needed no guidance and its reins hung on its neck as Sojan saw to his weapon.

The mercenary's hair was long and held by a fillet of leather. At the back of his large saddle were two substantial bags, secured by straps and thongs. A long, leather container of water followed the outlines of his saddle and behind this a thick, crimson cloak. All his worldly goods were carried with him. At the left-hand side of his saddle was an intricately decorated shield which had seen much use.

Sojan himself was tall, broad-shouldered and slim-waisted, with smooth muscles rippling beneath his jerkin. He was the perfect fighting man, keen eyed and wary. From his youth he had been trained in the arts of war. His father, a War Prince of Katt in the far West, had raised Sojan, his brothers and his sisters, in all the arts valued on Zylor as well as the art of the shield, which the people of Katt were almost alone in using.

But when famine came to Katt and the fields refused to bear food and the rain refused to fall, the War Prince sent his children abroad to fend for themselves, for he knew Katt was doomed, all her wealth gone on buying grain to feed the people. Some of these children became teachers of writing, reading and mathematics, but most earned their living by their swords and other weapons.

Sojan had fought under the banners of many War Kings but only leaders who brought with them justice and law. Those were the qualities he had been taught were worth fighting for. He had become a hero in the West and been offered great rank and treasure, all of which he refused, preferring the simple life of the mercenary. Now he crossed the Great Zylorian Desert with one purpose in mind.

"And," he thought to himself, "no petty ruffians will distract me from my determination."

Behind him in the distance now lay the bodies of the thieves, their swords and valuables remaining with them, for no mercenary of Sojan's kind deigned to take wealth from the dead. Soon he had all but forgotten the fight as he rode on, thinking what lay ahead under the blue-green sky of the planet.

Chapter Two
The War King

Two days later Sojan caught a glimpse of something on the horizon, just as Zylor's second sun was rising. The mercenary shielded his eyes, but decided he had witnessed some kind of minor hallucination.

Then, suddenly, Sojan again saw a distant shape glittering and pale red in the distance and knew at once what it was. He had ridden for many weeks to find the marble walls of Vermlot, the capital city of the mighty warrior nation of Hatnor, the greatest of all Zylor's warrior states. It had to be Vermlot.

A rich city was Vermlot; rich not merely in treasure but in fighting men and weapons of war, in her battle-fleet, her beauty and her splendour.

Sojan had seen only roughly drawn pictures of Vermlot, heard descriptions of her but never actually looked on her fabled towers and battlements, so as he drew closer to the city he found the breath drawn from his body by the extraordinary size and colours of the capital. Red-gold marble sparkled as the small sun set, casting long, black shadows across the plain, and the large sun rose, casting shorter shadows forming a lattice which almost obscured sight of the magnificent architecture. The towers within the walls were multi-coloured, seeming to sway in a wind, the effect of the competing suns which Sojan was entirely used to. The closer he got the more solid the city seemed to become until, by the time he reached the gates, Vermlot rose high above him, her walls tiered and set with dozens of openings from which defenders could aim their weapons.

The great Yeste Gate of Vermlot was a sea of silken banners, with guards on every tier above, making Sojan gasp so that he was almost unable to answer the challenge of the armoured guards who looked down at him, bidding him to halt and state his business.

"I am Sojan of Katt, called Sojan Shieldbearer, and I come in peace. As for my business, it is to offer my battle-skills, my sword, my loyalty and my life in service of His Majesty the great War King of Hatnor."

"And your trade, if not the obvious one?"

"I am an honourable mercenary, pledged to serve an honourable master. My only possessions are the clothes I wear, the beast I ride and the weapons I carry. I have ridden half a world to offer my services to your great War King, whose courage, wisdom and moral uprightness are known even as far away as distant Katt."

There was a pause as the guards scrutinized him and conferred briefly amongst themselves, then the massive platinum-bound gates opened wide enough to admit him and Sojan rode into the busy wonder of the city, gasping at the vast variety of everything he saw. There were merchants of every sort shouting their wares, people dressed in every manner of styles and colours. There were beautiful women looking down from galleries and balconies, proud warriors swaggering with hands on sword-hilts, drovers leading dray-myats who drew great carts piled high with the produce of distant farms. Nobles, commoners and slaves from every part of the great Hatnorian Empire.

Sojan had never seen such richness and variety and dismounted to ask the way to a decent inn where he might rest and find refreshment. As he walked the great boulevards and twisting streets of Vermlot his strange protective weapon, the shield his father had given him, aroused much interest, most of it polite but, as he neared his destination, one braggardly warrior chose to step in his path and mock him, apparently challenging him.

Sojan was surprised by the warrior. He was unused to such rudeness once within the walls of a friendly city. He tried to pass on, but the warrior continued to block his path, pointing at his shield and guffawing. The man had obviously overheard the exchange between Sojan and the guards.

"Oh," he bellowed, "what a brave mercenary he is indeed! He has travelled half a world to give us his protection, for, with his great piece of metal in front of him, which he can hide behind, he will be able to withstand all Hatnor's enemies! Perhaps he cannot fight without it? That's so, is it not, Sir Mercenary?"

This was clearly a challenge. Weary as he was from his long ride, Sojan drew himself up. At which the other, watched by a curious crowd, climbed a few steps and stood leaning on a pillar, looking down at him now from a balcony. His bearded face bore an unpleasant sneer. "Eh, mercenary? Is that not the truth?"

Sojan looked up to meet the others' greenish eyes. The mercenary spoke grimly and quietly but his tone was cold and his words were acid.

"I do not like your attitude," he said. "And I like your words less. I am a guest in this city and would expect the politeness normally offered a guest, but if you would fight me, then I suppose I must accommodate you. Draw your sword—if you know how to use it! And defend yourself! Perhaps it is you who will be cowering behind this shield before I have finished with you!"

The warrior stiffened and his face flushed: he put one hand on the balcony rail and vaulted into the street below, drawing his long vilthor as he did so.

Sojan unslung his round shield and drew his own long blade.

The warrior struck first, aiming a wicked slash at Sojan's legs, but the mercenary jumped high in the air, using his shield to block the blow. The warrior thrust this time and again the shield met his sword. Another thrust, similarly parried. Another. And still Sojan blocked him, without once making use of his own sword. As they fought back and forth along the narrow street, a thin smile appeared on Sojan's features. The warrior lunged, lunged again. And Sojan sheathed his own vilthor now, using only the shield to parry the warrior's thrusts while carrying the attack with his weapon's rim. The warrior looked astonished and his sword-thrusts became increasingly vicious and wild. Yet still not once had Sojan resorted to his own vilthor, making the warrior look ridiculous to the watching crowd who were now laughing and applauding, clearly on the mercenary's side.

Sojan paused. His adversary saw his chance and slashed at the mercenary's exposed limb. Sojan dodged with an almost dancing agility and brought his shield down with a bang on the warrior's head, stunning him. Still the warrior came on, however, and there was a dull thud as his sword connected with the shield's boss. At this, Sojan stepped back, slung his shield onto his saddle and drew his sword, taking the attack to his opponent.

The Vermlotian slowly lost ground until with an almost contemptuous flick of the wrist Sojan disarmed him.

Then, from a second storey window a figure dropped, first to the balcony of the first storey and from there to the ground. The figure removed his cloak with a flourish and with an echoing smile on his handsome face came forward with drawn sword.

"I fancy you'll not take my blade from me so easily, Sir Mercenary!"

This time Sojan had found an opponent he could, indeed, not readily defeat. The man was as quick as the proverbial cobra. His sword wove an invisible circle around Sojan's guard. Sojan accounted well for himself but not once could he find a chance to reach his shield. The newcomer had him at his mercy! Before he knew it the mercenary's sword flew from his hand to land ten feet away and he was defenceless!

"Yield?" questioned the victor.

"I yield," answered the mercenary. "You are a great swordsman, sir! To whom have I the pleasure of admitting defeat?"

"Perhaps you *have* heard of me," smiled the other, sheathing his vilthor. "My name is Nornos Kald and I am the elected War King of Hatnor."

"Sir," declared Sojan with a deep bow, "I, who came to enlist in your service and offer aid to your cause, begin by fighting you. I crave your forgiveness."

Nornos Kald laughed easily. "Never mind, Sojan Shieldbearer. You did very well against my warrior here. To best him as you did is a test indeed and I feel that I would do well to enlist your services." He signed to a servant who waited in a doorway. "Come, you will be my guest until I have need of a mercenary."

And with that the War King of Hatnor, who, except on state occasions, lived the life of an ordinary noble until such time as Hatnor was in a position of conflict, clapped his arm around Sojan's shoulder and smiled. "Here," he told the servant, "Oumlat! Take Sojan to one of the best guest rooms and see that he is well looked after."

Dazed by this sudden turn of fortune, the mercenary allowed himself to be led away into the palace of Nornos Kald.

Chapter Three
The Air Pirates

For a Zylorian week or so Sojan enjoyed the privileges of a favoured guest. He enjoyed the best food and wine and was tended by servants who answered his every wish. He accepted this hospitality with good grace, using the days in which to relax and to practice his battle skills while at night he rested, enjoying a deep sleep.

Then, just as he was finishing his breakfast, a warrior arrived to tell him that Nornos Kald wished to see him. Immediately, Sojan rose and followed the man to the War King's apartments.

"I summoned you, Sojan," Nornos Kald said, when they were alone, "because you are to accompany me on a journey. Our mission is to take Il-that, princess of Sengol, back to her father's country. I desire to bring Sengol into the Hatnorian alliance without bloodshed if possible and the king would think well of it if his daughter was personally escorted home by the War King himself. You had better prepare your weapons and be ready to move from your quarters by dawn tomorrow."

This news delighted Sojan. He had become bored while he awaited his War King's orders.

The great Royal Airship was escorted by ten aerial cruisers, heavily armed with Hatnorian air-guns which worked on the simple principle of compressed air, with a range of over half a mile. They were ready to take to the air early the next morning. The ships rose majestically, hovered for a few moments, and then, with motors purring, the great dirigibles veered off towards Sengol which lay far to the North.

Within three or four hours they had crossed the outermost boundary of Hatnor and her satellites and were winging their way at a steady eighty miles an hour over Veronlam, a country which owed no allegiance to Hatnor and which, although fearing the mighty Empire, was constantly stirring up petty strife between the minor Hatnorian nations. They had nearly reached the border of Veronlam when the soft purr of motors was heard and a shell whistled past them and exploded in their rear air container.

"Veronlam pirates!" yelled the fore-gunner.

Quickly the small fleet formed a protective barrier about the Royal ship. One airship was hit a dozen times in as many different places and hurtled downwards, flames roaring from the gas-bag and the crew jumping overboard rather than die in the flames.

Nornos Kald realised at once that to fight against so many would soon end in disaster for his fleet, and he ordered them to turn about and flee back to Hatnor. He decided to rely upon his speedier engines to aid them rather than their powerful guns.

The Hatnorian fleet circled and fled. Nornos Kald was the last to leave the battle and hastily turned about to follow his ships. But alas, it was too late, for three well-aimed shots in their main tank sent them spiralling slowly to earth to land with a sickening crash amidst a tangle of red-hot girders and flaming fabric. Being on the platform of the ship Nornos Kald, Sojan and Il-that were flung clear of the main wreckage, to lie stunned, almost as if in death.

Chapter Four
A Grim Welcome

Sojan did not know how long it was he lay amidst the wreckage of the Royal Airship, but when he awoke it was dawn. He knew that none could have escaped if they had been killed in the wreckage but nevertheless he spent a fruitless two hours searching for his companions—all he found were two or three charred corpses but none lived. Convinced that his companions were dead he took the only unbroken water bottle and set off in the direction of Hatnor.

After some hours of steady walking, Sojan's eye caught the gleam of white stone far to the South of his position. With a sigh of relief he began to walk quickly towards the gleam which grew soon into a patch and from that into a city, its walls towering fifty feet in places. Realising that he was still probably in Veronlam he knew that it would be useless to try to gain admission on the strength of his allegiance to Nornos Kald the War King.

Stripping himself of his Hatnorian Navy-Cloak and also his Navy-type gauntlets Sojan stood dressed as when he had first entered Hatnor, as a mercenary swordsman.

He easily gained admittance to the city of Quentos as mercenaries were always welcome to swell the ranks of any army.

"By Mimuk, friend, you're the third foreigner to pass through these gates today," the guard said, as Sojan was allowed to enter the city.

"The third. That's strange, is it not, guard?" replied Sojan. "Three strangers in one day! Mimuk, you must be joking!"

"I joke not, friend mercenary, remarkable as it seems two others have preceded you and one of them was a woman. Our warriors found them near the wreck of an airship. Some say the ones we captured were Nornos Kald himself and Il-that, daughter of Hugor of Sengol. Two prizes for good ransom indeed if it be the truth."

Sojan strode off in the direction indicated by the friendly guard.

Arriving at the tavern he hired a room and ordered himself a meal. Finishing his repast, he was horrified to find that the only money he had was that of Hatnor. If he tried to pass this he knew that the suspicions of the keeper of the tavern would be instantly aroused. What should he do? He had brought nothing with him to the tavern save his sword, shield and poignard and the clothes he wore. He reasoned that the only chance he stood was to try to slip quietly out of the door before the proprietor spotted him and ordered him to pay his bill.

As soon as the place seemed reasonably busy Sojan rose and slipped quietly towards the door.

Just as he thought he had reached the safety of the street a hand fell on his shoulder and the leering face of the landlord was brought close to his.

"Going so soon, my hireling blade? Methinks you would like to stay and sample some more of our victuals before you make your—er—*hasty* departure," he said with ponderous sarcasm. "Now pay up or my men'll make sure you pay for your meal—in blood!"

"You threaten me, by Mimuk!" cried Sojan, his easily roused temper getting the better of him. "You dare threaten me! Draw your weapon!"

"Hey, Tytho, Zatthum, Wanrim—come and save me from this murdering bilker!" cried the keeper of the tavern in mock terror.

Instantly three ruffians appeared in the narrow doorway and, drawing their blades, rushed at Sojan, causing him to release his grasp upon the unfortunate man and turn to face this new danger.

Zatthum went down in the first minute with an inch of steel marking its path through his heart. The remaining two were not so easily defeated. Back and forth across the narrow street the three fought, sparks flying from their blades, the clang of their weapons echoing amongst the rooftops.

Sojan was marked in a dozen places, but his adversaries were bleeding in as many as he was. With a quick thrust, a parry and another thrust the mercenary succeeded in dispatching the second man. Now only Tytho was left. Sojan allowed himself to be headed off and the man edged him completely round so that they were now retracing their path. With a mighty effort Sojan, who was still tired after his narrow escape from the airship, gathered his remaining strength together and made a vicious lunge in Tytho's direction.

Tytho cried out in pain when Sojan's blade found the muscle of his left arm, but did not relax his grip upon his own sword. Again Sojan was forced further back towards the gaping crowd which had collected outside the tavern. His shield saved him from the thrust designed to end the fight but he knew he could not last longer for he was rapidly tiring. Suddenly his foot caught in the trappings of one of the dead men's harnesses and he fell backwards across the corpse. A grim smile graced Tytho's face as he raised his sword to deliver the final thrust.

Chapter Five
Sentenced to Die

K ill him, *Tytho, kill him!*" the crowd roared in frenzied bloodlust. Sojan, entangled in the harness of the man he had slain, tried to rise but was stopped from doing so by a shove from Tytho's booted foot.

The hireling raised his sword again and the crowd leaned forward.

Suddenly there was a disturbance at one end of the street and the crowd quickly began to disperse. As it did so, Tytho saw that the City Patrol, scourge of the local thieves, was the cause of the crowd's disappearance. Looking hurriedly about him for a way of escape he found none; he dropped his sword and began to run, foolishly, *along* the street.

The leader of the Patrol raised his pistol. There was the slight hiss of escaping air and the running hireling gave a short cry, threw up his arms, stumbled and dropped on the cobbles of the street.

"What's happening here?"

By this time Sojan had disentangled himself from the harness of his late opponent and was standing, legs a-sprawl, hand to head.

"You've saved my life, sir!" he gasped. "These ruffians attacked me for my money. I succeeded in killing two but unfortunately became tangled up with this fellow." He indicated the body. "Tytho was about to finish me when you arrived!"

The leader laughed. "You certainly accounted very well for yourself," he said, "these three are among the worst of the type with whom we have to contend. Ruthless murderers, perfect swordsmen." Again he laughed, "Or almost perfect. You did us a service and I am grateful."

He surveyed Sojan's bloodstained and tattered clothing.

"You're a stranger here are you not?" he enquired, "a mercenary swordsman, perhaps?"

"Yes, I am named Sojan—they nickname me 'Shieldbearer' because I use this." Sojan pointed to his shield. He was hoping that news of his joining the Hatnorian forces had not reached the city.

"Well, Sojan Shieldbearer, how would you like to bear that shield and wield a sword in the Patrol?"

Instantly Sojan saw his chance. If he could get a post in the organised militia of the city, he might be able to contact his imprisoned friends.

"It has always been my ambition to serve in the Veronlamite Guard," he lied, "but to become a member of the great Patrol is a chance for which I had not dared hope."

"Then come with us and we'll enlist you immediately. And," the captain added, "get you a decent jerkin and harness."

Before he could become a full-fledged Patrolman, Sojan had to undergo a course of basic training. When this was finished, his duties were to patrol, with his men, a certain section of the city, and arrest any thieves, footpads or similar wrongdoers. The "justice" was rough indeed and was not appreciated by the population.

All the time Sojan listened out for rumours and from these rumours he gleaned that Nornos Kald and Il-that were imprisoned somewhere in the Prison of Zholun—a mighty towered building situated near the centre of the city. Sojan knew well that the Patrol's duties included patrolling the prison and acting as guards to "special" prisoners—and he was hoping that he would be given this assignment soon.

Sure enough, one day his hopes were fulfilled and he was assigned to guard a section of Zholun Prison.

With his eyes wide open, Sojan learned where the two were imprisoned.

"One is in the East tower—the other in the West. Nornos Kald lies in the East tower," a guard told Sojan one night after Sojan plied him with enough ale to get him drunk. "Our War King plans to attack Hatnor and hoped to enlist Nornos Kald's help in return for his life, but the Hatnorian refuses and is to die with the other prisoner. Their time is almost up. The day after tomorrow, when the two suns pass in unison, they will die by the sword."

Sojan had to work fast if he was to rescue his friend and their beautiful charge.

Chapter Six

The Prison Tower

Sojan's first loyalty was to Nornos Kald. He was by now well known to his fellow guards and easily contrived to enter the East tower wherein Nornos Kald was imprisoned. Stealthily he made his way to the metal-studded door of the cell.

"Nornos Kald," he whispered.

He heard the rattle of chains and through the bars of the door saw his chieftain's handsome face, drawn and pale through lack of food and sleep.

"Sojan!" exclaimed the War King. "I thought you died in the crash!"

"The wreckage hid me. I am alive and here to save you if I can. I was assigned to guard the West wing so it will be more difficult—however I shall try and get the keys. Until I return—have hope!"

And with that Sojan crept back along the gloomy passage. On return he found that the Patrolman on duty was talking to someone. He waited until the man had left and then walked into the little room which was being used to house the guards.

"Hullo, Stontor," cried Sojan, "what's up?"

Stontor looked worried. "It's my wife, Sojan, she's been taken ill and I can't leave my post."

Here was an unexpected stroke of luck. Immediately, Sojan saw his chance and took it.

"Well, you go and help her," he said. "I'll stay here until you get back. Don't worry."

"Thanks a lot, Sojan, you're a friend indeed. Here are the keys—shouldn't think there'll be much doing tonight." And with that he put on his cloak and ran down the long passage.

Hastily Sojan picked up the keys and made his way back across to Nornos Kald's cell. He unlocked the door and helped Nornos Kald from his chains.

"I was lucky—a coincidence—guard's wife ill—but the main trouble will be getting out of the city," he panted, as he turned the keys in the heavy padlocks.

Together they returned to the guards' room. Here Sojan left Nornos Kald. Then he made his way back to the West wing where it was a simple matter to get the princess from her cell. Silently they returned to Nornos Kald.

Keeping to the sidestreets and the shadows, the three sped towards the city gates.

Suddenly Nornos Kald hissed, "Stop! Stop, Sojan, there may be an easier way." He pointed to a flat area dotted with hangars and anchored airships. "With one of those we would have a better chance of escaping."

"But how?" enquired Sojan.

Again Nornos Kald pointed. "You see that small ship nearest to us—the one anchored down by a couple of ropes?" The ship of which he was speaking was fifteen feet above them, held to the ground by anchors attached to heavy ropes. "With luck we could climb the ropes and gain the ship."

"It will be dangerous," murmured the girl with a charming grin. "But I'll gladly risk it if you two will!"

Sojan answered her grin with one of his own. "That's the spirit!" He was growing to like this daring princess.

Chapter Seven
The Sky Chase

Stealthily the three padded along the side of the field, keeping well into the shadows all the time. A single guard lolled on the ground. Sojan crept behind him and, reversing his pistol, knocked the man unconscious.

With Sojan's and Nornos Kald's help, Il-that was able to climb the rope and they boarded the ship. As they clambered over the rail a light suddenly appeared from one of the cabins and an armed man swaggered on deck. He was followed by three others.

"Mimuk!" he cried. "What have we here?"

There was no time for words and, handing Nornos Kald his long dirk and Il-that his pistol, Sojan drew his sword, and engaged the man and his companions. Nornos Kald was close behind him. Back and forth across the narrow deck the six men fought, and the four crewmen were no mean battlers.

Nornos Kald, weak from his sojourn in Zholun Prison, still put up a good fight. Together they succeeded in killing two of their opponents—but the other two were, if not better swordsmen, much fresher.

The clash of steel echoed across the silent field, threatening to wake the world. Sojan was blinded by the sudden flash of a searchlight and taking advantage of this, his opponent cut past his guard and made a deep gash in his side. The pain was like fire and Sojan could barely restrain himself from crying out. He stumbled, almost falling to the deck, and with a cry of triumph the crewman raised his sword. A sudden hiss and a strangled gasp and he collapsed over Sojan. Turning his head he saw Il-that with the pistol in her hand.

"Thanks," was all he could say as he struggled to his feet and ran to help Nornos Kald.

While Nornos Kald threw the bodies overboard, Sojan started the engines. Below them they heard shouts of a Patrol and two searchlights were now levelled on the swaying airship. Soon they heard cries as the bodies of the crewmen were found.

With two sword strokes Nornos Kald cut the anchoring ropes and the ship rose swiftly into the air. There was a coughing roar and the propellers began to turn. The searchlights followed them; all around them shells whistled.

Suddenly, behind them, they saw that three battlecruisers of the fastest and heaviest type had risen to follow them.

"More speed, Sojan, more speed!" cried Nornos Kald. "Make for Sengol, it's nearer."

With a glance at the compass, Sojan turned the ship's nose towards the North. Nearer and nearer came the battlecruisers, guns popping softly. Il-that, a true daughter of a warrior king, climbed into the gunner's rear-seat and aimed the guns of their own ship at the pursuing cruisers. She pressed the triggers and the twin muzzles of the gun gave a jerk, a hiss, and there was an explosion. What all a gunner's skill could not easily have accomplished, Il-that had done with luck—brought down a cruiser in its most vulnerable spot—the main gas-bag. Flames roared from the fabric and the ship lost height. Faster and faster it went as the earth pulled it downwards. The engines roaring to the last it crashed with a flash of orange-and-crimson flame. But the other two ships had still to be accounted for and Il-that was not so lucky this time.

For two hours the chase continued, neither gaining, and all the time the shells from the Veronlam craft were getting closer as the gunner perfected his aim.

"They will catch us soon," cried Il-that, who still sat in the rear-gunner's seat, "they seem to be drawing closer!"

"Then we shall have to land and hope that we're not still in Veronlam," yelled Nornos Kald above the shrieking wind.

"It will take a long time for us to do so, sir," Sojan told Nornos Kald, "we have no anchors, and to release the gas in the gas-bag would mean that while we lost height we should also lose speed."

"Then there's only one thing we can do!" cried the Emperor, "and that's this!" Raising his sword he cut deep into the nearest gas-bag. He was thrown to the deck as the contents rushed out and almost at once the ship began to drop, dangerously fast. The three stood by the side, ready to jump. Again Sojan was impressed by the girl, who showed no fear at all.

With a hard jolt the ship touched the ground, bumped along it, and stopped. Over the side the three companions went and ran over soft moss to the sheltering shadows of some rocks as the Veronlamite searchlights began to stab into the darkness.

But it was easy to hide in the rocks and the caves sheltered them when the Veronlamites landed and made a vain search for them.

For the next three days, moving mostly by night, the three oddly matched people managed to stay clear of the Veronlamite searchers, hiding among the rocks and strange fern forests of the terrain. Sojan seemed to have an instinct for knowing when and where to hide.

By the fourth morning it was evident that they had crossed the border and it was an easy matter to walk to the nearest Sengolian city and thence continue by airship to the capital, where the king gratefully took his daughter.

"We of Sengol have always felt friendship to Hatnor," he said, embracing the War King and the man who had become his closest friend and lieutenant, "but with this brave deed you have ensured our alliance will endure forever!"

And on the airship home Nornos Kald echoed these sentiments when he clapped Sojan on the shoulder. "We were fated to meet, Sir Shieldbearer. Ah, what adventures we shall have together!"

Chapter Eight
Mission to Asno

Motors purring, captains shouting orders, the rustle of the canvas gun-covers being drawn back, gay flags, flashing steel, flying cloaks of many hues; a Hatnorian war-fleet rose rapidly into the sky.

On the deck of the flagship stood a tall, strong figure—that of Sojan, nick-named "Shieldbearer," second in command to the great War King of Hatnor himself—Nornos Kald.

At his side was a long broadsword, upon his back his round shield; his right hand rested on the butt of his heavy air-pistol—an incredibly power-ful weapon. Clad in a jerkin of sky-blue, a divided kilt of deep crimson and boots of dark leather, over his shoulders his jingling war-harness, he was the typical example of a Zylorian mercenary, whose love of bright garb was legendary.

The great war-fleet was destined for Asno—a country far to the North of Hatnor where the king, so the spies told, was raising an army of mercenaries to attack Yundrot—a colony of the Hatnorian Empire.

To stop a major war, Nornos Kald had decided to send a mighty fleet to crush the attack before it was started. Having other business, he had assigned Sojan to take his place. The War King was determined to make sure that no attack should take place against Yundrot, whose population was famous for its love of peace.

Only too pleased at the chance to enjoy the pleasures of battle, Sojan had readily assented and was now on his way to Asno in the hope that a show of strength would stop any plans of invasion. For the first time, the entire fleet was under Sojan's command.

Soon the fleet was winging its way over Asno, a land of snow and ice, of fierce beasts, its great tracts of ice-fields uninhabited by any civilised beings.

In another hour they would be over Boitil, the capital city.

"Gunners, take your positions!" Sojan roared through cupped hands and picking up a megaphone—for there was no radio on Zylor—shouted the same orders, which went from ship to ship until every gunner was seated in his position, guns loaded and ready for firing.

"Drop two hundred feet!" Sojan roared again to the steersman. These orders were repeated to the other captains, who in turn shouted them to their own steersmen.

"Prepare hand weapons and fasten down loose fixtures, check gas-bag coverings, every man to position!" Sojan shouted when the ships had all dropped two hundred feet.

"Slow speed!" The ships slowed into "second-speed."

In Zylorian naval terms there are five speeds: "Speed No. 1" is fastest possible, "Speed No. 2" is a fifth of this slower, and so on. When a commander gives the order to slow when travelling at Speed No. 1, the ship automatically adjusts to Speed No. 2; if going at No. 2 and told to slow, it changes to No. 3.

Now they were over the outskirts of the city, dropping lower and lower until Sojan thought they would touch the very towers of Boitil, scanning the squares and flying-fields for signs of the army. Halfway over the city a message was passed to Sojan that a great army camp had been spotted—just on the outskirts of the city. At the same time someone yelled for him to look, and doing so he saw that a fleet almost as large as his own was rising from flying-fields all over the vast city. Somehow this fleet had been successfully hidden from Hatnor's spies!

Sojan cursed the enemy. Was this a deliberate trap? He had to assume the worst.

"Prepare for battle!" he shouted.

As one, the safety catches of the guns were pushed off.

"Shoot as you will!" Sojan ordered.

There was a muffled "pop" and the hiss of escaping air as the explosive shells of the Hatnorian craft were sent on their mission of destruction. Almost at once the enemy retaliated.

Two Hatnorian ships, one only slightly damaged, the other a mass of roaring yellow-and-blue flame, dropped earthwards. The Hatnorians retaliated, sending bursts of deadly fire into the enemy fleet.

Meanwhile, Sojan had sent a fast air-boat speeding back to Hatnor to warn of Asno's treachery. They had hoped to avert war but had instead found themselves fighting for their lives!

For twelve hours the great air-battle was fought, developing into ship-to-ship duels as the opposing sides became mixed. Bit by bit the battle moved Southwards until it was over the great ice wastes.

Sojan was astonished by the considerable numbers of craft Asno had been able to assemble. They had obviously persuaded many of the privateer fleets to throw in their lot with Tremorn, Asno's War King. This battle had been planned for a long time. No doubt rumours of an attack on Yundrot had been deliberately seeded to lure the fleet into this fight away from their own territory. The plan had been to destroy the Hatnorian fleet, leaving the nation vulnerable and unable to resist an attack.

But expert handling of their craft, superior marksmanship and a slightly superior weight of numbers on the part of the Hatnorian fleet was slowly but surely weakening the Asnovians. Sojan, now with a gun mounted on the officer's platform, was taking an active part in the battle. His uncanny ability to hit almost whatever he aimed at was taking great toll and keeping Hatnorian morale high. Everywhere now the enemy's ships were hurtling earthwards, crashing in an inferno of flame, or merely bumping gently along the ground when a gas-bag was slightly punctured.

At last, one by one, the privateers began to slip away from the field, leaving only the Asnovians to defend their capital. The other privateer ships, seeing their companions escape, disengaged and followed them. The individual hireling ships, manned mainly by mercenaries, flew in every direction but that of Asno, while the Asnovian craft turned and headed for their home base.

In tight formation, under Sojan's brilliant strategy, sped the Hatnorian fleet, following a close formation and turning to No. 1 speed. Any ship they overtook was ruthlessly shot down; but half a dozen or so were lucky and escaped them.

In three hours they were back over Asno, leaving the city unharmed but bombing the troop emplacements with incendiaries until nothing remained of the great camp but smouldering fabric and twisted steel.

Now, through the south gate of the city, streamed forth ragged bands of hired soldiers, bent on escaping while they could. The planned attack on a Hatnorian colony had not even begun. A just reprisal on Nornos Kald's part. A reprisal carried out in full by Sojan. But his business was not finished and, landing on part of an undamaged airfield, Sojan ordered the frightened commanding officer to take him to King Tremorn of Asno.

"I bring a message from my Emperor!" he cried when he was in the vast chamber which housed the king's court. All around him stood frowning nobles and servants, anxious to hear Sojan's terms. In contrast to all the great display of royal pomp around him, the War Captain seemed almost bizarre, wearing his simple mercenary clothing, his strange shield on his back. Great pillars supported the roof and brilliant tapestries hung from the ceiling. Murals on the walls depicted scenes of battles, on land, water and in the air, and the proud expressions of the painted figures offered another contrast to the reality of defeat in the audience chamber.

"Speak your message," ordered the king. "What are your terms? I admit that I am beaten!" Almost under his breath he added: "For the present!"

"For all time, sire, while a member of the Nornos family sits on the throne of Hatnor!" Sojan replied. "Now, do you wish to hear my terms?"

"Speak!" The king made a weary, defeated gesture, refusing to meet Sojan's clear gaze.

"The first is that you acknowledge allegiance to Hatnor and pay a tribute of five hundred young men to train in our armies every tenth year. The second is that you disband any army you still have, save for policing your city. On signs of attack, you will notify the Empire, who will come to your aid.

"As a member of the Empire you will be subject to all laws and trading terms of the Empire and in times of major war shall enlist two-thirds of your fighting strength in the armies of Hatnor and the remaining third if called upon. You will not make war-ships or weapons of war, save hand weapons, for your own use, but all existing warships and larger arms shall be sent direct to the capital. Do you recognise these terms?"

The king paused and, turning to his *major-domo*, whispered a few words to him. The man nodded.

"Yes, I recognise your terms." He sighed.

"Then sign your name and oath to this document and seal it with your royal seal. Upon the breaking of your word, the lapse shall be punished according to the magnitude."

Sojan handed the paper to a courtier who carried it to the king. The act of bowing to a king is unknown upon the planet Zylor; instead the subject places his right hand upon his heart to signify complete allegiance.

So it was that Sojan achieved his purpose. But more adventures were yet to come before he could return to his palace at Hatnor.

Chapter Nine
Revolt in Hatnor

S ojan, Sojan!" the call rang across the clear Zylorian sky as a small scout-ship veered towards the larger warship, the flagship of Sojan, second-in-command to the War King of Hatnor—Nornos Kald.

"Who are you?" Sojan's lieutenant roared through a megaphone.

"I bring urgent tidings from the court of Nornos Kald—the land is in turmoil!"

"Come alongside," the lieutenant responded.

As the scout-ship drew alongside, an armed man jumped from it and rushed up the ladder to the platform whereon Sojan stood.

"Sojan! While the fleet has been at war, revolution has swept through the land. It was all part of the same plan. Nornos Kald has been deposed and a tyrant sits on the throne of Hatnor. There is a price upon your head and upon the heads of all whom you command.

"Flee now, Sojan, while you have the chance. Trewin the Upstart controls the city and half the Empire. The other half is in a state of unrest, unsure whether to support one faction or another!"

"I cannot flee while my War King rots in chains—tell me, who still cries 'Loyalty to the Nornos family'?"

"None, openly, Sojan. A few are suspected, but they are still powerful nobles and even Trewin dare not arrest them without cause."

Sojan's face became grim and he clenched his hand upon his sword hilt.

"Lun!" he cried. "Order the fleet to turn about and adjust to Speed 1!"

A look of surprise crossed his lieutenant's face. "We're not running, Sojan?"

"Do as I say!"

"Turn about and adjust to Speed 1!" Lun shouted through his megaphone.

At once the great fleet turned gracefully about and adjusted, speed by speed, until it was flying at maximum velocity. There were puzzled looks in the eyes of many of Sojan's captains, but they obeyed his order.

"Tell them to set a course for Poltoon," he ordered Lun. Lun did so and soon every ship was heading South—to the steaming jungles and burning deserts of the Heat Lands.

"Why do we sail for Poltoon, Sojan?" asked Lun.

But Sojan's only reply was, "You will see," and he resumed his earnest conversation with the messenger who had brought him the news.

On the third day they were sailing at No. 1 speed over a vast belt of jungle, seemingly impenetrable. But Sojan's eyes, less atrophied by civilised living, caught what he had been looking for—a patch of green, lighter than the dark green which predominated.

"STOP!" he roared. "Stop and hover—no one is to drop anchor."

The flying machines of the Zylorian nations are usually very similar to our airships. The gondola is supported by steel hawsers depending from the main gas-bag. The propeller is adjustable and can be slung either fore or aft of the ship—it is usually slung aft. They are steered by two methods, a rudder aft plus manipulation of the propeller. A normal-sized warship usually mounts five guns—two very powerful ones fore and aft, a smaller one on the captain's platform and two mounted on a platform on top of the huge gas-hull. The gunners reach this platform by means of ladders from the deck to the platform. This position is extremely dangerous and if ever the gas-container is hit it is rare for a gas-bag gunner ever to escape.

The ships stopped to hovering position as ordered and while they waited, Sojan had his ship drop downwards, nearer and nearer to the little patch of green which became a small clearing, just large enough to land one ship, but for a fleet of over fifty ships to land here was impossible. With a slight bump the ship dropped to the ground and the anchor was thrown into the soft grass. Sojan ordered that the gas-bags be deflated. They could always be inflated again as every ship carried a large supply of compressed gas-cylinders.

Now the ship was only a third of the size and was dragged into the undergrowth which was not at all thick. Sojan told his crew of eight to get to work and chop down all the small growth but to leave the huge forest giants standing. This they did and very soon the clearing widened and as it did so a new ship dropped down until the fifty were all deflated and covering a large area of ground under the trees. The cabins made excellent living quarters so there was no difficulty about housing the men. Rations were also plentiful and a spring of fresh water was nearby.

"I know this part of the country well," Sojan told his men that night, "the inhabitants are for the most part friendly. While they are not civilised, they are not savages and I believe they will give us some help. But now we sleep and tomorrow we shall rouse the tribes!"

Next morning, Sojan with a small party of his men set off for the village of his barbarian friends.

The chief greeted him warmly and was interested in Sojan's need for soldiers.

"You know me and my people, Soyin," he said, using the nearest Poltoonian equivalent of Sojan's name. "We all love to fight—and if there's a bit of loot thrown in, who's to say 'no'?"

"Then I can depend on you?"

"By all means—I shall form a council immediately and recruit as many of my fellow chiefs as possible. Between us we should muster a few thousand fighting men."

By Zylorian standards, where most nations are comparatively small to Earth nations, a thousand men is quite a large number.

"Then have them ready by the third day, my friend," Sojan replied. "Blood will stain the usurper's robes before the month is gone."

Chapter Ten
The Hordes Attack

The day of the invasion was drawing nearer and Sojan began to work harder and harder in the training of his barbarian horde. The Poltoonians were enthusiastic, for they had been on good terms both with Hatnor and Sojan. Spies brought word that there was more and more unrest in the outlying provinces of Hatnor, whose peoples were seeing increasingly what the rule of Trewin the Upstart meant in day-to-day reality.

"The time is ripe to strike," Sojan told his captains and the wild chiefs. "We must invade now or our cause and our self-respect will be lost and we will never again have the opportunity to win Hatnor back from the usurper and restore Nornos Kald to his rightful throne!"

His airships, camouflaged by the mighty trees of the steaming Poltoonian jungle, were provisioned and ready to do battle. His captains were word-perfect in his plan of invasion. Everyone had his orders and knew how to carry them out.

A day later a horde, consisting of thousands of mounted barbarians led by Sojan himself, moved towards the North—and Hatnor!

Two days later, the faster-moving airships rose into the air like a swarm of hornets armed with incredibly powerful stings. As they passed the horde, the ships slowed to minimum speed and followed, flying low, just above them. In another day they would arrive at the boundaries of Hatnor—and the blood of all who opposed them would run in the gutters.

Sojan was sure that very little innocent blood would flow as the army would be on his side. It was the criminal population, promised everything by Trewin, who had planned this revolution for years, egged on by a few evil nobles, who had risen and overthrown their elected War King while the bulk of his army was defeating those who had been persuaded to lead them into a trap in the outer province.

There would always be unrest in any regime. Sojan knew this. But at present there was no cause for the people to grumble about their ruler. As so often happened, the unrest had been caused by a power-seeker intent on turning a nation into a blood-bath for his own selfish ends.

Now in a few short weeks the once happy people groaned beneath the tyrant's yoke, no man, woman or child able to count themselves safe from his oppression.

Sojan was determined to get rid of the usurper and do everything in his power to free his friend and War King Nornos Kald. He looked back with pride from where he rode his myat at the head of the horde. They had not been hard to train, for they were magnificent fighters, but they had been harder to organise. Now they were ready.

Not only men made up the barbarian army, their womenfolk rode beside them, armed with knife, sword, shield and spear. In their left hands they carried charm sticks to keep their men and themselves from harm. Most of these women were extremely beautiful and the armour they wore did not detract from their good looks in any way, rather it enhanced them.

No longer under cover of the trees, the horde moved chiefly at night. Sojan did not want Trewin to suspect anything until they were as close as possible to the Hatnorian border.

At last they reached the outer boundaries of the Empire and found little opposition here. But Sojan did not relax. It would be later, when news of their invasion reached the city of Iklon, that the fighting would begin. Sojan was finding it difficult to keep the barbarians in order; they had decided that anyone was an enemy who was not fighting with them and they were confused by Sojan's forbidding them to loot the settlements. But after a council meeting with the chiefs he was sure that they would be reliable, at least for a time.

Two days later found them at the gates of Iklon. Gates which were securely locked and guarded.

The barbarians were all for laying violent siege to the place, but Sojan realised that Iklon could hold out against such tactics for an eternity.

"You are forgetting our ships," he said, "we have the rest of the Hatnorian airforce under our control. The people of Iklon will not last as long as they hope!"

A few hours later Sojan's flagship sailed gracefully down for him and, with the pilot's skilful manipulation of his gas canister, climbed up again when he was aboard. Then the flagship returned to where the rest of the fleet waited.

Sojan raised his megaphone and called instructions to the nearest ships. Soon orders were shouted from ship to ship and the fleet set its engines in motion.

A few hours later the flagship and a dozen or so of the larger battlecraft broke from the main fleet and dipped downwards towards the great city square. Aboard were hundreds of soldiers, the most reliable of the barbarian horde, and as soon as the ships reached the ground, not without some opposition, they swarmed out across the square to engage the rather frightened militia who barred their way.

Next the streets surrounding the square were filled with wild cries. Strangely woven banners were raised against a background of flashing steel. The ships overhead could hear the muffled poppings of air-pistols and rifles. It was impossible to use the heavier artillery against the troops below and it became quickly obvious that they were not needed.

Into the square the barbarians poured. Soon it was impossible to tell friend or foe as the fighting surged back and forth, spreading outwards into the streets, into the very houses themselves. Meanwhile more of Sojan's troops were landing outside the city. Attacked from the inside as well as at their walls, the tyrant's men were uncertain where to concentrate their forces and while they wavered, the barbarians took the opportunity to batter in one of the minor gateways and clamber over the inner wall.

With a huge roar the Poltoonians burst into the city and met the half-hearted defences of Trewin's men.

The streets were slippery with blood, echoing with the ring of steel and the cries of the wounded.

Sojan was in front, hewing and hacking with his great blade, his strange shield held before his face and upper body, his long hair streaming behind him and a grim smile upon his lips. "To the Palace, to the Palace," he cried. "Take the Palace and the battle's won!"

But before they were forced to fight for the final prize, Iklon's ruler, a mild-featured little man whom Trewin had forced to join him, came rushing down the steps of his residence screaming for the end of conflict, throwing himself to his knees and begging Sojan for his life.

Much to the surprise of the barbarians, Sojan laughed and raised the little man up. "You broke your oath to your War King whose only crime against his people was to bring them peace! What should your punishment be?"

"I—it—it's for you to determine, great War Prince. I had no choice but to obey the Usurper. He holds my daughter in prison. It is how he made so many of the Empire's nobles obey him. I do not ask you to spare my life but I beg you to save hers."

"If I save her, will you swear another oath, to follow the orders of Nornos Kald or, until he is free, to follow mine?"

"I will great prince."

"You must also pay a tribute to my allies, the Poltoonian Horde. I will instruct them to cease from violence if you will agree."

"I do so agree!"

"Then I will take what are left of your men and fleet and add it to my own. I will instruct the Horde to leave you in safety."

And so it was with each of the cities and nations Sojan reconquered. Like a tidal wave, the army surged over their enemies in the direction of Hatnor.

So swiftly did armies and cities fall that it soon became apparent that Trewin the Usurper was holding most of his nobles to ransom in one way or another. By the time they reached the Empire's capital, they received almost no resistance. Leading his men up the great steps of the Imperial Palace Sojan raised his sword in triumph. "Soon Nornos Kald will be free to take his place at the head of his War Council!" cried the mercenary-turned-Prince.

His men cheered and surged forward. But the doors would not open to their thunderous knocking. Sojan ordered the battering rams brought up.

Once—twice—thrice—the battering rams crashed against the ancient timbers. There was a cheer as the main door flew open, but the cheer was suddenly stifled. Sojan and his men drew back in horror.

Chapter Eleven
A Warrior's Justice

There stood Nornos Kald, their War King, worn and in rags, a filthy stubble on his face. And surrounding him, a body of Trewin's personal guard. Behind them stood Trewin himself, stroking his blue-black beard.

"Come another step closer, Sojan, and I'll be forced to kill your precious War King!" he called.

Sojan and his men were in a quandary, what were they to do? It was check, if not checkmate, for them.

An idea sprang into Sojan's mind.

Aiming a pistol at Nornos Kald, he pulled the trigger. The Emperor fell to the ground with a moan and lay still.

"There, dog, I've done your dirty work for you!" Sojan laughed.

In a rage Trewin fired blindly at Sojan. The Swordsman flung himself to the ground and the bullet whistled by to catch one of his men in the shoulder.

Lifting his own pistol, Sojan fired twice. Trewin, in the act of fleeing up the staircase, flung out his arms and toppled down the great stairway, blood trickling from his mouth. He landed with a thud at the feet of his guards.

With a cry, Sojan, his sword glistening in the light of the torches suspended around the hall, charged for the astounded guards who, without thinking, threw down their weapons and fled.

Nornos Kald picked himself up from the floor with Sojan's help.

"A clever move, Sojan," he grinned, "but it took some clever shooting, too."

He examined the hole which Sojan's bullet had made in his coat.

"It was a minor risk, sir. If I had not taken it, the city would even now be in the hands of Trewin."

"At the moment it seems to be in the hands of your Poltoonian barbarians," laughed the War Lord. "Let us go to the rescue of our fellow countrymen."

Peace had come once more to Hatnor.

Chapter Twelve
The Purple Galley

To describe accurately the shining pageantry, the gorgeous fabrics, the colours, the varieties of people and the myriad flashing weapons in that great hall would be near-impossible. The gleaming white stones of the mighty chamber, hung with vivid tapestries of red, black, gold, yellow, orange, green and purple, reflected the equally scintillating colours of the uniforms and dresses of the men and women who stood before the throne of Nornos Kald, Chief Noble of the Empire and elected War King.

But there was one uniform missing, one tall figure which should have been there was not, one sword did not flash in the great hall.

And the faces of the nobles were sad—for the missing man was Nornos Rique, prince of Hatnor—the War King's son.

"My people," said Nornos Kald, softly and very sadly, "my son has been missing for thirteen days now and still no news of him or the Princess Sherlerna. Has anyone *anything* to report—you, Sojan, have you found any traces of my son?"

"No, sire, although I have searched the whole empire. We have agents everywhere attempting to glean news. If there were as much as a rumour it would help us but I can only conclude that your son is not in the Hatnorian Empire!"

"Then we must seek him elsewhere. Find him, Sojan! Take the men you require—and return with my son! If it is possible then you are the man to discover where he is!"

The sun was just setting when a weary and travel-stained rider guided his myat into the small collection of stone-and-wooden buildings which was the border town of Erom. He had ridden for days, stopping only to eat and gather a few hours' sleep when he could no longer stay awake.

His clothes were good and were mainly made of durable hide. His weapons nestled in well-oiled sheaths and scabbards, his shield was covered with canvas. It was easy to see that here was the typical soldier of fortune—a Zylorian mercenary.

He dismounted at the small tavern and called through the door which was ajar.

"Hey there! Is there a stable for my animal and a bed for me?"

"Yes, my lord," came a woman's voice from the tavern and a girl of about eighteen appeared in the doorway. "Hey, Kerk!" she called. "Fetch a blanket for this gentleman's myat and take him to the stables!"

"This way, my lord," said the battle-scarred veteran who came to do the woman's bidding. "What's trade like?" he added with a grin as they neared the wooden building which served as a stable for the beasts of the whole village.

"Not too bad," the mercenary smiled. "As long as men are men and their tempers are the same then I'll never be out of a job. There was an uprising in Hatnor some months ago. That was a good scrap if ever there was one!"

"Aye, I heard about it from another gentleman who came this way soon after it happened. Didn't say much, though—most untalkative type if you ask me! He wasn't a Hatnorian—nor a Northerner for that matter, that was easy to see!"

"What do you mean?" The mercenary was obviously interested; more than casually so.

"He was a Shortani man, you can't mistake 'em."

"Shortani's a big continent—did you hear him say what country in Shortani?"

"Wait a minute. I believe he did say something." The old man paused and tugged at his grizzled beard. He frowned, thinking hard. "Yes, I've got it—it was raining at the time. Like it does *most* of the time in these parts," Kerk laughed—"Never seems to stop it don't . . ."

"Yes!" the mercenary was impatient. "But what did he say?"

"What? Oh, yes. The country. Well, *he* said, when he got here, that it was 'never like this in Uffjir,' Yes, that was it."

"Uffjir, hmmm, that's right on the farthest side of Shortani. And even then he may not have been returning there. It probably isn't anything but it seems strange for an Uffjirian to travel so far from his tropical lands, especially in winter. What did he look like, this man?"

"Oh! The usual type, you know. Small, a bit fat, wore one of them fancy jewelled swords which snaps as soon as you cross it with a good bit of Turani steel. Why, I remember when I was a young 'un—that would be a bit before your time. We didn't have none of them newfangled flying machines in *those* days, I can tell you. *We* had to do all our travelling by myat—or more likely on our feet . . ."

"Yes!" The mercenary was almost crying with impatience by this time. "But can you describe the Uffjirian?"

"Well, he had a *beard* if that's any good. And it was curled up a bit—looked as if he'd put oil on it. Wore fancy clothes, too, no good for travelling but expensive—yes, they were certainly expensive. He was a nobleman by the look of him—hired a whole crowd of the village men and they all went off together somewhere. They ain't back yet."

"Have you any idea where they went?"

"Only the direction. They went off in the opposite direction to the one from which you came. Mounted, too, and although they wouldn't admit it, every one of them has a sword hidden in his blankets. They can't fool *me*, I have to look after their myats!"

The myat had been rubbed down and was in his stable by this time, attended by the two men, one an aged veteran with over a hundred years of fighting behind him and the other equally a veteran with not much more than twenty years behind him. They lived short lives on Zylor for most men died of a sword thrust by the time they were seventy or eighty. Their natural life-span of 120 years was rarely reached.

That night, the mercenary sat in the corner of the tavern, drinking and cleaning his heavy pistol. There were two other visitors at the tavern. A young man of seventeen years or so and his father. They were friendly men and found mutual interests with the mercenary in that they were both veterans of the Findian/Kintonian wars. The mercenary had fought for the Findians and the man—Orfil—had fought on the side of the Kintonians. But there was no bad feeling between the men for at that time Orfil had also been a mercenary. Now he was a merchant—dealing in precious jewels—and he and his son were travelling to the Aborgmingi, a small group of islands in the Shortani Sea. The mining of precious stones was unknown there, he said, and he found it worth his while to travel the distance over land and sea to sell them as they obtained prices which were over five times as much as those in Fria, his own country.

"Ride with us," he invited, "there is always a greater amount of safety if there is a greater amount of men and I would be glad of your company."

"I ride towards Shortani," said Sojan, "but whether I shall for long depends on circumstances."

The merchant knew better than to ask what "circumstances" they were for privacy means life on Zylor and those who ask too many needless questions are liable to find themselves in an alleyway keeping close company with a knife!

The three men retired to their respective rooms and the mercenary was glad to get some rest. Wearily he sank onto the not-so-soft bed and lay down to sleep.

In the morning he awoke at his accustomed hour and attempted to rise. He could not, for his hands were bound. He was strapped to the bed and the only thing he could move was his head. Looking down at him with a smile on his face was—Orfil the merchant, and his son. Only his "son" had donned her skirts again and was an extremely pretty girl!

"Well, my nosy soldier, you've put your nose into one game too many this time!" laughed Orfil. He seemed to be enjoying a great joke. The girl behind him was not so amused. Her whole bearing was tense and the hand that gripped the pistol at her side gleamed white at the knuckles.

"Perhaps I should introduce myself," continued the man, "my name *is* Orfil. I am the Captain of the Spies Guild in Rhan. This lady prefers to remain unknown, although where you're going the gods will know it anyway!"

"You're going to kill me then?"

"Yes."

"And am I permitted to enquire 'why'?"

"Certainly. I am afraid that I shall be forced to murder you—though I regret it, sir, for I like you. You see, you have been enquiring just a little too pointedly to be harmless. I suspect that you are more than a common mercenary—that perhaps you are in the pay of Uffjir. Should that be so, then it will be more of a pleasure to kill you!"

"I am no Uffjirian, you oaf! And I am not involved in any intrigue. I seek my War Lord's son who disappeared some time ago! Think not that I would sink so low as you!"

The smile vanished from the Rhanian's face and his right hand clenched on his long sword.

"Then I am sorry! You see Nornos Rique is in this right up to his lance-tip!"

And with that, he raised his sword. The girl turned away, and just as Orfil was about to deal the death thrust, the door opened slowly and he saw the face of the Uffjirian nobleman. Behind him were half a dozen burly swordsmen.

"Vit take you, Parijh!" cried the spy and then to the girl, "Quick, get behind me and open the window. I'll hold them back. There are myats awaiting!"

And with that he rushed upon the Uffjirian who for a moment was so taken aback that he could hardly defend himself from the furious attack of Orfil's sword.

"Quick men," he yelled, "seize him, kill him, don't let him escape!" But the narrow doorway would not permit more than one man to enter at a time and Orfil easily pushed Parijh back and swung the heavy bar into position as the door shut.

"No time to slay you now," he panted as he clambered over the window ledge, "perhaps some other time . . ."

The girl had by this time scrambled from the window and was waiting with the myats. The soft thud of their hooves was drowned by the yells of the man from Uffjir and the surly answers of his companions.

Silence fell as the men gave chase to Orfil and the girl. The mercenary still lay strapped to the bed. The door was barred from inside and he had begun to think that he would soon starve to death when someone knocked on the door.

"*Get me out of here!*" he yelled.

"Is there anything the matter, sir?"

This was too much even for a hardened warrior. "Yes there is!" he roared. "And if you don't let me out right now—I'll tear the place down with my bare hands!" A rather vain boast considering his position.

Murmurs at the door and the retracing of steps down the creaking staircase.

He waited expectantly, hearing occasional voices. Then there were tramping feet on the stairway and in a few moments the door fell inwards, closely followed by two men with a battering log and behind them old Kerk.

"I *said* there was something up!" he exclaimed triumphantly.

It was a matter of minutes to untie the mercenary, for him to gather up his accoutrements, to pay Kerk and to find and saddle his myat. Then he was off, down the long forest track, following the trail of Orfil and his pursuers.

For three hours he followed a trail which was easily found. Once or twice he thought he heard movements in the forest but, although he kept his hand ever ready on his sword, he was not attacked.

Then, just as he turned the bend in the trail, they were there: the Uffjirian's men, lined across the narrow path, swords drawn and pikes at the ready.

But the mercenary was trained to quick thinking and at the same moment as his heels dug into the myat's flanks, he drew sword, unhooked shield and brought his lance to bear as he thundered down upon his foes, his crimson cloak flying behind him like the vast wings of the *sucha* bat and a blood-curdling war-shout on his lips!

Taken aback, they wavered, but at the Uffjirian's yells behind them, pushed forward to meet the charging lancer. Down went one with a brilliantly tufted shaft protruding from his throat. The lance was wrenched out of the mercenary's hands and his steed reared and snorted, flailing with its cloven hooves. His face alight with battle-lust, he ducked beneath the guard of another man and dealt him a cut which put him down shrieking and calling to some unknown god in an agony of death. He whirled his steed about, hoping to gain a little ground by retreating, but it was too late, for he was surrounded by a solid ring of pikes and blue steel. He caught blow after blow on his shield and the flat of his sword. One man lunged upwards with his heavy pike and the myat snorted in pain before his deadly hooves beat the pikeman down.

Leaping from the wounded myat, the lone swordsman found himself surrounded by four of Parijh's men. He bled from a dozen superficial cuts and still he fought with the skill and ferocity of a trained *crinja* cat. Then there was a gap in their ranks and he was through, rushing for a tethered myat twenty yards away.

Howling like were-wolves, they followed him across the glade and reached him just as he cut the tethering rope of the myat with his sword and leaped into the high saddle. They attempted to slash at his animal's legs but a swift arc of blue steel drove them back. As he passed the body of the man whom he had first slain, he stopped and wrenched the lance from the corpse and then he was away, down the long trail in the direction Orfil had taken. All his would-be captors heard was a grim laugh which echoed through the tall trees of the forest.

Turning in the saddle, the mercenary saw them run to their mounts and Parijh come from behind, scolding and cursing—for amongst other things, the fine beast the mercenary had taken had belonged to the Uffjirian!

And it soon proved its worth for he easily outdistanced them and was again following Orfil's tracks—a trail which was to lead to the weirdest adventure in his whole career.

Chapter Thirteen
The Sea Wolves!

Two days after his fight with the Uffjirian's men, the mercenary rode into the port of Minifjar in the country of Barj.

There were several ships in the harbour: merchantmen mainly, but here and there rose the tall prows of warships.

Although their aircraft are chemical-motor powered, the Zylorians have not found an engine capable of moving their ships, or for carrying them very far and, since steam or electricity are also unknown, they still rely on sails and oars for motive power, their atmosphere being differently constituted.

Most of the ships were equipped with both sails and oars but two of them were built for sails only. From every one of them, long barrels poked from strategic ports, for it was only a suicidal madman who would sail anything but the calm waters of the Asnogi Channel and the Shortani Sea unarmed.

There was one ship, a galley, which stood out from the others. Its tall prow rose triumphantly above the rest and its sails and paintwork were predominantly purple. Purple, like black on Earth, is the colour of death on Zylor, so it attracted much attention from the inhabitants of the small town.

The mercenary sought out the only presentable inn and bought a meal and a bed for the night.

As he lugged his equipment, wearily ascending the flight of narrow stairs, he looked up and caught a glimpse of a familiar face—that of Orfil of Rhan's girl companion.

Evidently she had been watching him. The warrior kept a wary hand on his sword and resolved to make sure that his door was firmly barred that night.

But soon after he had dumped his belongings on the dirty bed, he heard the rattle of harness and, from his small window, he saw the spy and the girl leaving the walled entrance of the inn. They had none of their possessions with them which told the mercenary a great deal. They had gone for reinforcements.

Sitting on the edge of the bed Sojan pondered what he should do.

He had decided that it would be wiser to leave, when there came the sound of myats' hooves and a squad of Barjite Cavalry, fully armed with lances, swords, long rifles and pistols, clad in uniforms of blue, red and green with shining breastplates, helmets and leg greaves of bright steel, clattered to a halt outside the inn.

"Thank Vit!" the mercenary murmured. For he recognised the captain of the mounted men as an old friend, who had fought beside him in an expedition Barj had made when bandits had been raiding their caravans of merchandise.

"Red!" he cried, opening the window. "Red, you son of a *crinja* cat!"

Red, or as his men knew him, Captain Jeodvir, Vollitt's son of Chathja, turned. Then, as he saw who called him, a wide grin took the place of his previously astonished expression and he passed a hand through the shock of hair which gave him his nickname.

"Sojan! What're you doing in this particular bit of Hell?"

"And you? One of King Vixian's crack lancers commanding a coastal patrol?"

"The king doesn't like me any more, Sojan," laughed the warrior. "Not since I pressed for better pay for the cavalry and nearly started a civil war at the last council!"

It was Sojan's turn to laugh. "You couldn't plead for better conditions for the underpaid infantry, I suppose?"

"What? And have them get the idea that they're up to cavalry standard!"

The rivalry between infantry and mounted divisions in Barj was very real and at times became a threat to the internal peace of that nation. The brawls between the better trained cavalry (generally inheriting the right to become an officer) and the recruited infantry were cursed in every town from Erm to Ishtam-Zhem, the capital. But Sojan was not concerned with this, he had an ally now, no need to run, he could stay and fight like a man.

"Looking for a fight, Red?" he said.

"Dying to be killed, why?" enquired Red, using an expression which was currently popular among fighting men.

"Because I have a feeling that we will be in one soon!"

"Good, I'll tell my men to be prepared."

"Thanks, I'll need some help, I think."

"Unusual for you to admit *that*!"

"Shut up, I'm coming down."

In the courtyard of the inn, Sojan told Red what he knew about Orfil and what had happened to him since he left the court of Hatnor to search for his ruler's son.

And as he finished, Orfil and a band of some twenty mounted men in seamen's clothes, rode into the courtyard. The captain's squad consisted of ten men. They were outnumbered almost two-to-one. The seamen had no lances but the cavalry had left their rifles, pistols and lances with their myats' saddles and other equipment. Now they were armed only with long *vilthors* and small battle-axes.

It took Orfil less than a second to take stock of the situation and with a curse, he bore down upon the group, yelling a blasphemous battle-shout so full of evil that it made Sojan's hair tingle. His men followed him. They were hardened sea-wolves. All of them by rights were fodder for the executioner's axe. Scarred, wild-eyed men in exotic clothes of many hues and lands. Black, green, white and red. From every nation on Zylor, they bore weapons which were equally varied: battle-axes, maces, pikes, hooked swords and broad-swords, vilthors and blades resembling scimitars. All were there, and many so strange they could not readily be identified as weapons.

Sojan blocked Orfil's lance thrust with his own long sword and unslung his shield from his back in a hurry. But not soon enough, for Orfil's lance stabbed again and flung the mercenary backward against a wall. Luckily, the lance tip broke on Sojan's breastplate and Orfil swore to his dark gods as he wheeled his steed about and attempted to cut at Sojan with his broadsword. But now Sojan stumbled to his feet again, back pressed to the wall, shield up and blade screaming as he cut past Orfil's guard.

But Orfil was swept away as the fight eddied back and forth across the court-yard. There, a blue-green man of Poltoon went down with a lancer on top of him, stabbing again and again. Near him a huge red man, bearded, with one of his small horns broken and splintered, staggered towards his tethered steed spitting blood from a punctured lung—he never made the myat. A lancer was crushed by sheer weight of numbers as four howling, long-haired black men from Shortani bore him down and almost tore him to pieces.

Everywhere was chaos and Sojan hardly knew who it was he fought, there were so many of them. Finally he singled out another red giant who whirled a shrieking twin-bladed axe around his head and laughed through his black beard all the time. He bled from a flesh wound on his left arm and his face streamed blood from a superficial sword cut, but he never seemed to tire. Sojan caught a blow of the axe on his shield which dented it so much that it almost broke his arm. Discarding the shield he skipped nimbly away from the arc of blood-stained steel, ducked beneath it and ripped upwards with a thrust that caught the giant in the throat and threw him groaning to the cobbles before Sojan lost sight of him as a fresh wave of sea-spoilers pushed towards him.

The war-shout of his people was upon Sojan's lips and it rose above the screams and curses of the men, spurred Red and his men on to greater feats of magnificent swordsmanship until the sailors were driven back. Slowly, very slowly, they gave ground and just as victory seemed in the hands of Sojan and his allies, from the courtyard walls dropped scores of well-armoured axemen.

It was impossible to defend themselves against this sudden onslaught and the last thing Sojan heard as an axe haft fell on his helmet and blackness followed blinding light was:

"Take them alive. They will suffer more tonight!"

Chapter Fourteen

Sojan at Sea!

Sojan awoke with a piercing pain in his head which quickly disappeared. Looking about him, he found that he was lying on a comfortable couch in a well-furnished room which seemed to have an indefinable "something" wrong with it.

Then he realised what it was. Every article of furniture was clamped to the floor and the windows were small square openings in the walls, just below eye-level.

He was in a ship's cabin! Obviously one of the ships in the harbour. That was why the men who had attacked him had worn seafaring garb. Which ship though? He didn't know. Doubtless he would find out soon enough. Could it be the purple ship of death which swayed at anchor in Minifjar Harbour? It was likely. This business was mysterious enough for anything.

He walked over to the porthole and looked out. No, the purple ship could be seen from there. Then what ship was this?

He went back to the couch after trying the door which he found locked as he had expected.

He waited an hour—a long hour—until the bar on the door was lifted with a creak and the door swung open.

To his surprise, he found himself staring into the face of Parijh, the Uffjirian who said:

"Welcome aboard the *Sea Crinja*, my friend!"

But the man who stood behind Parijh caught the adventurer's attention most of all. It was his War King's son, Nornos Rique of Hatnor!

"Shiltain!" swore Sojan when he saw him. "What—?"

"Explanation later, Sojan, we were lucky to rescue you. Right now you're not very welcome. My fault, I suppose, for giving no hint that I would be going—but there was no time."

"But how did I get out of Orfil's hands?"

"It's a long story—too long to relate here. Meanwhile, we sail for the Sea of Demons!"

"What?"

"We're sailing dangerous waters, Sojan, for we play a dangerous game in which the whole planet is at stake. Do you want to come on deck?"

"Thanks."

The three men climbed the long ladders to the poop deck. Nornos Rique shouted orders as sails were set and men moved to their oars. All the men were well-built fighting men.

Sojan looked back to where the huge purple galley swayed at anchor like a dead ship becalmed in the terrible weed jungle of the Black Ocean. She gave no signs of following and soon the sails were billowing, oars creaked in unison and they were on the open water, bound for the mysterious Sea of Demons.

Like all ships, there was continual movement aboard. Men scurrying up and down the rigging, guns oiled and cleaned, the shouts of the mate giving orders.

The ship comprised three decks. Two raised fore and aft and a middle deck which was little more than a raised platform over the oarsmen's pits on port and starboard. In the centre of this deck there was another slightly raised platform measuring about thirty feet upon which was the single mast. At the base of this mast a drummer sat beating out a steady rhythm which was followed by the oars who took their timing from the drum.

On this platform, also, was the heavy artillery and something which Sojan had never seen before—harpoon guns, twelve of them, five aside and another two fore and aft.

It was obvious that peaceful trading with the tribes along the Shortani coast was not entirely the object of this particular voyage.

Suddenly, Sojan remembered his comrades.

"What happened to my friends?" he asked.

"They're all aboard the *Purple Arrow*, that cursed ship of death you saw in Minifjar Harbour," answered Rique. "You see, Sojan, we only had time to free you before we were discovered. My men and I swam across and boarded her silently last night. We finally found you and, judging by your snores, you were in a drugged sleep. There were four others with you but they were so much dead weight that we could only take you and secretly leave knives in their shirts with which to aid themselves if they have the chance. I'm sorry, Sojan, but it is too late to go back for them now even if it were practical."

"You are right, of course, Rique," answered Sojan, "but I would that I could help them!"

Now the tall *Sea Crinja* was in open waters, beyond sight of land. Bound for the terrible Sea of Demons where few ships ever sailed—and returned. And, in the days they sailed towards their destination, Sojan pieced together the ominous tale of the Old Ones and how the Priests of Rhan sought to conquer Zylor with their evil aid.

It seemed that word of the plot was brought to Uffjir first. This country lies due North of Rhan on the Shortani coast and is generally better informed about the Island of Mystery as it is sometimes called than is the rest of Zylor.

The Uffjirian monarch, King Ashniophil, had feared to make public the news as it would very likely force the Rhanian Priesthood into swifter action. Instead, he had sent a messenger to enlist Nornos Rique's aid as, if the worst ever happened, Hatnor was the most powerful country on the whole planet. Nornos Rique, naturally, had not thought it wise to notify his father at once as he knew the other's aptitude to make quick, but sometimes hasty decisions and this is what Uffjir was trying to prevent.

Unfortunately, at the time of the messenger's coming, the Princess Sherlerna had been with Rique and had overheard everything. She threatened to betray Nornos Rique to the Rhanians unless he paid her a fabulous amount of money.

Knowing that even when she had the money, she would be dangerous, Rique decided to go into hiding. He had to kidnap the girl and ride for Rhan in an effort to come to terms with the rulers or, if this failed, destroy or capture their leaders and their strange unhuman allies.

After several detours, he finally reached Minifjar but not before the princess had escaped and fled to Orfil who had promptly ridden for Minifjar himself where a ship (one of the purple fleet of the Rhanian Theocracy—or Priest Rulers) awaited him in case just such an emergency as this should occur. The mercenary's questions had aroused his interest when he had overheard them at the inn and he had taken Sojan prisoner. Only to be foiled by the Uffjirian messenger who was acting as rear-guard for Nornos Rique.

The rest Sojan knew.

Now it was a race to get to Rhan first.

Chapter Fifteen
The Sea of Demons

It was a race to get to Rhan first. The *Purple Arrow* would take the comparatively safe way there by sailing down the coast of Poltoon until quieter waves were reached (namely the Poltoonian Ocean) and back to Rhan via these waters.

The *Crinja*, however, would attempt to sail through the Demon Sea, cutting off a considerable part of the distance. They knew little of what they had to fight against. The *Arrow* did not know of their plan and was relying on the greater speed to catch the *Crinja* and either destroy her or beat her to Rhan and have her destroyed there. If the *Crinja* could reach Rhan first, she would have several days' start and the fate of the world would be decided in those days. Why the *Arrow* had sailed later, they knew not, but guessed that they were waiting for someone.

It was a day's sail until they would reach the Demon Sea and in that time, Sojan got to know his companions better.

Parijh, the Uffjirian, proved to be a humorous man. Cheerful in the face of every danger they had had to meet. When necessary, he was an excellent swordsman but preferred to keep out of what he called "unnecessary brawling." This often gained him a reputation of cowardliness but, as he said, it was an asset rather than otherwise, for what better opponent is there than the one who underestimates you?

Sojan had to agree with this statement and a strong feeling of comradeship and mutual respect grew between them as they sailed ever nearer to the Sea of Demons.

Nornos Rique himself captained the *Crinja*. Rique was a tall man with a face that, though not handsome, had a dependable and rock-hard ruggedness and eyes of steel grey.

The mate was, as is usual on Zylorian naval craft, either privateer or part of an authorised Navy, a cavalry captain by the name of Andel of Riss who, although inclined to make independent decisions without consulting anyone first, was a good man in any kind of fight, and worth four of any one in the crew, who were all fine hands and who admired him and respected him as only seamen can respect a man. They would also prove this in a fight with man or the elements.

The custom of placing cavalry men as seconds-in-command of ships is not as strange as it seems and the custom evolved thus:

At one time in the not-so-ancient history of Zylor a strong rivalry developed between seamen and landsmen. It became so bad that if a war came, the land forces could never rely on the naval forces—and vice versa.

It was the idea of assigning landsmen to learn the ways of the sea and naval officers to get to know the cavalry and infantry that saved them from chaos, and nowadays the two forces worked together in perfect harmony.

Later, on the evening of the third day out of Minifjar they were sailing a sea which was similar to any other sea but which, according to the maps, was the feared Sea of Demons.

"We'd better anchor here and sail on at daybreak," Nornos Rique decided, and he gave the order to drop anchor. The anchor chain rattled down for several minutes before stopping with a jarring clank.

"Water's too deep, sir! Anchor won't take!" yelled Andel.

"Then we daren't drift. Ship oars and set sail on your course."

"Yes, sir!"

Night fell bringing an atmosphere of decay and death which could almost be smelled or touched. But apart from this, nothing happened save a faint scraping from time to time along the side of the boat which was attributed to some heavy sea-weed or a piece of drift wood.

The twin suns rose and the green dawn came, sending shadows and streamers of cloud scurrying over the horizon. The sea was green and shone like dark jade with some of jade's intangible qualities.

Oars smashed into it, ploughing it in bright foam-flecked furrows, and the monotonous beat of the drum began.

Sojan and his comrades ate breakfast in an atmosphere of gloom.

"It's this confounded sea!" suddenly roared Andel, rising from his chair and crashing his fist into his open palm. "Vit! By the time this voyage is over, there'll be men's lives lost and most likely we'll all be on the bottom!"

"Calm down, Andel, we'll deal with any danger when we get to it," Nornos Rique said.

Andel grunted sullenly and subsided.

Two depressed hours followed until:

"Vit take us!"

This oath was followed by a piercing scream which tailed off into a choking gasp.

The four men rushed on deck. Most of the crew were at the starboard rail, staring downwards to where red foam was flecked with white.

"Turn back, sir, you must turn back!" One hysterical seaman turned from the rail and rushed towards Nornos Rique screaming.

"Calm down, and tell me what happened!"

Fear was in the man's eyes. A terrible fear bordering on madness. He babbled out his tale.

"A—a *thing*, sir—it crept up on Mitesh and—oh, sir—it grabbed him by the throat and jumped overboard!"

"Is that all?"

"It's enough, sir!" murmured another of the men.

"What did this 'thing' look like? Who saw it clearly?"

"I did, sir."

It was the man who had commented a second before.

"Well?"

"It was a kind of green and brown. Scaly. By Vit, sir, it looked as a man might look if his mother had been a fish!"

"You mean this animal was—human?"

"Not *human*, sir. But it had a man's body sure enough. And his face was pointed, like, sir. And his *eyes*—his eyes were green, like the rest of him, and seemed to rot you when he stared at you!"

"All right. Thank you. Take this man below and give him something to drink!"

"Yes sir. Do we turn back?"

"No! You all knew there was danger!"

"Danger, yes sir, but not from—from *devils*!"

"Get below—we sail on!"

Back in their cabin, Sojan spoke.

"I've heard old folktales, Rique, about occurrences such as this one. Now I know why the ancients called this the 'Sea of Demons.'"

"Do you think they are organised in any way?"

"I've never heard of them being anything *but* in large numbers! If they're intelligent they'll almost certainly be organised in tribes of some kind."

"Perhaps this was a warning, then?"

"I think it might have been."

"We'd better set all guns in readiness. Those harpoons will come in useful. I had them mounted in case of meeting any of those large saurians that inhabit the Poltoonian Ocean. But it looks as if they'll be needed for a different 'game' now!"

The ship's oars began to creak again. But was the beat of the drum less sure? Were the oars a heartbeat slower? It seemed to the men standing on the poop deck that this was so.

Towards the middle of the day, the atmosphere of death grew and suddenly from the sea on four sides of the vessel the weird inhabitants of the Sea of Demons rose, squealing and hissing. Once more they attempted to board.

But this time the sailors were ready and the guns sent forth a steady stream of deadly missiles, driving the shrieking horde into the sea.

"They went quickly enough!" yelled Andel jubilantly.

"Too quickly. They'll be more wary next time and they'll be back at night for sure!"

And night did fall and with it strange sounds which rose from the water and chilled the blood of the men on board.

But again this time the crew were prepared and their searchlights stabbed the gloom, picking out the grotesque inhabitants of the Sea of Demons.

The crew moved forward, their yells mingling with the strange hissing cries of the sea-people. Sabres flashed in the searchlight glare and the blood of seamen and the man-like monsters mingled on the deck, making it difficult to get a footing.

The ship was a contrast of glaring light and total blackness. Men leaped from shadow into blinding glare or disappeared into murky darkness. Men's breath was steaming in the cold night air. Men's battle-cries pierced the shadows where light failed. And Sojan and his companions were in the thick of it, their swords lashing this way and that at their unhuman adversaries. Sojan's war-cry spurred on the men and slowly, then swiftly, they pushed them back and the body of the last monster to invade their ship crashed over the rail to splash into the murky waters below.

There was an audible sigh from the sweating men.

"We've pushed 'em back once, lads, and by Vit, we'll push them back from here to Rhan if needs be!" cried Sojan. With the thrill of victory still in their hearts, their pulses tingling with conquest, the men's voices rose in assent.

A brief count found two sailors suffering from wounds where the talons of the sea-people had ripped them, while three more men were missing, obviously dragged down by the sea-people.

"We should reach Rhan in a day," said Nornos Rique.

"Or the bottom," broke in Andel gloomily.

But the monotonous day ahead was broken only by the screaming of sea-birds as they passed the outlying islands of The Immortal Theocracy of Rhan as it was called. This "immortal theocracy" was now little more than Rhan itself and a group of four islands inhabited mainly by primitive tribes, most of whom dwelt in the interior, anyway, and had probably never heard of Rhan.

As they neared Rhan, Sojan felt misgivings. Would they succeed in carrying out their plan? Or would their perilous journey be in vain?

It was with these odd questions in his mind that he followed his friends down the gangplank and through a series of narrow lanes to a private house owned by a society known to those few holding positions of trust in the Hatnorian Empire as the "Friends of Hatnor." These "friends" were generally native Hatnorians carrying forged or, as in some cases, real papers giving false names as well as assumed nationalities.

Three long knocks and two short ones three times repeated gained them admission.

As they walked along the narrow corridor to the main living room they began to feel just a little more secure, even though they were deep in the heart of Jhambeelo, the enemy's city.

But as the door swung open and friendly light flooded into the dark corridor they were taken aback!

"Hello, Sojan," grinned Red. "I don't think I've met your friends?"

"By Vit! Red, how did you get here before us?" cried Sojan.

"Simple. I flew!"

"What? No airship could make the distance."

"You're quite right. I didn't come by airship. Banjar, here, brought me!"

For the first time the comrades noticed what appeared to be a hunchbacked, rather tall, man with piercing blue eyes and aquiline features. Golden-haired, he possessed a complexion of a darker gold. Sojan was astonished. Could this be one of the fabled Golden Men of Zylor?

"To snap the bow in half," said Red, using a term common on Zylor which means roughly—"To cut a long story short," "Jik, Wanwif, Selwoon and myself succeeded in staving a rather large hole in the bottom of the *Purple Arrow*. Naturally enough, it was not long before we were beginning to regret this as water was rising steadily in the hold. Then, as we were all good swimmers, I thought that the only way to escape drowning would be to enlarge the hole and get out that way. So in turns we widened the hole and, with a great deal of difficulty, pulled ourselves under the keel of the boat and up into the open water. We lost Wanwif, I'm sorry to say. He didn't make it.

"Well, after that we found that we would have been better off drowning in the ship as there was no sight of land. I learned afterwards that we were in the Black Ocean and this didn't help as the stories I've heard of the Black Ocean are anything but cheerful. But believe it or not, after swimming in a Westerly direction for an hour or so, we were picked up by a little fishing vessel, oared only, manned by some natives of Yoomik which is the largest of the Rhanian group next to Rhan itself.

"The people looked after us but soon we got weary of hanging around their village and decided that an exploratory trip into the interior of the island would be the only thing to break the monotony. We trekked for several days until coming upon the village of Banjar's people—the Ascri.

"The Ascri at one time were enslaved by the Rhanian Priesthood and still bear a grievance against them. It was Banjar who, when he had heard that I believed you were going to Rhan, suggested that he fly me there. We landed at night and made our way to Rhan. Banjar's people are advanced in many of the crafts and sciences and they have an asset which helps them tremendously. Show Sojan and his friends your asset, Banjar!"

Banjar grinned and stood up. Unfolding a pair of huge wings.

"My people, I believe, are descended from the ancient winged mammals who used to live on Zylor. Just an off-shoot of evolution, I suppose. But one which has proved of great help to my folk who can travel great distances at great speeds and although we are few in number, we can elude any enemies by leaving the ground and escaping that way. As my friend says, 'It is a great asset'!"

Formal introductions were made and food eaten but when this was finished Sojan spoke to Red.

"Have you managed to find out anything which might prove useful to us, Red?"

"I have indeed, my friend, I have found out something which, with your courage and skill and a great deal of luck, will save the world from chaos!"

Chapter Sixteen
Prisoners in Stone

Red's plan was simple enough. Members of the secret society of the "Friends of Hatnor" had found an ancient plan of the Great Temple which was both chief place of worship and the centre of the Priesthood's rule in Rhan. There were three tunnels leading into it. Old sewers, long since disused. Two were cul-de-sacs, having been walled up. But in the last, the walling had been a hasty job and the bricks used to seal it had collapsed. However, these tunnels were still guarded at the other end. Some said by Palace Guards—but others said simply that they were guarded by "something." Even if the foe was human it would take an incredibly brave man to venture the rotting tunnels.

"Why not an army?" asked Andel. "Surely a great many men would be safer than one?"

"Safer, yes, but certainly not so secret. Every action we make must not be detected by the Priesthood—otherwise we are lost. We can only make a very wild guess at what power these Old Ones wield and it is our aim to stop them using it—not bring it down upon our heads—and the rest of the world's heads, also."

"I see," said Parijh, "then let me be the one to go. I offer not out of heroics—which are extremely bad taste in any case—but I am more accustomed to stealth than these sword-swinging barbarians with me." He grinned.

"Ho! So that's what we are, are we?" roared Andel. "I'll have you know . . ."

But the comrades would never hear the rest of Andel's forthcoming witticism for Red broke in: "Be a bit quieter, Andel, or you'll have the whole of the Rhanian Soldiery on our heads!"

"Sorry," said Andel.

"No," continued Red, "I think Sojan should go. He is better for the job than anyone else. He has barbarian training, he is cat-footed, lynx-eyed and can hear a sword sing in its scabbard a mile away. I think he will succeed in getting through more than any other man in our company!"

"Then it will be I, that's settled," said Sojan with satisfaction. "When and where do I start?"

"You start now, and I will lead you to the entrance of the tunnel. I suggest that you carry a rifle, an axe, your shield and your long sword. Half-armour would be advisable, also."

"Then I shall take your advice." Sojan laughed and proceeded to don borrowed half-armour. This consisted of greaves for his limbs, a breastplate and helmet.

Then he was ready and prepared to follow Red down winding backstreets to a small turning near the Great Temple. Here, Red lifted a rusted cover to reveal an equally rusted ladder leading down into darkness.

"Good luck!" was all he said as Sojan slipped down into the gloom and sought about for hand- and foot-holds on the age-worn rail. Then the lid was replaced and Sojan found himself in utter darkness.

Down he fumbled, sometimes missing footing where one of the metal bars had rusted away, once nearly falling when his groping hand instead of closing on solid metal closed on damp air. But at last he was on the uneven floor of the disused sewer, peering into the gloom. He followed the wall along for what seemed an age, stumbling over fallen bricks and refuse. At last he sensed an obstruction ahead and he unsheathed his sword and felt the reassuring butt of his heavy pistol in his hand. On he went, past the fallen wall until—suddenly—there was no more tunnel. Or so it seemed. His right hand, which had been groping along the wall, touched nothing. But after the first brief shock he grinned to himself. This was the turn of the tunnel. Soon he would meet the Guardians.

And meet them he did for, with a soul-shaking shriek, two of the mysterious guardians were upon him. Huge reptilian things, red-eyed and red-mouthed with teeth reaching a foot long and razor sharp.

Sojan, shocked by their sudden attack, took a step backwards, hitched his rifle to his shoulder and fired straight into the mouth of the foremost beast. It shrieked again but still came on. Hastily he dropped the rifle and replaced it with his heavy axe and long sword. But before the beast reached him it had stumbled and fallen with crumpling forelegs, writhing in a fit of agony which ended with one abrupt shudder of death.

The other monster was checked for a moment, sniffed the corpse of its companion and then voiced another spine-chilling shriek which was half hiss and half human cry. Sojan met it with sword lashing and axe whining through the air about his head. Back went the monster but it returned in an instant, clutching at Sojan with its claws which almost resembled human hands—though hands with six-inch steel talons on the ends of each finger. Sojan stumbled backwards, his axe cutting and hacking at the hideous thing, his sword slashing into its throat again and again until at last it was down in a death agony that lasted minutes.

Pausing to wipe his weapons clean of blood and to pick up his rifle, Sojan moved on down the tunnel, feeling a little more cheerful now that he knew his foe and had conquered it.

And, abruptly, he was at the end of the tunnel and a similar steel ladder, in better condition, leading upwards. Warily he clambered up. Rifle, axe and shield strapped across his broad back and his sword firmly clenched in his teeth.

There was a metal cover here, too, and he lifted it cautiously to be blinded for a moment by the sudden gleam. He had been so long in darkness and the semi-darkness of the tunnel that he blinked hard for several seconds until his eyes became accustomed to the light.

Silently he eased his body through the narrow hole and just as softly replaced the cover. He was in a lighted corridor with torches on either side. The corridor was short and had a door at each end. Which door? He decided immediately to take the door leading farthest away from the tunnel. At least he would be a little deeper into the Temple and nearer the Inner Room in the centre which housed the Old Ones.

Gradually he pushed the door until it swung open. He thanked the Gods of Light that they had not been locked.

Down another corridor he sped, cat-footed as ever, wary hands on sword and rifle, his armour glinting in the torch-light and his shadow looming black and huge on the wall.

Most of the priests would be at rest, he knew, but it was equally certain that guards would be posted at strategic points and absolute caution was necessary. He had a rough plan of the Temple printed in his mind but the maze of corridors which he was following and which ran deeper and deeper into the heart of the Temple were complicated and were probably of more recent origin for the map had been very old.

But cautious as he knew he must be he was certainly not slow. For every heartbeat counted. He had to reach the chamber of the Old Ones somehow and discover who—or what—they were and what their motives were for allying themselves with the evil Priesthood of Rhan.

The murmurs of voices. The laughs of men. The clank of sword-scabbard against armour. At last, a guarded entrance. Was he near the strange sanctuary of the Old Ones?

The men's backs were to him. This was not the time for heroics, for a cry would mean discovery; and discovery he must avoid. He raised his rifle and brought it down on the head of one guard while with his other hand he chopped at the back of the other man's neck. They both collapsed without a murmur. Looking up and down the intersecting corridor to make sure he had not been seen, he grabbed the two bodies by their loose clothing and pulled them back into the shadows. No time to hide them. And no time to hide himself. For the clank of steel-shod feet resounded down the corridor. He hugged the wall and prayed to his ancient gods that he would not be discovered.

Sojan heard the steps come nearer and nearer, and then, miraculously, fade away again. Risking discovery, he peered round the wall and saw another passageway. Down it strode two guards of the infamous High Priests of Rhan, the rulers of the place. Cat-footed as usual, he followed them. This corridor was not very well lighted but, unlike the others, it had doors set in the walls.

Sojan hoped that one of these would not open.

Suddenly the priest stopped.

"Wait here," Sojan heard him say. No time to think, now, he must act. Into the nearest apartment and pray to Vit that it was unoccupied.

Luck! The rooms were empty. These, Sojan could see, were the apartments of the High Priests. No monkish sparsity of furniture here. The rooms were lavishly furnished and decorated. Grinning, Sojan bounced down onto the bed and breathed a prayer of relief. Then he was up again and taking in his surroundings. On one wall hung several of the long flowing robes which the High Priests wore.

One of the customs of these men was to go veiled—to give them a little more security from the assassin as well as an air of mystery, Sojan guessed. As individuals they could also slip from the Temple and mingle with the people without fear of being recognised. This was one of the reasons why the people of Rhan were so easily kept in subjection by the evil Priest Rulers.

But there was a chance, though Sojan knew it was a slim one, that he could don one of these robes and enter the Inner Chamber and meet the mysterious Old Ones face to face.

Quickly he slipped into the robe, stuffing all but his sword and pistol under a nearby couch and hoping that they would not be discovered. The weapons he kept were well hidden by the folds of the robe and he could keep his armour on.

Out now, and down the passage, past the lounging soldiers who sprang to attention and saluted him with their untypical Rhanian salute—clenched fists against temples and a short bow from the waist.

Sojan acknowledged the salute by a curt nod of his head. The veil hid his features entirely, and if he was unmasked by some mishap, only the other High Priests would know whether he was a fraud or not. So, comparatively safe, Sojan moved along the corridor towards the huge, metal-studded door which was the portal to the Inner Chamber.

It was unlocked, and the guards on each side of it stood away respectfully as Sojan opened it.

At first he could see nothing, the room was lit by one torch which cast shadows everywhere. Then, from the corner of the large chamber, a voice spoke. It was a voice of infinite weariness, full of lost hope and the knowledge of an eternity of despair.

"Why trouble us again, Priest? In the past we did your bidding willingly, not knowing to what evil uses you put our power. Then we were locked away here. You threaten us with destruction and tempt us with promises of freedom. What are we to believe?"

Sojan realised that instead of the evil forces he had expected, here were prisoners; slaves rather than allies of the Priesthood.

"I'm no priest," he said, "if I knew who you were I might help you even!"

"Is this another trick, Priest?" murmured the voice, although this time there was a little hope in it.

"No trick. I'm the sworn enemy of the Priesthood of Rhan. I represent the rest of Zylor, who have no wish to become enslaved by the Rhanians and their horrible 'religion.' Yet rumour has it that you are allied with them." He squinted into the darkness. "Who or what are you?"

"He holds us in his power. We were forced to do his bidding. We are the first inhabitants of Zylor. We lived here before ever the shining ships of humanity sprang from distant worlds in a desperate attempt to reach other habitable planets. They thought that the end of their world had come. As it happened their world did not die, but it was too late then, they had taken all their knowledge out into space with them, and in the long passage across the galaxies much of their knowledge perished, for the journey took centuries to complete.

"By the time the new generations reached this planet, their ancestors had died and Man had to start again, almost from the beginning. These men, who called themselves 'Lemurians,' lived peacefully with us for many hundreds of years and we helped them as much as possible, for we are a very ancient race and had more knowledge than even the ancestors of the Lemurians, although of a different kind—for while Man concentrated on improving his material condition, we concentrated on improving our minds and could control mighty elements with our wills. Eventually the Lemurians became frightened of us and sent us away (there were only a few of us living in far-flung settlements then; now we are even fewer)."

"But how did you become the slaves of these priests?" asked Sojan. "What happened?"

"Although there were many men who feared us and called us Things of Evil and similar names, there were others who began to worship us for our powers, calling us gods and setting up altars and Temples to us.

"Just as some men are foolish and susceptible to flattery, so some of our number were equally foolish and began to think that perhaps they *were* gods after all. They dwelt in the Temples and had sacrifices made to them and took part in meaningless rituals. The priests soon found their weaknesses, however, and decided that they could rule the people if they frightened them by telling them of the wrath of the gods, the end of the world, the good of their own particular branch of religion and the evil of the others. Divide and Rule was their principle and that was how we and the rest of the humans were controlled. By deviously setting one cult against another they succeeded in capturing us and imprisoning us." There came a long, sad pause, then:

"I was one of those foolish ones . . . Our contemporaries have long since left this planet in search of another, uninhabited by Man. It has become clear to us that with Man we cannot live in peace, at least not with freedom.

"You may have read in your history scrolls of the mighty Theocracy which dominated the world at one time. Rhan is now all that is left of the Theocracy—a remnant of a great and terrible nation!

"A century or more ago the people rose against their oppressors, country by country, until the evil Priesthood was driven back, further and further, to seek refuge on this island, the original capital of the old Imperial Theocracy. It was here that the cult, based on worship of us, was spawned and, if you can help us, it is here that it will die. Otherwise a new Age of Winter shall cover the world in a cloak of death! They know how to torture us. They will make us do these things, even though now we think we can resist. And this time, too, will bring that false promise of freedom. And this time, too, will come our grasping for false hope, and this time, too, will come betrayal. Then will come a short period of rest until we are ready to be tortured again. Until, eventually, we succumb and do their work without the threat of torture or the promise of freedom but only so that we shall not have to fear either!

"This time they have sworn to keep their promise to us of freedom, O, Man! Freedom after thousands of decades. Freedom after eons of despair. We would follow our brothers, we would travel the infinite depths of Space and Time were we once released. We would see Suns and Planets, green things. Seas and Plains. For us these things are worth more than life. We are *of* them more than Man—for we, like the planets and stars, and the grass that grows forever, are almost immortal. We have no bodies, as Man knows bodies, no senses as Man interprets senses—we are Minds. You can see that the temptation is great! We were not strong-willed to begin with. We were flattered by Man's petty ceremonies. Now that he offers us Light and Freedom again. He lies and we all know we have no real choice but we *must* accept." A long pause and then, tinged with just a little real hope:

"Unless there is another way."

"There may be another way," Sojan said. "If you will but tell me *how* you are imprisoned, perhaps I can release you!"

"There are certain minerals, rare and almost unknown, which have the properties of lead compared to radium. Radium cannot harm or pass through lead. Similarly, although we can pass through most minerals and life forms, we are imprisoned if we enter a certain precious stone. We can enter it, but by some strange trick of nature, our beings cannot pass back through it. Thus we were enticed centuries ago, into these blocks of *ermtri* stone. The only way in which we can escape is by someone outside boring shafts into the blocks and thus cutting channels through which we can pass.

"Do you understand?"

Dimly Sojan did understand, though his brain was shaken by the effort of trying to imagine beings so utterly alien to Man, yet in some ways akin to him. For the first time in his adult life his hand trembled as he picked up the torch and cast its light towards the centre of the hall.

There on an altar, covered by a crimson cloth, rested five large blocks of some dark, cloudy blue substance.

The substance was not hard in the way a diamond is hard. It had a softness to it and resembled blue jade of the purest quality. Yet it was not jade. It sparkled like diamonds. Even in legends, it was a stone of which Sojan, who had travelled across almost the whole of his planet, had never seen nor heard.

"I understand," he said, "but what tool will cut it?"

"Steel, sharp steel will bore into it. Have you steel?"

"Yes."

"You seem surprised."

"Only that so much time has passed since the time your people knew only stone and bone for tools . . ."

"Will it hurt you?"

"No, it will leave no impression."

"If I succeed in freeing you will you promise to help us?"

"We give you our word. We have told you how our word cannot easily be broken."

"Then I will do what I can."

Wiping sweat from his forehead and hands, Sojan moved towards the blocks. He drew his sword and clambered up onto the altar. If the sword broke and the guards came in he would be left with his favoured weapon snapped into slivers!

Placing the sharp point of his blade on top of the first block, he turned it round and round. Feeling it suddenly bite deeper into the strange substance. He became aware of a weird tingling which seemed to flow up his sword and into his body. He could not define it but it was not unpleasant. Suddenly there was a dazzling burst of green-and-orange brightness and something seemed to flow from the hole that he had bored, flow out and upwards, lighting the room. He heard no words, but in his mind there was a great sense of joy—of thanks. Then, one by one he took the point of his sword to the other blocks and watched as they broke under the influence of the same strange power. And then came a crackling force of incandescence as the green and orange brightness flowed from them.

Slowly these flames took on a slightly more solid shape, until Sojan could make out eyes and circular bodies. It came to him that by effort of will alone these creatures could form themselves into any shape they desired. These, then, were the Old Ones. Perhaps in a million, million years, Man too would have succeeded in being able to form the atoms of his body into whatever shape he chose. Perhaps, with the goal defined, sooner. Perhaps, these beings once were Men? That would explain the strange kinship Sojan felt for them. A kinship which his Lemurian ancestors no doubt felt also, before their witnessing of such alien powers changed their finer feelings into those of fear and hate and they learned how to imprison these advanced beings in that strange blue stone.

"Before you leave," Sojan begged, "I crave one request as a price for your release."

"Anything! But you must instruct us. We cannot act without your directions."

"Then when I have left this building and my friends and I are safely at sea, destroy this terrible place so that the power of the priests will be shattered for all time and such an evil can never rise again!"

"Gladly we grant you this. We will wait here until you are at sea. But tread carefully, we cannot help you to escape and the priests have power we cannot control any more than can you."

Thanking them, Sojan turned about and left, sword in hand. But in his exultation he had forgotten the soldiers outside and they stared in amazement at his naked blade and the sweat on his face. This did not seem to them to be any kind of High Priest with whom they were familiar!"

Taking quick stock of the situation, Sojan spoke to them.

"I—I had a little difficulty with one of the bolts on the interior," he lied, "I had to use this sword to loosen it . . ."

With a puzzled look, the men bowed and saluted, but there was doubt in their eyes.

"A priest would not go unveiled for anything," he heard one of them murmur as he entered the room which he had left previously. "He doesn't seem a priest to me! Here you, stop a minute!"

But Sojan had quickly drawn the bolt to give him at least a little time and was hastily donning his weapons again. The men began to bang on the door and more men came to see what the noise was about.

"That's no priest," he heard someone say. "The High Priest Thoro is conducting the Ceremony of Death in the Outer Temple! He won't be back for hours!"

"Batter down the door you fools," came a voice that was obviously that of one in authority, probably another High Priest.

Anxiously, Sojan looked for a second exit. There was only a curtained window.

He parted the curtain, and looked outside. It was still dark. He looked down. A courtyard scarcely ten feet below. *With luck,* he thought, *I can jump down there and escape as best I can.* He put a foot on the ledge and swung himself over, dropping lightly to the grass of the courtyard. In the centre of the courtyard a fountain splashed quietly—a scene of peace and solitude. But not for long. He saw a face at the window he had so recently quit.

"He's down there," one of the soldiers shouted.

Sojan ducked into the nearest doorway, opposite the room he had left. He ran down a short, dark corridor and up a flight of steps. No sign of pursuit yet. Panting heavily he ran in the direction he knew an exit to be. It would be guarded now, he knew, for the whole Temple was by this time alert. And so it was. With his usual good luck, Sojan had succeeded in making the exit unchallenged. But there would be no such luck here, with five huge soldiers coming at him.

Chapter Seventeen
The Unlucky Ones

Again Sojan had no time for heroics. His pistol came up and two of his would-be killers went down. The other three were on him now and his sword cut a gleaming arc about his head. His battle-axe shrieked as if for blood as he carried the attack towards his foes instead of they to him. Nonplussed for a second, they fell back.

That falling back was for them death! Now Sojan had some kind of advantage and he made full use of it as he drove blow after blow, thrust after thrust into the men.

Bleeding himself from several wounds, Sojan came on, down went one man, then another. Now the last warrior, fighting with desperation, hacked and parried, and sought an opening in Sojan's amazing guard.

None came, the man sought advantage too often, became desperate and lunged forward—and almost pinioned himself on Sojan's blade. Back he tried to leap, clumsily. A perfect target for a whistling, battered axe to bury itself in helmet and brain.

Leaving his axe where it had come to rest, Sojan fled the Temple. His heart pounding, he finally reached the house where his friends waited.

"Come," he cried, "I'm successful—but we must make the ship immediately, all of us, else we all die. I don't know what they intend to do."

His companions realised that there was no time for an explanation and followed him wordlessly.

A frantic race for the docks. One brief skirmish with a City Patrol. And then they were on board. Up anchor, out oars, cast-off.

And as the ship sped from the harbour they looked back.

There came a blinding flash and then a deep, rolling roar as the great temple erupted in a sudden burst of flame. Then, as they peered at the city, there was blackness again. The temple was not burning—there was no temple now

to burn. It was being *dissolved*! Its substance dissipated like some kind of miasma, keeping its shape but growing larger and larger!

Then, as they watched, Sojan and his friends saw five streaks of blue-and-orange flame rise out of the heaving miasma which seemed to strive with its own intelligence to keep its shape. The five blazing streaks shot skyward and rocketed upwards and outwards—towards the stars! As they left the miasma began to lose any semblance of shape. Whatever mind had controlled it now failed. And Sojan knew that the priest-kings of Zylor no longer ruled Rhan—or any other place on the planet. With one last convulsion, the miasma roared, was silent and then vanished. For a moment it seemed the sea boiled before it, too, grew still.

And Sojan sighed, sheathing his battered blade, certain now that the Old Ones had kept their word.

"What was that?" gasped Nornos Rique rubbing his eyes on his sleeve and staring again at a scene which had grown suddenly peaceful.

"The Old Ones," smiled Sojan. "I'll tell you a tale which you may not believe. But it is a tale which has taught me much—as well as giving me a valuable history lesson!"

The voyage back was not a boring one for Sojan's companions as they listened to his strange story.

But what of the Purple Galley you ask, what of Orfil and the princess who betrayed Rique? That, readers, is a story which is short and sad. They, too, attempted to sail through the Sea of Demons in pursuit of Sojan and his companions.

But they were not so lucky.

Chapter Eighteen
The Plain of Mystery

The wind tore at the rigging of the tiny air-cruiser as it pushed bravely into the howling storm.

Four men clung to the deck rails whilst a fifth strove to steer the tossing gondola.

"Keep her headed North!" yelled Nornos Rique to Sojan.

"At this rate we'll be tossed on to Shortani unless the wind shifts!" Sojan yelled back.

Parijh the Shortanian grimaced.

"I've been meaning to go home for some time!" he called.

"You'll be home for your own funeral unless someone gives me a hand with this wheel!" cried Sojan.

Sojan, Nornos Rique, Parijh, Andel and Red, the five men who had saved their planet of Zylor from the evil Priest Rulers of Rhan some months ago, were returning to Hatnor after being the guests of honour at several banquets held to celebrate their triumph. Sojan, Rique, Andel and Red had been uncomfortable about the whole thing, only Parijh, always glad of the limelight, had enjoyed himself thoroughly.

The storm had sprung up quickly and they were now battling to keep the little dirigible into the wind which drove them steadily Southwards.

"Wouldn't it be better to land, Sojan?" Andel shouted.

"It would be, my friend, if we knew where we were. There's every likelihood of getting out of this trouble into something worse."

Suddenly there was a loud snapping sound and the wheel spun throwing Sojan off balance and onto the deck.

"What was that?" yelled Parijh.

"Steering's gone! We can't attempt to repair it in this weather. We'll just have to drift now!"

The five trooped down into the tiny cabin. Even there it was not warm and they were all depressed as they shivered in their cloaks and attempted to get some sleep.

Morning came and the storm had not abated. It lasted all through that day, the wind ripping into the ship and sending it further and further South.

"There's never been a storm like this in my memory!" Nornos Rique said.

The others agreed.

"Further North," said Andel, "they're quite frequent. Lasting for days, so they say."

"That's true," said Sojan.

By midnight of the next night the storm finished and the sky cleared of the clinging cloud. The stars, their constellations unfamiliar to Earth eyes, shone brightly and Sojan took a quick bearing.

"We're over Shortani all right," he muttered. "Well over. In fact, I believe we're near the interior of the continent."

Beneath them the scene was one of peace rather than that of death and mystery. Great plains, watered by winding rivers, lush forests, rearing mountains. The mountains seemed almost to take organic shape and loomed proudly over the landscape like gods looking down upon all they had created. Here and there herds of strange animals could be detected for the moons were very bright. They were drinking and did not look up as the airship glided silently above them.

In the morning Sojan and Andel set to work on repairing the broken steering-lines whilst the others looked down at the peaceful-seeming country beneath them.

All the time they worked they drifted further and further into the interior.

"If we drift much further, Sojan, we won't have sufficient fuel to get us out again. Remember, we only had enough for a short journey!" Parijh called up to him where he was working on the steering gear.

"Vit take us! I hadn't thought of that," cried Sojan. "But there's nothing we *can* do until this steering is fixed. Work as fast as possible Andel or we'll be stranded here!"

But repairing the steering wires and readjusting the rudder, especially sitting in the rigging with only a flimsy safety line between you and oblivion, isn't easy and it took Sojan and Andel several hours before the motors could be started up again.

"There's not enough fuel to make it back to Hatnor," Sojan said. "But if we're lucky we'll be able to get to civilised country on the Shortani coast!"

Now there was nothing they could do but hope and the men relaxed, watching the wonderful scenery beneath them and speculating on what kind of people, if any, lived there.

Red, who played a Zylorian instrument called a *rinfrit*—a kind of eight-stringed guitar, sang them a song, based on an old legend about these parts. The first verse went something like this:

"There's many a tale that has been told
Of Phek the traveller, strong and bold!
But the strangest one I've ever heard—
Is when he caught a shifla *bird."*

"What's a *shifla* bird?" enquired Andel curiously.

"Oh, it's supposed to be as big as an airship and looks like a great flying lizard."

His companions were amused at this story, and all but Sojan, who was looking over towards the West, laughed.

"Don't worry too much," said Sojan calmly, "but is that anything like your *shifla* bird?"

And there, rising slowly from the forest, was the largest animal any of the adventurers had ever seen. Earth men would call it a dragon if they saw it. Its great reptilian jaws were agape and its huge bat-wings drove it along at incredible speed.

"It seems there was some truth in the legend," muttered Red, licking dry lips and automatically fingering the pistol at his belt.

"There's always some truth in legends," said Sojan, "however incredible."

The thing was nearly upon them now, obviously taking their cruiser for some kind of rival. It was as big as their ship although its body was about half the size whilst its wings made up the rest of its bulk. It was a kind of blueish grey, its great mouth a gash of crimson whilst wicked eyes gleamed from their sockets making it look like some dark angel from the Zylorian "Halls of the Dead."

"Drop, Sojan, drop!" cried Nornos Rique as the men stood for a moment paralysed at the sight of something which they attributed only to the story scrolls of children.

Sojan whirled, rushed over to the controls and pushed several levers which opened valves in their gas-bag and caused the ship to lose height quickly.

The *shifla* swooped low overhead, barely missing them and causing them to duck automatically. Suddenly there came a cracking of branches, the ripping of fabric and the harsh snap of breaking wood. The ship had crashed into the forest. The men had been so busy trying to escape from the danger above them that they had forgotten the forest beneath them.

Sojan lifted his arm to shield his face and flung himself backwards as a branch speared through the ship like a fork through a fish and nearly impaled him at the same time. Eventually the noise stopped and, although the ship was swaying dangerously and threatening to fall apart any moment, sending the men to destruction, Sojan and his friends found that they had only bruises and scratches.

Sojan's barbarian instincts came to the rescue. Cat-footed as ever he clambered out of the wreckage onto the branch which had almost killed him.

"Quick!" he yelled, "after me!"

His friends followed quickly, Parijh panting with the effort. They moved cautiously along the branch and finally reached the trunk of the tree. Down they clambered, easily now for the tree was full of strong branches and it was only a drop of four or five feet to the ground.

Sojan looked up to where the airship dangled, its great gas-bag deflated, the gondola smashed and torn.

"When that falls," he said, "we'd better be some distance away for it's likely that the engine will explode."

"There go our supplies and rifles and ammunition," said Nornos Rique quietly.

"We've got our lives—for the present at least," Sojan reminded him. "We'll have to head steadily Northwards and hope that we don't strike a mountain range. If we are lucky we can follow a river across a plain. Several plains adjoin civilised or semi-civilised territories, don't they, Parijh?"

"One of them runs into my own country of Uffjir, Sojan, but there's one chance in fifty of making it!"

"Then it looks as if we'll have to chance it, Parijh," Sojan replied slowly, looking over towards the East. "But at least we shall be able to ride. There—see?"

They looked in the direction in which he was pointing. About a mile away, a herd of myats grazed placidly.

"Fan out—we should catch them easily if we organise properly," Sojan called.

Slowly, so that they would not disturb the animals, Sojan and his friends closed in on the myats. Once trapped they were easily caught for, unlike most animals used as beasts of burden, myats were bred originally for the sole purpose of carrying human beings so that even wild ones were relatively docile.

Within a day their animals were captured and trained. The friends cheered up considerably now that they were mounted. They made good time, for these myats were particularly strong and fast, and they took direction from the twin suns.

Some days later Sojan caught sight of a strange gleam in the distance—as if the sun was glancing off a highly polished surface.

"Head in that direction," he called to his companions. "There seems to be a building of some kind over there!"

And sure enough, it was a building. A great glistening domed construction, rising hundreds of feet into the air. It was built of a similar stone to marble. But what exactly was it? And why was it standing alone in such a savage wilderness? Perhaps what troubled the companions more than anything was whether there were men using it now? And were they friendly or otherwise?

"The only way to find out who or what is in there is to go nearer," said Andel.

"You're right," agreed Sojan. "Let's go!"

They forced their steeds into a quick trot, growing increasingly astonished, as they neared it, of the building's enormous proportions.

They dismounted silently and made their way cautiously to the wide entrance of the place, which was apparently unguarded.

There were windows high above them, probably set in rooms situated at different levels in the building. Part of the roof was flat but most of it rose in the magnificent dome they had first seen. Although there were no signs of corrosion at all, the men got the impression that the building was centuries old.

"There seem to be no stairs in the place," mused Sojan, looking around him at the gleaming marble hall which they had entered. To his left were two sheets of shining metal, seemingly set into the walls for no reason. To his right was an archway leading into a room just as bare as the one in which they now stood. "Wonder what these are?" Red said, brushing his hand across one of the metal sheets.

Instantly there was a faint hum and the sheet of metal disappeared upwards, revealing a small indentation! Was it a cupboard?

Red stepped warily into the alcove, sword in hand. At once, the sheet of metal hummed downwards behind him.

"*By Vit! He's trapped!*" cried Sojan.

He brushed his own hand across the metal, but nothing happened. For several minutes he tried to open the metal door but it seemed impossible. How Red had done it, they could not tell.

Suddenly from the outside came a yell.

Rushing into the sunlight they looked up—and there was Red, very cheerful, grinning down on them from a window of the tenth storey, the one nearest the roof.

"How did you get up there?" called Nornos Rique.

"The 'cupboard' took me up! It's a kind of moving box which lifts you up to any storey you wish. Though I had to let it take me all the way up. There were lots of buttons to press, but I dare not press any of them. After I'd got out, the doors closed again. I tried to get back in but the doors at that end wouldn't move. It looks as if I'm stuck here for life."

He didn't look as if he was particularly worried about the prospect.

Comprehending, Sojan rushed back into the great hall and again passed his hand over the metal "door." It hummed upwards. He didn't step in immediately but waited for his friends to join him.

"The ones who built this place must have been wonderful engineers," remarked Sojan. "That's no great surprise now I recognise the language in which the directions for the operation of that thing were written—it's old Kifinian!"

"What?" exclaimed Parijh. "You mean that the ancestors of the Kifinians built this?"

"Obviously. They were famous for their engineering skills. It has to be Kifinian work. Otherwise how do you explain the language?"

"From what you learned at the Temple of Rhan, Sojan," mused Nornos Rique, "the ancestors of the entire planet, so far as human beings like ourselves are concerned, came from another planet thousands of years ago—perhaps this was built before the race spread and degenerated. But what could it be?"

"I think I know," answered Sojan. "Notice how the whole area around the building is entirely treeless—a flat plain—a few shrubs, now, and other vegetation, but for the most part flat. This place was a landing field for airships of some kind. We have, as you know, similar landing fields all over the civilised parts of Zylor. This building was no doubt a control station of some description."

Suddenly Red who had been standing by the window called to his friends.

"*Look, down there!*" he yelled. "*Savages, hundreds of them!*"

Below them swarmed a silent mass of strange near-human creatures. They all carried spears and short, broad-bladed swords. They were covered in tightly matted hair and had long tails curling behind them.

"We seem to have violated taboo ground, judging by their actions," said Parijh who knew this people better than the rest, for his race occasionally traded with them. "They won't enter themselves, but they will wait until we come out—as come out we must, for food."

"The best thing we can do," said Andel, "is to look around this place and see if there is any other way out."

"Good idea," agreed Sojan, "if you see any more of those metal plates, try to open them."

They split up and each explored a certain section of the floor. Soon they heard Andel call from the centre of the building. Rushing to the room from which he had called they were astounded to see a large, opened panel. This one revealed a kind of bridge spanning a drop which must have gone right down to the foundations. The bridge led to a huge, streamlined shell of gleaming metal fitted with triangular fins.

They stepped onto the bridge and moved in single file across it until they reached a door. Scowling faintly, Sojan deciphered the ancient hieroglyphics on it.

"Here we are," he said, pressing a button. "To Open." And open it did.

"It's obviously an airship of some kind," said Andel, who was the most mechanically minded of the five. "Probably a ship similar to the ones in which our ancestors came to this planet."

"You mean an airship capable of travelling—through *space*?" said Sojan.

"Perhaps," said Andel, "but also travelling from continent to continent probably. If only we knew how to operate it!"

They finally managed to find the control room of the ship. All around them were tiers of dials and instruments. Working quickly, now that the script was becoming more familiar to him, Sojan deciphered most of the captions on the instruments. Set on the main control panel were levers marked, "Automatic, Emergency, Poltoon," "Automatic, Emergency, Jhar," etc. The names were those of continents.

"We can't stay here all the time," said Sojan. "If we stay we will starve to death, if we go outside we die, we might as well risk it." So saying, and without waiting for his friends' advice he pulled the lever marked Poltoon and stood back.

There came a gentle hum as the door through which they had entered closed. Another hum grew steadily louder and the entire roof of the building opened out letting in the sunlight. Then a hiss and a rumble like thunder and Sojan and his companions were thrown to the floor. Still the rumble increased until blackness overcame them and they lost consciousness.

Chapter Nineteen
Ship of the Ancients

Sojan was the first to recover. Looking through the forward porthole he saw a sight which to him was terrifying. The velvet blackness of outer space, stars set like diamonds in its ebony beauty.

There was another rumble from the depths of the ship. With animal tenacity he sought to cling to consciousness. But it was no good. He collapsed once more on the floor of the ship.

He awoke a second time to see a blue sky above him and green vegetation beneath him. His friends rose on shaky legs.

"We're not much better off, it seems," grinned Sojan, cheerful now. "We're in the Poltoonian Wilderness. The nearest civilised land is Tigurn. See, over there are the remains of a port similar to the one on the Shortani plain."

He pulled another lever. Immediately the portholes disappeared and they had the sensation of moving downwards at great velocity. A high-pitched whine and they stopped. A panel slid open and a small bridge moved outwards over a drop of some five feet above the ground.

"There was probably a landing stage at this point," said Sojan with the air of an ancient professor delivering a lecture. "Anyway," he laughed, "we can drop the last few feet."

When they reached the ground they stood back.

Then the faint purr of machinery and the doors closed. Another sound, not quite so smooth—the chug-chug of an airship motor. The companions turned and saw several large airships of standard pattern circling above them. They flew the banner of Pelira, a country which had allegiance to Hatnor. Flying low, the captain of the airship inspected them, saw that they were not the strange monsters he had expected and landed his craft lightly fifty feet away from them. They ran towards it.

The look of astonishment on the captain's face was ludicrous. He immediately recognised the companions who, since their conquest of the Priest Rulers of Rhan, had become Zylorian heroes.

"What—what —?" was all he could get out at first.

"How're you fixed for fuel, friend?" laughed Sojan.

"We—we've got a full tank, sir, but how . . . ?"

"Then head for Hatnor," grinned the adventurer. "We'll explain on the way."

Chapter Twenty

Sons of the Snake God

Who seeks to set foot in Dhar-Im-Jak?"

A harsh voice rang across the harbour to the merchantman *Kintonian Trader*, which rode at anchor there.

The captain cupped his hands into a megaphone and roared back at the soldier.

"Sojan Shieldbearer, late of the court of Nornos Kald in Hatnor, mercenary swordsman! Seeking employment!"

"I've heard of him. Very well, we need good sword arms in Dhar-Im-Jak, tell him he may land!"

Traani, the captain of the *Trader*, called down to Sojan who sat sprawled in his cabin.

"They say you can land, Sojan!"

"Right, I'll get my gear together."

Ten minutes later, a tall figure stepped on to the deck of the ship. His long fair hair was held back from his eyes by a fillet of metal, his dark blue eyes had a strange, humorous glint in them. Over a jerkin of green silk was flung a heavy cloak of yellow, his blue breeches were tucked into leather boots. Upon his back was slung a long and powerful air-rifle, on his left arm he carried a round shield. From a belt around his waist were hung a long vilthor and a pistol holster. Sojan the Swordsman was looking for work.

Later that day, in an inn near the city centre, Sojan met the man to whom he had been directed when he had told the authorities of the harbour what kind of employment he was seeking.

"You're looking for employment in the ranks of the regular military, I hear? What qualifications do you have?" he said.

"I was commander of the Armies of Imperial Hatnor for nearly a year. In that time I succeeded in stopping a rising in Veronlam, a similar rising in

Asno, I organised the Poltoonian barbarians when Nornos Kald was deposed and restored him to his throne, I and four others were instrumental in utterly destroying the would-be conquerors of Zylor—the Rhanian Theocracy. I have been involved in several minor border wars, but of late things have quietened down and I thought that I would try my luck somewhere else. I heard of the impending war between the city states of Dhar-Im-Jak and Forsh-Mai and decided that I would like to take part."

"I have heard of you, Sojan. Your remark about Rhan jogged my memory. I feel that you would be a great asset to us. We need more professional soldiers of your calibre. As you know, both Dhar-Im-Jak and Forsh-Mai have been on friendly terms for hundreds of years, neither of us had any use for regular armies. Then about a year ago this new religious cult took over the ruling of Forsh-Mai and quickly formed an army of soldiers, spies, trouble-makers and all kinds of undercover men. We seem to have an epidemic of religious cults! The quickest way of turning friend against friend, eh? Only recently our own spies brought us news that, as we suspected, Forsh-Mai was preparing to march into Dhar-Im-Jak and take over our republic."

"Have you any idea when they intend to attack?"

"In two weeks' time, no less, I'm sure."

"Then we must work quickly. I would be grateful to know what kind of command you intend giving me?"

"I shall have to discuss that with my superiors. I will naturally let you know as soon as possible."

Edek rose, downed the last of his drink and, with a short nod, left the inn. Just as Sojan was rising, there came a scream from the alley. Sword out, he rushed for the door to see a girl struggling in the grip of several burly fighting men. They were obviously bent on kidnapping her and Sojan lost no time in engaging the nearest hireling.

The man was an expert swordsman, his thrusts were well timed and it was all Sojan could do, at first, to parry them. The man's companions were still holding the girl who now seemed to be making no attempt to get free.

The clash of steel was music to Sojan and a grim fighting smile appeared on his lips. Suddenly he felt a hard blow on the back of his head and he was consumed by darkness.

Chapter Twenty-One
The Castle of Kandoon

Sojan regained consciousness in a small room, barred on both door and windows. Standing over him were two men; one held a water jug in his hand with which he was dousing Sojan.

"So our hard-headed mercenary is at last awake, I see!" The tone was gloating. The man's face did not belie the impression his voice gave. His thick black locks and beard were curled and oiled.

Upon his fingers were heavy rings, his nails were tinted with gold. Sojan looked at him in disgust. The bejewelled fop signalled to his companion to throw some more water at Sojan. Instantly Sojan rose and knocked the jug flying across the small cell.

"If your manners were as fine as the silks you wear, my friend, I should take you for *some* sort of man!"

The fop's face twisted for a moment and he half raised his hand. Then he smiled and dropped the hand to his side.

"We'll allow the wolf some time in which to cool the heat of his temper as water seems to be no use," he murmured. "Come, Elvit, let us leave this place—it smells!"

Sojan signalled to the guard who was locking the door.

"What place is this, friend?"

"You're in the Castle of Kandoon, swordsman, we caught you nicely, didn't we? That ruse in getting a girl to pretend that she was being captured was Lord Kandoon's idea. He's a clever one. You'd be better off to be a little more civil to him, he is thinking of employing you."

Several hours later, Kandoon returned with the same escort.

"Now, Sojan," he smiled, "I can understand your annoyance at being locked up in this place—but it was the only way in which we could—um—convince you of our sincerity when we offer you fifty thousand *derkas* to take command of our armies and lead them to glorious victory for the State of Forsh-Mai. We, the Sons of the Snake, will conquer all. Everything will be yours. What say you, man, is that not a fair proposition?"

"Aye, it's fair," Sojan's eyes narrowed. He decided to bluff for a while. "*Fifty* thousand you say?"

"That and any spoils you can take for yourself when we loot Dhar-Im-Jak!"

"But what's this 'Sons of the Snake' you mention? Do I have to join some secret society to wield a sword for fifty thousand *derkas*?"

"That is a necessary part of our offer, Sojan. We are, after all, doing this for the glory of Rij the Snake, Lord of the World and the After World, Master of Darkness, Ruler of the . . ."

"Yes, yes, we'll forget that for a moment. What does it involve?"

"First a meeting of all the major disciples, myself, the General-in-Command (who will take orders from you while the conquest is in progress), my *major-domo*, the two priests who invent—hem—who spread the Truth of the Snake."

"But why this mumbo-jumbo—if you want to conquer your enemy, why not just do it? I can't understand what you're trying to do."

"Then briefly I will explain. The two cities have been at peace for hundreds of years. Men and women from the states have intermingled with each other, families have intermarried until we are virtually a single nation. Apart from the names and boundaries, we are practically the same people. We need an excuse, man, don't you see? We can't send a soldier to march against his brother or even his son unless he thinks that there is something worth fighting for. This, my dear Sojan, is a Holy War." He raised a cynical eye to Heaven. "Quite legitimate. We are—how shall I put it?—spreading the Word of the Snake God with the Sword of Justice! Part of our indoctrination campaign, actually, that last bit."

"Religion might have been invented to justify war and for no other purpose," mused the mercenary, his quick mind working. "All right! I'll join."

Sojan had hit on a daring plan. "When do I become an initiate?"

An hour later, Sojan stood in a darkened room. In front of him was a long table and at it sat men clad in robes decorated with serpents.

"Let the ceremony begin," he intoned.

Now was the time to act. They had given Sojan back his sword along with his other equipment and he now drew it. With the blade humming he downed the two nearest fighters. Three left, three wary men and led by one who had been described as the finest swordsman in Shortani.

Luckily only two of the men were swordsmen—the other was almost helpless. In the fore Kandoon, cowl flung back and his face a mask of hate.

"Trick me, would you," he hissed. "We'll show you what we do to dogs who try to turn on Wise Kandoon!"

Sojan felt a lancing pain go through him and he felt the warm blood as it trickled down his left arm. With renewed energy he launched himself at Kandoon who was taken off guard for a moment. Clean steel pierced a tainted heart and the man toppled backwards with a short death-scream.

"Those who assume mercenaries long for war are, as ever, misguided. The best of us believe in peace above all else. Maybe I've taught a few greedy fools a valuable lesson."

And collecting his myat from where he had stabled it, Sojan Shieldbearer rode on.

With the fake "Sons of the Snake God" exposed for what they were, what amounted to civil war was averted and the two cities resumed their friendly relations. Once again Sojan had done a major service for the cause in which every honourable soldier believed.

Chapter Twenty-Two
The Devil Hunters of Norj

The last rays of Zylor's second sun were just waning when Sojan reined his myat and stared down into the green valley below.

He glanced at the crude map before him.

"This must be the Valley of Norj. It seems to be unexplored according to the map. Strange that no one has ventured into it."

Strange it was; for, even in the dusk, Sojan could see that the valley was lush and green. A river wound through it and brightly plumed birds sang from the branches of tall trees. A seeming paradise.

"It will make an excellent place to camp," thought the mercenary as he guided his mount downwards.

Later that night, he set up his camp in a small natural clearing in the forest. His myat was tethered nearby and his campfire glowed cheerily. The night was warm and full of forest smells.

After eating his meal, Sojan climbed between his blankets and was soon asleep.

It was just after midnight when the strange noises awakened the warrior.

There they were again—a peculiar hissing screech and the pounding of hooves; the cries of—men, and vicious cracks of whips.

Sojan raised himself on one elbow, hand reaching for his sword. The myat stirred uneasily and swished its great tail from side to side.

The noises drew nearer and then subsided as they fell away towards the West of the valley.

Sojan did not sleep any more that night but kept a watchful eye open. The rest of the night was uneventful and in the morning, Sojan cooked himself a big meal which was meant to last him the day, for he intended to investigate the noises he had heard, the night before.

Riding slowly, with eyes always scanning the ground, Sojan soon found the tracks that the inhabitants of the valley had made. There were two distinct sets of tracks. One similar to those of a myat although with subtle differences, seemingly lighter. The others were entirely unfamiliar. Three-toed tracks like, and yet unlike, those of a bird—and considerably larger. The beast that had made them was obviously a quadruped of some kind, but other than that Sojan could not tell what kind of animal had made them—there were few four-legged birds he could think of—and none of the ones he had heard about was as large as this.

There had been at least ten riders, and it seemed that they had been chasing one or perhaps two of these bird-beasts. Probably some kind of hunt, thought Sojan, yet what kind of men were they who hunted at the dead of night?

Sojan rode on, following the tracks in the hope that he would find some clue to the mystery. He came across a steep inclination, the tracks ended here in a flurry of mud and blood. Then the tracks of the beasts the men had been riding continued. They had ridden for a short while parallel to the bluff and then forced their animals to ride up it.

Sojan did the same. His heavier mount slipped occasionally and nearly slid back but eventually it had carried its rider to the top. From there Sojan saw a strange scene.

A battle of some kind was going on between two groups of men. Near a squat black-stoned tower, five men, one mounted, were endeavouring to check a horde of armoured warriors who rushed from the tower. Beasts similar to Sojan's myat but lighter, hornless and almost tailless stood waiting.

The mounted man held the tethering reins of the other four animals while he cut at two of the armoured men with a battle-axe held in his right hand.

Although the mounted man was clad in armour, the other four were dressed only in jerkins of coloured cloth and divided kilts of leather. They were unshod and carried no sheaths for the weapons, mainly swords, with which they defended themselves. It seemed to Sojan that they were attempting to escape from the armoured warriors, one of whom, dressed more richly, and darker than the others, stood in the rear and urged them on in a language which was at once unfamiliar yet strangely familiar to Sojan's ears.

But there was no time to ponder over this now; the men needed help and Sojan, in a more curious than chivalrous mood, intended to aid them and perhaps find some answer to the mystery.

His long spear was out, his shield up and he forced the myat into a wild gallop down the hill, screaming to his gods in a barbarian war-shout.

His savage thrust caught the first of the armoured warriors in the throat and stayed there, the spear jerking like a tufted reed in a storm. His sword screamed from its scabbard as he pushed deeper into the mêlée of cursing men.

Taking his chance to escape while the enemy were still confused, the other men quickly mounted their beasts. Sojan was still in the thick of it, sword lashing everywhere and dealing death with every stroke. One of the riders looked back, saw the mercenary still engaged and spurred his own beast back to where Sojan fought.

Grinning his thanks to Sojan he covered the mercenary's retreat with his own slim blade then followed.

Howling, the warriors attempted to pursue on foot. They were brought back by their leader's frantic cries and scrambled round behind the building.

The armoured rider called to Sojan in that familiar, yet unintelligible tongue, and pointed towards the East. Sojan understood and turned his myat in that direction. Behind them the pursuers were whipping their steeds in an effort to overtake them.

Deep into the forest they rode, leaving their enemies far behind. For perhaps three hours they detoured until they reached the end of the valley where a sheer cliff rose. Brushing aside some shrubbery, the armoured man disclosed an opening in the base of the cliff.

Ducking their heads, the six rode through, the last man carefully replacing the camouflage.

The passage ended in several connecting caves and it was in one of these that they stabled their mounts and continued on foot to the cave at the far end. Here they slumped into chairs, grinning with relief at their escape.

The leader, the man in armour, began to speak to Sojan who stood bewilderedly trying to understand the language in which they questioned him. Vaguely he began to realise what it was—it was his own tongue, yet so altered as to be scarcely recognisable. In an hour he could understand most of their speech and in two he was telling them how he had come to the Valley of Norj.

"But I am curious to find out who you are—and why men hunt giant four-legged birds at midnight," he said. "Who were the men from whom you escaped?"

"It is a long story to explain in a few words," said Jarg, the leader, "but I will first attempt to tell you a little of the political situation here, in Norj.

"There are two distinct races living here—men like ourselves and another race whom I scarcely like to define as 'men.' Ages ago our people reached this valley after a long sea voyage and trek across Shortani. We came to this valley and settled in it and it was not for some time that we learned that another people lived at the far end of the valley. A race of grim, black-haired and black-eyed men, who hunted at night with steel-tipped flails and who remained in their castles during the day. They did not trouble us at first and eventually we became used to the hunts, even though they sometimes passed through our fields and destroyed our crops. We were secure, we thought, in the valley and there was no man curious enough to venture too near the black-stoned castles of the Cergii.

"But soon men and women—even children—of our people began to disappear and the hunts became more frequent for the Cergii had found a new sport. They had a different quarry to the Devil-birds which they breed and release at night to hunt with their whips. It was then that the mangled bodies of our tribesmen began to be found . . . Lashed to death.

"They were capturing our people—and hunting them! So it was that we declared war upon these beasts, these whom we had never harmed nor attempted to harm.

"Over the years traitors to our race went over to the enemy and became their warriors. You saw some of them today. Our once great race dwindled and became fugitives, living in caves and, if captured, the quarry of the Hunters of Norj. Still we carry on warfare with them—but it is hit-and-run fighting at best. The four you see here were captured recently and it was more by luck than anything that I managed to bribe a guard to release them. I came last night with weapons and myats—you see the breed has changed as has our speech. Unfortunately the timing was imperfect and the first sun arose before we could make good our escape. We were seen and would all be dead or captured had it not been for you."

"There must be some way to defeat them!" demanded Sojan. "And if there is a way—I swear that I will find it!"

Chapter Twenty-Three
Hounds of the Cergii

Sojan and the stern-faced fighting men of Norj, some sixty in all, stood in the main cave, waiting for nightfall.

Plans of Sojan's attempt to overcome the Cergii had been discussed and Sojan and Jarg, the leader, had reached a decision.

The Cergii were few, it seemed. About ten in number. They were immortal, or at least their life-spans were incredibly long and the race had gradually dwindled to ten evil sorcerer-warriors whose only pleasures were their midnight hunts.

At dusk, Sojan rose, went over the final plan with his friends and left, heading Eastwards, towards the castles of the Cergii—some twenty in all, mostly in an advanced state of decay—only one of which housed the Cergii and their Norjian slaves and hirelings.

The tiny Zylorian moons gave scant light and Sojan found it difficult picking his way through the rubble of the ruined outbuildings.

There came a faint scuffling behind him; a sound which only a barbarian's senses could have heard.

Sojan ignored it and carried on.

Even when the scuffling came nearer he ignored it. The sudden blow on the back of his head was impossible to ignore, however, and a blind sense of survival set him wheeling round, hand groping for his sword hilt before blackness, deeper than night, swam in front of his eyes and he lost consciousness.

He awoke in a damp-smelling cell, lit only by torchlight which filtered through a tiny grille in the wall. The cell was obviously on a corner for the large barred door was not in the same wall as the grille.

Peering through this door was an unkempt warrior clad in dirty armour and holding a spear.

With half-mad eyes he glared short-sightedly at the mercenary. His mouth gaped open showing bad teeth and he chuckled loudly.

"You're the next game for the Hunters of Cergii," he cackled. "Oh! What a feast the beasts will have tonight."

Sojan ignored these words, turned over and attempted to ease the pain in his aching head.

After many hours in which he attempted to get some rest, Sojan was jabbed roughly awake by the guard's spear butt.

"What is it now?" he enquired as he raised himself to his feet and dusted off the straw in which he'd been sleeping.

"Heh, heh!" cackled the man. "It's almost midnight—time for one of our little hunts!"

Sojan became tense. He had a plan based on the knowledge that if he was captured he would most certainly be forced to partake in one of the hunts of the Cergii as the quarry.

"Very well," he said, trying to sound as frightened as possible.

The courtyard was dark and gloomy, one moon showing through a gap in the ruins. The strange smell of an unknown animal came to Sojan's nostrils and he gathered that these were the "hounds" of the Cergii that Jarg had told him about.

He heard the stamping of the myat's hooves and the jingle of harness and, as his eyes became accustomed to the darkness, made out the vague outlines of tall mounted men.

"Is the quarry ready?" called out a voice as dead and cold as the ruins around them.

"Yes, Master, he is here!"

"Then tell him he will be given quarter of an hour's start—then we will be upon his scent!" the voice went on.

The guards stood aside and Sojan was off—along a route already planned nights ago. His plan was a daring one and one which called for a great deal of courage. He was acting as a human snare for the Hunters.

Down a narrow forest trail he ran, the trees and grasses rustling in the cold night breeze, the sound of small animals calling to each other and the occasional scream as a larger animal made its kill.

The air in his lungs seemed to force itself out as he ran faster and faster. The time was getting short and he had several more minutes yet until he could reach the planned spot.

Sounds—not the sounds of the forest, but far more ominous—began to reach his ears. The snap of cracking whips and thundering hooves as the Hunters and their silent hounds rode in pursuit.

Faster and faster Sojan ran, keeping his eyes open for the landmark which would afford him comparative safety.

At last, just as the cracking of whips and pounding hooves seemed to be on top of him, it came into sight. Past the tall rock he ran, into a tiny gorge flanked on each side by towering rock walls.

Up the side of the cliff he scrambled as the Hunters entered the gorge. Then:

"Now!" roared Sojan, and as he did so sixty death-tipped arrows flew down and buried themselves in the bodies of Cergii riders.

Their curses and frantic screams were music to Sojan and his friends as they fitted new arrows and let fly at the sounds.

Yelling the great battle-shout of his ancestors Sojan leaped down the rocks again, a long sword in his right hand.

A shadowy rider loomed out of the darkness and an evil face, white teeth flashing in a grin of triumph, aimed a blow at Sojan with his own blade.

Sojan cut upwards, catching the rider in the leg. He screamed and tumbled off his steed, putting it between himself and Sojan.

He came upright, limping rapidly in the mercenary's direction. Sojan ducked another savage cut and parried it. Down lunged his opponent's sword attempting to wound Sojan's sword-arm. He again parried the stroke and counter-thrust at the man's chest.

Following up this move with a thrust to the heart, the mercenary ended the evil hunter's life.

Most of the Cergii were now either dead or mortally wounded and it did not take Sojan and his friends long to finish off the job they had started.

"Now for the hirelings!" yelled Sojan, goading his myat in the direction from which they had come; his sword dripping red in the moonlight, his hair tousled and a wildness in his handsome eyes.

The sixty riders thundered down the narrow forest trail towards the castles of the dead Cergii, Sojan at their head, shouting a battle-cry which had been voiced at a dozen great victories for the men whom Sojan had led.

Straight into the courtyard they swarmed, catching the soldiers entirely unawares.

Dismounting, they crashed open the doors of the castle and poured in.

"Guard the doors!" yelled Sojan. "And all the other exits—we'll finish off every traitor in the place!"

His first call was in the dungeons—for there he knew he would find the man who had been his jailer during the previous day.

The half-crazed warrior cringed when he saw Sojan enter sword in hand. But one look at the tall mercenary told him he could expect no mercy.

Drooling with fear he yanked his own sword from its scabbard and swung a blow at Sojan which would have cut him in two had it not been deflected by Sojan's blade.

Coolly Sojan fought while his opponent became more and more desperate.

Slowly the warrior was forced back as Sojan's relentless sword drove him nearer and nearer the wall.

His madness gave him immense stamina and gradually he began to fight with more skill.

"Heh, heh!" he cackled, "you will soon die man! Think not that you escaped death when you escaped the Cergii!"

Sojan smiled a grim smile and said nothing.

Suddenly the maddened warrior wrenched a spear from the wall and hurled it at Sojan. It plunked heavily into his left arm causing him to gasp with pain.

Then his eyes hardened and the warrior read his fate in them.

"You'll die for that," said Sojan calmly.

Almost immediately the warrior went down before a blurring network of steel and sought a fresh incarnation with an inch of steel in his throat.

Sojan returned to the main hall of the castle where his friends were finishing off the rest of the Cergii's warriors.

"Well," he laughed cheerfully, "I must be off!"

Jarg turned. He saw the wound inflicted by the madman's spear.

"You can't ride in that state, Sojan!" he cried.

"Oh, it will heal," Sojan smiled. "It is only a superficial cut! But you have work to do, restoring your farms now that the Cergii are vanquished. I should like to stay—but this is an interesting continent with lots to see. If I hurry I might be able to see it all before I die!"

With that he strode from the room, mounted his myat and cantered off, up the steep track which led him out of the valley of Norj. No doubt many more adventures lay ahead for Sojan, either in this incarnation or another.

"There goes a brave and honourable man. What he promises he performs! What he cannot do he does not say he will do," murmured Jarg as he watched him disappear over the hilltop. "Would that there were more like Sojan Shieldbearer."

And so he rode into the legends of Zylor, a man who lived according to that age-old code of honour which has ensured the peace and justice of all the planets Sojan's ancestors settled: a man for whom death was no barrier and who would live forever, ready to do battle with the forces of greed and tyranny wherever they occurred. Would he ever return to Hatnor and his friends there, to fight beside them, laugh with them and find further strange adventures in their company? That perhaps we shall never know, but we can be sure that Sojan—or one with Sojan's brave soul—would find what it was he loved and be content if not on Zylor then on another of the many planets of our astonishingly varied galaxy.

Together with various friends of my teenage years, I would write several other short stories set on the same planet or in the same universe as Sojan's. I also wrote Harold Lamb-influenced historical stories for boys' "annuals" such as The Searchlight Book for Boys *and for Amalgamated Press papers in which Barry Bayley or myself were almost the sole text contributors by that time. We were both admirers of the old American pulps of every kind and this was reflected in our work.* Tarzan Adventures *was the nearest thing we'd ever had in England to a juvenile US pulp. Sadly,* Tarzan Adventures *did not last much longer after I had left and the editor who took over from me believed that fantasy stories and readers' departments were "unwholesome" reading for boys, rejecting any further stories submitted to him in the fantasy genre and dropping most of the departments and other features. For a few years the nearest I would come to writing similar fiction would be short historical stories in* Robin Hood Annual *and other sister publications, as well as scripts for historical adventure strips like* Karl the Viking *and* Olac the Gladiator. *Slowly I made a transition from juvenile weeklies to adult monthlies until in 1960 I would be asked to create what is now the Elric series for the magazine* Science Fantasy.

Michael Moorcock

Under the Warrior Star

Joe R. Lansdale

Dedicated to the great creators of
Planet adventure and sword and sorcery:
Edgar Rice Burroughs, Otis Kline, and Robert E. Howard.
Goodbye to nostalgia.

Chapter One
My History

I write here on yellow pad among the bones of the dead. The wind whistling through broken glass.

My name is Braxton Booker. This vast and empty underground structure, where I now sit, recording my experiences, is really where my story began, and now it is where it ends. But, to better understand what has happened to me, I'll move to an earlier beginning, and tell you about the events of my life that made me the perfect person for this strange adventure.

Not that I expect you to believe me. Providing anyone ever reads this. The bottom line is it is all so fantastic. If someone were to tell me what I am writing on my pad, or give it to me to read, I would think them either a liar or mad. But my experiences weigh on me like the tumbling stones of an avalanched mountain, and recording my adventures somewhat lifts that weight from my soul. So, here it is.

In a nutshell, when I was eleven, living in a small town in East Texas, my father, fearing that I was becoming a loner, and that I lacked confidence, introduced me to an elderly man who taught jujitsu and fencing. His name was Jack Rimbauld.

Rimbauld was elderly, five eight, weighing about one hundred and thirty pounds, soaking wet with change in his pocket. His age and size and appearance were misleading. He was the toughest, quickest, most physically capable man I ever knew. He had studied all over the world in his youth, both the physical arts and the arts of education. He was a warrior and an intellectual. He had settled in our small town to retire, for whatever reason. In time, we became not only student and teacher, but friends.

I never asked why he had come to live in East Texas. Never considered it. I was a young man and caught up in the skills he was teaching me. Each day after school I went to his home with great enthusiasm. The sight of the big fencing room and the matted room next to it were like the Holy of Holies for me.

I knew very little about my teacher beyond those training rooms and his library, where we often sat after class and he spoke to me of better understanding my skills. He wrote poetry, haiku mostly, but other kinds of poetry as well. He requested that I read them and try my hand at them. I tried. I also attempted the Japanese art of flower arranging, and the tea ceremony. I wasn't very good at any of that. My tea was sour, my flowers drooped. My poetry thudded.

He taught me meditation, and I swear I once saw him, sitting cross-legged on a mat, hands on his knees, eyes closed, slowly lift off the mat and hover there quietly for a full minute or so. Another time, I was looking right at him, and then he was gone. I heard him behind me. He had moved across the room by some weird means of teleportation. He told me it was just a trick of the mind. That he had never moved, but that he had in fact put the idea in my mind that he was behind me. Another time, in his office, he was at his desk and I was sitting in a chair across from him. The door opened, and in Jack walked, closing the door behind him.

This time, when I looked back at the man behind the desk, Jack was still there. There were two of him in the room. Slowly, the Jack behind the desk faded, and the Jack in the doorway smiled, turned, and walked right through the closed door. I stood there blinking for a long moment, not believing what I had seen.

When I rushed into the mat room, he was sitting there on one of the mats, cross-legged. The look on my face made him laugh out loud.

What I remember most about that, though, was right before the second Jack had entered the room, the Jack behind the desk had shaken my hand.

I had felt his touch, as sure and solid as if he were there.

He tried to teach me this power of mind over matter. It was difficult work. I didn't entirely understand it, though when I'm not caught up in the whirlwind of life, I make an effort to improve my ability. So far, my ability is me sitting cross-legged on the floor trying not to think about a cheeseburger.

But the combat arts, there I thrived.

If Jack Rimbauld had a family, I never heard of them. If there was someone dear to him, other than myself, I was never given an indication.

Looking back on it now, remembering certain things he said to me, I have the belated impression that he may have had some dark secret in his past. That, however, is nothing more than a guess, and comes in hindsight, and is ultimately unimportant to my story. Back then, I only knew that he was Mr. Rimbauld, maestro, sensei, friend and mentor.

I remember him saying to me, "Brax. You have an impulsive nature, and a temper. Neither serve a man well in the long run. The mind and the spirit and the body must be welded together by the tightest of glue."

This meant very little to me at the time.

I took lessons five days a week in fencing and jujitsu for three hours a day until I was twenty, and then three days a week in both arts until I was twenty-two and Jack became ill, and shortly thereafter, died, surprising me by willing me not only his collection of swords, but his home and library and a fairly substantial savings. How he came about this money, I don't know. I never saw him teach another soul, other than myself, and I never knew of him to have a job or to go off to work. Perhaps these answers lie somewhere in the volumes of handwritten composition books he left me.

Before his death, he had taught me all there was to know about the sword, and not any one kind of sword, but all manner of swords and knives, and even some training in archery and spear casting. Anything with a point I could use with considerable skill. I was no slouch at jujitsu, either, and earned a third-degree black belt under his tutelage. He also spent time introducing me to books, and loaned me numerous volumes of rare editions of novels by the world's greatest authors. He was my education, and he was like a second father to me. I respected the information and skills he gave me.

Because of those skills I made a great mistake, and then those same skills saved my life. So, I owe Jack Rimbauld much praise, and I owe myself criticism for bad judgment. In the end, however, I would not undo what happened.

Though there are events leading up to my situation that are interesting, and under other circumstances might even be considered thrilling, they pale in comparison to the amazing events that came after. The events that I expect will be difficult for you to believe.

Because of that, I'll condense the early adventures, and simply say that I made the Olympic fencing team, and might have won a gold medal, if one of my comrades and I had not gotten into a quarrel over a young lady with long blonde hair and very nice figure.

He ended up with the girl. But it was not enough for him, and he, like in the old days, challenged me to a duel using sabers. I was foolish. I no longer cared about the girl, or at least not that much, but I did care—too much—about my pride. I accepted his challenge, and soon found it was not just a duel of skill, but that he fully intended to strike me down.

With a parry and a stroke, I cut him deeply in the face and shoulder, and dropped him. It was a frightful wound, but he wasn't dead. Being young, and foolish—and I am not far off that youth now, but in experience I am much older—I fled for fear of arrest. I most likely could have made a good legal defense, claiming accurately that he had tried to kill me and I was only defending myself. But at the time, it didn't occur to me. I was frightened.

What a funny word. Frightened.

Now, after all I have been through the idea of being frightened by merely wounding a man in self-defense strikes me as little more than amusing.

I ended up in Alaska. There I was able to hide and use a false name and not need anything much in the way of identification. I worked on a fishing boat briefly, and then ended up helping a fellow named Carruthers fly supplies, and I suspect stolen goods, to different locations in Alaska.

In over a period of a year I learned to operate the small prop planes, though I never acquired a pilot's license. I didn't need one. Carruthers had his own landing strip and flew his own flight plans and there was no one to stop him.

Alaska is truly the last frontier.

On Earth.

But somehow I was tracked by the law, and when I found out they were coming to get me, I panicked and stole one of the planes. I did all right until I was over a great patch of wilderness, flying low, and ended up with an eagle smashing into my propeller. It did damage. The plane went down. I tried to glide it to a landing, but when the plane hurtled earthward, it was as if I and the entire world were in a centrifuge.

I lost control. As I went down I thought of my parents, both dead some years back from a car wreck, and I thought of the girl I had lost to a man who had once been my friend. I thought of the Olympic opportunity I had missed, and I thought of my old mentor Jack Rimbauld.

I thought of a dog I had when young.

No more cheeseburgers.

And then the plane hit.

Chapter Two
The Invisible Project

When I awoke I was warm. It was night and the main body of the plane was on fire, and pieces of it were scattered along the ground. I had been thrown free, and had somehow survived, perhaps because the plane had skidded on its belly in soft mud near a large body of water. I could see the marks of that slide imbedded in the shoreline near the water. I wasn't sure how I had managed that landing, or if I had. Perhaps it was nothing more than blind luck.

The impact had not only thrown me out of the plane, it had knocked me unconscious. And now, as I came slowly awake, saw the debris, felt the heat from the aircraft burning near the edge of the water, I was certain that I had broken more than a few bones.

In that estimation I was at least partially correct. I could see a bone in my leg jutting through a rip in my pants; it suck out like a jagged stick. The sight of it made me sick. I tried to pull myself up, so that I could rest my back against a large tree. I managed this, but passed out shortly thereafter. I blinked awake once, and saw a shadow moving along the shore in the firelight. And then the author of the shadow presented itself.

A grizzly bear.

I reached in my pocket for my clip knife, which was a little like pulling a toothpick, considering the size and strength of a bear, but it was not my nature to give in to anything without a fight. My old instructor, Jack Rimbauld, had established that in me, and it held to my being as tight as the skin on my bones.

In the process of drawing the knife, I realized my little finger on my right hand was twisted at an odd angle. It hurt to drag the knife from my pocket, but I managed, and was able to flick the blade open.

The bear turned its head toward me. It was outlined very well in the firelight. It sniffed the air. It was perhaps twenty feet away from me. It began to lumber slowly in my direction. I tried to pull myself even more upright against the tree trunk, but I was all out of energy.

Then I saw movement off to my left. Someone was coming along the edge of the bank, several people, in fact. Awareness of this was followed by a queasy feeling, perhaps the result of shock. The next thing I knew the world was blinking in and out and there was a popping sound that I recognized on some level, but for some reason could not put a proper thought to it. Later I would determine it came from rifles being fired in the air.

I passed out.

O nce, I awoke and found myself being bounced along on some sort of support, covered in a warm blanket. I only had this awareness for an instant, and then I plunged back into blackness.

I don't know exactly how long I was out, but when I awoke completely, it was bright and the air smelled of disinfectant. I lay in a hard bed with crisp white sheets. My leg was in a cast. So was my hand and little finger. I pulled back the sheet and saw that I was bandaged all over. I had more wounds than I realized.

I had been awake for only a few moments when a man came into the room. He was tall and thin and balding, except for a white tuft of hair that stood up on his head like a comb on a rooster. I thought he looked like a mad scientist. I wasn't entirely off in this judgment.

Leaning over me, he smiled, and gave me a container of water with a straw. My mouth was dry as the desert, so I sipped. He sat in a chair by my bed, waited patiently while I drank. He said, "So, are you feeling a mite better?"

I said that I was, and then, "Where am I?"

"Now, that is something I have to admit I'm not going to answer completely."

It was a surprising statement, and I said so.

"No doubt it's confusing," he said, "but let me put it this way. This is a private facility, financed by a large number of rich, private investors. You are underground, son."

"Underground?"

He nodded. "That's right. Deep down. A few of those who work here, having lost interest, at least temporarily, in surviving like a mole, went above for a break, heard the plane crash. They went in search of the explosion, and found you. Good thing too. A bear was about to put you to the taste test. We ran it off by firing shots in the air, and we brought you here, doctored you up."

"Who is we?"

"Me and a hundred employees, fifty of them on site at the moment. I suppose you could say I'm the head honcho here. The question now is what to do with you."

I wasn't sure what he meant by that, so I lay silent.

"You rest and I'll think it over. By the way, you may call me Dr. Wright. What shall I call you?"

"Brax," I said. "That'll do."

I didn't leave that room for several days. Finally, I was allowed to visit Dr. Wright. He had an office down the hall from my room. The room I was in was one of three rooms that provided hospital beds. There were a lot of other hallways that led to I knew not where.

I was given a motorized wheelchair and a large man dressed in black with a large black pistol on his hip. He was my escort. He made sure I went where I was supposed to go, and when he let me in Dr. Wright's office, he remained outside, the door closed.

Dr. Wright sat behind a big desk in a rolling leather chair. I could see mounted on the wall behind him a pair of crossed sabers. This, of course, caught my eye right away. He noticed, said, "You like swords?"

"I love swords," I said.

"You know how to use them?"

"Quite well," I said, and gave him my history. I planned to leave out the part about my problems in the lower states, but for some reason I let it all spill out. Maybe I was tired of the whole hide-and-seek business I had been conducting for the last year or so. Whatever my inner motives, I held nothing back.

"So, that one incident led to the plane crash?" he said.

"Yes," I said.

Dr. Wright nodded. He turned and looked at the sabers. "I was once quite good myself. That was a thousand years ago."

"What exactly is it you do here?"

"If I told you, I'd have to kill you," he said, and the smile that came across his face was narrow and hard, as if it had been pinned there.

"That wouldn't be good," I said.

"No. No," he said. "It wouldn't."

I lost track of time, but gradually my leg healed and so did my hand. I never really knew if it was day or night, being underground. My world was a world of electric lights. I was allowed the opportunity to move around on crutches, and sometimes I was allowed to venture down to Dr. Wright's office. I think he enjoyed the visits as much as I did, and he supplied me with books to read, and once we even played chess. I beat him the first time because he seemed distracted, but no time thereafter. It was a little like my relationship with Jack Rimbauld, but without the physical activity, and though Dr. Wright was pleasant enough, there always seemed to be a point at which he became reserved and unwilling to give more of himself emotionally.

One day, as we hovered over the chessboard, he said, "I suppose I can tell you something of our work here."

I didn't say anything, not wanting to show too much interest, but I didn't want to show lack of interest either. I lifted my head and tried to look no more curious than a puppy that has heard a noise.

"Have you heard of quantum physics?" he asked.

"Yes."

"What do you know about it?"

"That it's called quantum physics, and I believe it's mostly theoretical."

"No, it's not theoretical at all. There are many things about our universe that can be discovered by the study of it."

"I think I heard something about it having to do with, among other things, parallel dimensions."

"That's one thing, yes. One of many amazing things. What we're doing here, with our studies, and they are purely independent, and paid for by individuals so wealthy that their wealth cannot be measured, is we're creating a universe in a laboratory."

"A universe?"

He smiled at me. "That's right."

"You telling me this. Does it mean I'm going to be killed?"

"No. I don't think so."

"That doesn't seem certain enough."

"I'm certain," he said. "But it is top secret, and I'm not supposed to tell anyone, but it gets lonely here."

"With a hundred people?"

"With a hundred people who are scientists first and foremost. You, you have a good mind, but you have other interests. And, to tell you the truth, I have a proposal for you. I'm somewhat reluctant to mention it, but you seem like a young man that just might like the possible challenge."

"Possible?"

"Yes," he said. "Because if it doesn't work, you may die, or perhaps worse, be consigned to some place beyond our understanding, a kind of limbo."

"Sounds almost religious."

"If the creating of a universe is not an attempt to play God, what is?"

He leaned forward, supporting himself with his elbows on either side of the chessboard. "Our operation is top secret, and . . . Well, I'm going to make the jump. I'm going to go ahead and tell you. As I said, it is financed by a large number of rich individuals, but those rich individuals do not spend a dime."

"Pardon," I said.

"They are shills. Fronts to what is in fact a government operation that is not on the books, and is therefore . . ." He grinned at me. "Not a government operation. It is an invisible project, an attempt to not only create a universe but to control it. Theoretically, many believe that if you can create a universe, then you can travel to that universe, and within are worlds that can be used for exploitation. The profit, creating one universe after another, could be beyond understanding, beyond reasoning."

"That seems like a considerable jump in thinking," I said.

He laughed a little. "I'm making it sound considerably more simple than it actually is. But to be frank, if I were to explain it completely, and in a scientific manner, you would be lost."

"I believe that," I said.

Dr. Wright nodded. "We have a problem. No volunteers to make the jump."

"The jump?"

"Into our new universe."

"You've actually created the universe?"

"We think so. The scientists we have here have been working on the project with me for twenty-five years. And, the truth is, to the layman's eye, there's not much to show. Because of that, we are on the verge of being shut down. Perhaps violently."

"Why violently?"

"Because, young man, as I said, we do not exist. And the main government has discovered the secret government's project. Citizens find out about us, the religions zealots find out about what we're doing here . . . Well, we would not only lose financing, we might, in fact, lose our lives. The whole project, knowledge of it, those involved, would have to be erased. Overnight, the most amazing discovery in the history of science would end. And we, who do not exist, would continue not to exist. Only for real."

Dr. Wright leaned back in his chair and studied me for a long moment. I thought the story sounded fantastic, but considering I was in their underground world, I was more than a little inclined to believe him. At least partly.

"All of the men and women who work here have families," he said. "They rotate in and out, spending part of the year at home, part of the year here."

"You're saying they all have something to go back to."

"I am."

"And you're saying I do not."

Dr. Wright slowly nodded. "From what you've told me, that seems to be the case. Your parents are dead. No close family. Wife or girlfriend. Not even a pet. You could go back, of course, possibly work out your problem, and go on with your life. It's also possible you could spend a few years in jail, if not for the injury you gave the young man, then for stealing an aircraft."

Dr. Wright gave me the adoring uncle look. "What I'm offering here, however, is something that is unique."

I understood then. Understood why he had been so friendly. He and his nonexistent organization saw me as nothing more than a lab rat.

Chapter Three

The Jump

I was angry and insulted, and when I went back to my room, my first thoughts were of escape, but then it occurred to me, I would be escaping to . . . Where?

Dr. Wright had befriended me, hastily winning my allegiance to benefit his plans, to show progress so his facility would not be closed down, even destroyed. It was underhanded, but the truth was, I saw it all as a new and amazing opportunity. A chance to try something that had never been tried. After my sojourn in Alaska, flying planes, living by my wits, to return to the lower states, to possibly spend time in prison, or to go about everyday life, a nine-to-five job, was not appealing. Like my old mentor, Rimbauld, I was an adventurer at heart.

To be part of something never before done . . . I found that vastly appealing. A day-to-day government project would never openly allow an outsider to put him- or herself in jeopardy. Here, however, in a place that was not supposed to exist, it could happen. I decided right then and there, as I sat in the darkness of my room in a soft chair, that I would make it easy for Dr. Wright. I would volunteer.

My guess was, there was a good chance that if I did not volunteer, I would be made a volunteer. There was no way in the world that he planned to let me go, to be a potential blabbermouth that might reveal not only what was being done here, but its general location.

I did not have, and had never had, a real choice.

And I didn't want one.

A day later Dr. Wright took me to the laboratory and showed me what was there. When I say laboratory. It was a room the size of warehouse. There were busy men and women in white coats. There were computers with blinking lights on long wooden tables, and there were vials of this and that, and all manner of colors pulsing through tubes, and there were wires, red, blue, green, yellow, and the tubes and wires led to a glassed-in room at the far end of the lab. It was not a small room, but neither was it huge. There were rooms with windows, and looking through one of the windows, I saw spinning colors and stars and little bright planets, and dead center of it all, a prominent solar system revolving around a large star the color of a fresh egg yolk, which Dr. Wright identified as a sun. The room, that little universe behind glass, was breathtaking.

I was dazed, to say the least. I felt like a god looking in on that universe, those stars and worlds, that solar system, that bright yellow sun.

"It's a little like fine-tuning artillery, this traveling about," he said. "We have used mice up until now, trying to close in on that planet next to that sun in that solar system."

He pointed with his finger. "We now believe we can send a human visitor to that planet. We created that universe quite recently, but in the time of the universe itself, billions of years have passed. Life may have formed on those planets. Certainly, we believe the world close to that particular sun is hospitable. Different from what we know here, but maybe not too different. There are other solar systems, and other suns, and other planets, but from what we have researched, and perhaps guessed at a little bit, we feel that one dead center of it all is the most likely to house life, maintain a visitor."

"When you say a visitor, I assume you are no longer talking about mice," I said.

"No. Not mice. You."

"Once I'm there, provided I make it. Can I return?"

"If we send you successfully, we can bring you back successfully. A timer. We brought three of the five mice back."

"What happened to the other two?"

"Can't say."

"Can't, or won't."

"Can't."

From the moment I learned that Dr. Wright planned to use me as his guinea pig, and I assumed against my will if I chose not to agree, I looked at him differently. But I decided not to let it show. I wanted to go.

"How does it work?" I asked.

"Come."

I followed as he led me along a hall, into a room, over to a long metal table. There were computers on it, blinking lights and moving dots across their screens. It made no sense to me. On the table there was a little ball of metal, open in spots; it was shaped in the manner of fingers clutched loosely into a ball, with gaps between the fingers. The gaps were filled with hard glass or plastic, strips of windows.

"The mice traveled in this?"

"Yes."

"No space craft? I don't get it."

"You're not traveling through space, you're traveling . . . Ah, how to explain, son. You are traveling through dimensions, through time, and space is of no consequence. If the mice went, and came back, then the air on the particular planet where we plan for you to arrive can be breathed. We learned that."

"What planet?"

"The planet we call Fourth From The Sun. Meaning the particular sun in the particular solar system inside the universe we've made. The mice went there, and most of them survived."

"The ones that didn't survive. They went elsewhere?"

"No. They went to the same place. But they didn't come back."

"Did the vehicle come back?"

"Once, yes. It was empty. The other time. No. It didn't return."

I thought about that a moment. "All right, I presume that you do not intend for me to fit in that little ball."

He smiled at me and guided me toward a room that connected to the laboratory. Inside he closed the door. On a pedestal was a ball like the mice had traveled in, but it was, of course, huge, and there was a set of stairs that led up to it. Across from it was a glass, and it showed into the room containing the created universe I had seen before. Looking at it, it was amazing to think that that microcosmic universe housed stars and planets and suns, and maybe, life.

Dr. Wright walked up the steps and touched the ball. The silver fingers opened slowly. There was a seat inside with straps. There were a few simple controls.

"Is it like flying a plane?"

"You fly nothing. These switches," and he touched a red one and a yellow one, "are for opening and closing the ball. Once you arrive, you have one switch to set." He pointed at a larger yellow switch. "And then, it doesn't matter if you're inside again or not. You can be anywhere, and it will gather you up."

"Gather me up?" I asked. "How's that?"

"Once you're there, when the mechanism decides to return you, it will gather you into atoms and pull you inside the ball. It will find you, like a mother hen collecting her chicks. You need do nothing. Your atomic structure will be broken into fragments, so that it can make the journey back unharmed, and when you arrive, they will be pieced together again. Then, you touch a certain switch if all goes well, and you can open the ball, and come out. It's that simple."

"How long will I have there?"

"Here, your time gone could be seconds, minutes, days, a few weeks. Possibly a year. No way to tell for certain. But your time there, on that world, in that solar system, inside that universe . . . It could be a lifetime."

And then it struck me. The mice had traveled there and come back, and the life span of a mouse, compared to a human, is quite brief.

I said, "Did the mice age?"

"No," he said, smiling slightly. "We think that may be a peculiar side effect of the transfer. A freezing of the physical; an end to aging. From what we can

tell from the mice, they have ceased to age. And they seem even more spry. None of this has worn off. Perhaps in time it will. But not so far. Not a bad side effect."

"Why?"

Dr. Wright shook his head. "I don't know. We don't even have a theory. It's a mystery."

"And you don't know that humans will be effected the same, do you?"

"No," he said. "We don't. But it seems highly likely."

"Of course," I said. "There were the two that didn't come back."

"True, Brax. Quite true."

As he escorted me out of there and back to my room, I thought: He has not even asked my last name, not once. And then I thought: Unless I made the round trip, there wasn't really any reason for him to know.

I t was three days later when I awoke to find that through the slot in the door they had slipped me fresh clothes. Jeans and tee-shirt, fleece-lined jacket, socks and tennis shoes. I put them on, and an hour later I was brought breakfast. When I finished I was conducted by my guardian back to the room with the large ball in it. The last three days had been used to show me what I needed to do, which was minimal, and what I might expect, which was merely speculative. The only ones who might be able to explain that to me with any authority were the rats who had gone and come back, and they weren't talking.

Inside the ball I strapped myself in the chair. Dr. Wright said, "It will seem to spin. It isn't spinning, and it isn't moving, but it will feel that way. When you arrive, you should make sure the ball is in a safe place. It should, if all goes well, bring you back, as long as it isn't damaged. Do you understand?"

Of course I had heard this for the last few days, but I nodded as if it were the first time the information had been imparted to me. Before I pushed the button to close the door, which was almost all of the left side of the device, I noticed that Dr. Wright was teary eyed. I was uncertain if he felt some concern for my safety, or if he was merely excited to find that his human guinea pig had been so willing and so cooperative without him having to push the hard sell.

"Brax," Dr. Wright said. "I wish you all the luck there is."

He produced a broad belt with a little case fastened to its side, and gave me a fat pocket knife. It was one of those knives with all manner of gadgets attached. Awl, scissors, spoon, two different blades, as well as some devices I didn't recognize.

"You may need these things," he said. "They will all travel with you, will materialize with you when you come to a stop, wherever that may be."

"Provided it's not the middle of a star or underwater," I said.

"Yes, there's that," he said. "But remember. The mice came back."

"Most of them," I said.

He nodded. "The case on the belt contains first aid materials, some other odds and ends. It might come in handy."

I put the knife in the pack and fastened the belt.

"Before I go," I said, "I want you to know this. I know full well that I wouldn't have left here alive had I not chosen to go. Or at least someone would have tried to prevent me. I wouldn't go down easy. I just wanted you to understand I knew what my options were."

"Accident laid you in our hands," Dr. Wright said, and his voice was choked up, as if a knot had been tied in his throat. "I didn't want it this way, but the organization who sponsors us. They leave us little choice. And if we fail, or if the laboratory, our experiments are closed down, then I would suffer the same fate you might expect for yourself. I knew that going into this project. I had a chance to get out. I didn't take it."

"The difference is you chose to be here," I said. "But I will offer you this consolation, Doctor. I want this. I want it bad. I don't like not having a choice, but in this case, it's the choice I want to make."

"You're an odd one, Brax."

"This world is too tame for me, Dr. Wright."

"Then let's hope the next world excites you more."

I smiled at him. "Enough small talk. Let's do it."

I touched the button on the device. Dr. Wright left the room. A moment later all the colors of the universe leaped through the ball and the planets and stars charged toward me like bullets.

Then all was a swirl of darkness, and then the darkness was splattered with white stars. Then they were gone. There was a feeling as if my ears might break. I saw my hands, resting on the small console in front of me, come apart in a billion flakes of colorful energy. I tried to lift my arms, but they appeared to be dissolving. And then they were gone, and my memory of The Jump, as Dr. Wright called it, ended.

Chapter Four
Giants and Monsters

I was whole again. I lifted up my hands and inspected them. Everything seemed okay, all the fingers were in the right place. I patted myself down. A superficial examination proved me to be sound and able bodied. The belt with the pack Dr. Wright had given me was still strapped on me. I was a little dizzy, but other than that, I felt fine.

The ball was wrapped in a green color and the green color was full of light. It took me a moment to adjust, but I soon realized it was foliage around me; a big mass of leaves and boughs, and the leaves were easily the length of an average man's body, two feet or more across. The arrival, the impact after materialization in this mass of greenery, had cracked a band of the machine's see-through covering. It hadn't broken the clear plastic loose, but it had put quite a mark on it; it ran all the length of the glass, like a giant dueling scar. Maybe something similar had happened to one or both of the missing mice. One mouse got out, and something got it. The other mouse may have had its device damaged, and that's why it and the device failed to go back.

All I knew was I was a human mouse, and so far, so good in the physical department. As for my ride? At this point it was debatable. I had no idea how badly it had been damaged, or how little damage it took for it to be nonfunctional.

The leaves were pressed tight as a coat of paint against the clear parts of the ball, dotted with large dollops of dew, or recent rain. The light shining through the leaves made them appear artificial, almost like some kind of ornament.

I set the return button, and then pressed the hatch release. When I did, the powerful, but unseen hinge that was one side of the ball sprang open and knocked the leaves back and the light from the sun shone in bright as a spotlight.

I unfastened my seat belt and got out of the ball, and when I was clear of it, it automatically closed and sealed with the quickness of a snapping turtle. There was no way to open it now. Not until it was ready. I wouldn't be going back inside until it dissolved me again, or whatever it was it did, and returned me to Earth. Provided it was still working.

Before me was a long stretch of brown ground that sloped off at one end. The ground was smooth for the most part, but there were bumps and rolls here and there. I moved away from the ball, and glanced back. The leaves that my machine had pushed aside, now that it had closed, were slowly wrapping themselves around it again. They did this until the only way you might see my traveling machine was to know it was there. And even then, it was doubtful. The sunlight was resting on the leaves, but unlike the view from inside the ball, the leaves appeared dark from the outside.

I looked up.

Above me were limbs and leaves. They climbed high, high, high. It was as if I were trying to see the top of a mountain. Light came through in gaps between the boughs. The gaps were enormous. Some of the limbs were the size of entire redwoods in California.

I walked where there was plenty of light shining through a break in the boughs and vegetation in the manner of great leaves and long needles and flowers, all of which were easily the size of rowboats and all kinds of colors. Through the gap, I could see the sun, and assumed it was the star that had been pointed out to me in the laboratory. Now, here I was on the Fourth Planet from that sun.

The sky was as blue as a Robert Johnson song.

I ambled along, and soon I was walking along the dark brown surface with no limbs above me. I felt as if it should be hot, but it wasn't. I also realized that I felt really good. The air was terrific, so sweet and full of oxygen, I felt a little euphoric.

I walked for a long time. When I looked back, I realized that where I had landed was well in the distance. I turned and walked some more, and then the ground thinned on both sides, became narrow before me.

The land kept tapering. Soon, I could see a clutch of bushes. A moment later I realized they were not bushes at all. They were little growths off of what I was walking on, and what I was walking on wasn't ground.

I was walking on a mostly barren limb, except for that little eruption of greenery. My ground was in fact a limb larger than any tree I had ever seen. I finally came to where it forked and broke off in a jagged manner, most likely due to natural causes.

I carefully looked down.

The earth was miles below. I could make out rivers, like blue lines, and above the rivers, mountain peaks, even a few spotty clouds surrounding the mountains, as if someone who was about to pack it up and move it all were in the process of packing everything in cotton.

I turned around and looked back at the tree. The trunk of the tree was very thick around. It went for a far distance in either direction before it curved on either side. It was filled with massive limbs and all those big leaves, needles and flowers.

Next to that monstrous, strange tree, far away on either side, were other trees, and next to them were more, on and on, beyond vision, into the depths of an unknown world. Between the trees were patches of light and shadow, spreading left and right, climbing high and expanding broadly, and like all the trees, it too was festooned with all manner of different leaves and needles and flowers, and some had round and oblong, multicolored fruit, like Christmas decorations, large as beach balls.

I was standing on one giant limb projecting from one monstrous tree that was merely one of many in a massive forest that rose higher than the mountains and clouds, and yet the air was thick and easy to breathe. I wasn't a scientist, but I knew enough to feel that this world violated certain base assumptions of scientific fact. It wasn't that I felt it lacked science, merely that when created, certain laws of physics had been altered in the creation.

So large were the trees, and so close to one another, the limbs so even and so wide, it would not be difficult to walk from one tree to another. I even determined that the bark of the trees was jagged, and could be grabbed and climbed like a mountain face. Vines hung from a large number of the limbs like ropes, and at a glance, I saw something monkey-like scramble up one and disappear into a wad of foliage.

It was overwhelming, and for a moment, so amazing, I felt as if my legs might fold out from under me and I would collapse.

Gladly as I had come, I now wondered what I was to do here. Then the words Dr. Wright had spoken to me about time here being different than time at home struck me.

I could be here on this fourth planet from this massive sun, for a long, long time.

If the ball no longer worked, if it no longer had the power to break me apart and gather me up in all my pieces, and throw me out of this miniature universe, through dimensional barriers, through time and space, back to my world, then this world of trees was my world forever.

As was often the case with my life, I had made a hasty, impulsive decision and thought it good at the time. I wasn't so sure now.

Of course, there was another factor.

If I had not made the decision, it would have been made for me.

A moment later, standing there on the tip of the branch, all of this running through my mind, my concerns were abruptly lost to me when I saw the most extraordinary sight. A sight that made me believe what I had seen so far was minor in comparison.

Between the large trees, some distance away on another smaller limb, I saw a man moving swiftly. He was on foot and was covering considerable ground (or to be more precise, tree) in great hopping strides, like an excited grasshopper. He was a small man, perhaps five feet in height, and he was lean and dark as the bark of the trees around him, his hair was long and red as a vicious wound. Short as he was, he was large chested, long legged, and long armed. His only clothing was a loincloth. His feet were bare.

He rushed out on the limb, stood on the edge of it, and leaped from it, caught a dangling vine, swung across a vast gap, and landed on the base—again, quite some distance away—of the massive limb on which I stood.

I could see that he had a bow slung over his shoulder, and a quiver of arrows, and he also had what appeared to be a long spear slung by a cord of some kind over his back. He carried a long blue metal sword in his hand. When he spied me, he sort of crouched, as if I were a problem.

I didn't move.

In the distance I heard a sound akin to bamboo being knocked together by a violent wind, saw behind the man there was a stir between the trunks of the trees, where a thick growth of what in fact did look like bamboo grew along a patch of intertwined limbs. The tall green and brown stalks knocked together like angry children banging oversized chopsticks, then from between the long reeds something burst into view that seemed to be out of the imaginings of a lunatic. For a moment I considered the possibility that I might in fact still be lying on that Alaskan shore, my back against a tree, the plane I had stolen in ruins. Or perhaps I was in the spinning ball, somehow lost in limbo, as Dr. Wright said I might be, and my head was stuffed with confusion and imagination as I moved eternally through . . . nowhere.

For what parted the reeds and came into view was what I can only describe as something akin to a praying mantis. It was astride a great blue and yellow, multi-legged critter that looked like a humongous aphid or beetle. There really is no word to describe it. The mantis's mandibles snapped at the air like old-fashioned ice tongs.

Behind it, came another, and another, until three of the mounted creatures were in view, and their mounts were scrambling over limbs and vines with an almost magical grace.

It didn't take a genius to understand that the man was on the run.

There was no way for me to know if the manlike creature was in fact the worst of villains, and the Insectoids, as I named them at first sight, were just and correct in the matter of their pursuit. But, I suppose certain cultural instincts involving man and bug took over, and of course, the fact that he was one and they were three was a deciding factor as well, although I was soon to discover that there were more than three.

At that moment, I didn't consider anything deeply. I just responded, as was my nature, and was soon running toward them. This seems to be a Booker trait. When we should be silent and observe, or run away, we become loud and charge forward, directly into the mouth of trouble.

I was soon aware of the fact that I had incredible energy. Not just adrenaline, but as I ran I found that I was almost leaping. At first I thought it might be due to a lighter gravity, but soon realized it was another reason altogether. My muscles felt extraordinary. I'm not sure what the journey, the transmitter, or the planet, or this universe, had done to me, but it was as if I had been given an enormous transfusion of muscle, and power.

As I ran, the man gave me a look, but soon turned his attention to the mantises and the beetles. If that wasn't problem enough, the reeds parted again, and stepping from them, first one, then another, there were two beings perhaps twenty-five-feet tall. They were humanoid in structure, but broad in the hips and narrow in the shoulders, slumped somewhat with wide mouths that went almost ear to ear, and they had a third eye in the center of their broad foreheads. They were nude except for large net bags that hung around their waists. In the netting were three or four humans on each hip. Men and women and children. They were screaming in a high-pitched language that meant about as much to me as the song of cricket. It amazed me, big as the giants were, that they were able to support these human beings in mesh bags without showing any sign of strain.

The giants had massive feet with long toes. Their hands were enormous, oversized for their bodies; with fingers so long they had an extra row of joints. They carried in one hand what I can only describe as a giant scoop, and in the other a long, loose, open net. At the back of their necks, partially on the rear of their skulls, was a strange-looking, squid-like creature. Tentacles thrashed all about like Medusa hair. I couldn't determine if these things were in fact some kind of secondary creature, or just some structural accouterment that came with the giants at birth.

If that wasn't bad enough, the reeds rattled again, and two more of the creatures appeared, their waists dripping in netting filled with yelling humans.

The little man was brave. He stopped, stuck the sword in the limb at his feet, quickly swung the bow off his shoulder and flicked three arrows out between his fingers, laid them all against the bow, fired one right after the other, like bullets from a chamber.

One of the arrows went into the foremost giant, took an eye, the other lodged in the throat, and a third went into the chest. The last shot was about as effective as a porcupine quill in an elephant's knee. The eye and throat shot, however, yielded results.

The monster grabbed at the arrow, jerked it free, taking what was left of his eye with it, and then he grasped at the one in his throat. The blood was pouring from that wound like a crimson river. It had hit a vital spot, an artery, and the giant wavered and stumbled, and fell, dropping onto the netting and its contents, crushing them like overripe fruit beneath his massive body, squirting blood and innards from under him and in all directions, like lumpy jam.

The man who had loosed the arrows let out with a bellow. It was not a sound of triumph, but of heartache. He had killed one of his tormentors only to destroy a large number of his own kind. The death of his enemy brought the death of his kin. And by his own hand.

I was at his side now, and I snatched the spear off of his back with one clean move. He turned, as if to stop me, then saw me lunging forward with the spear, tossing it smoothly into the knee of one of the giants. It might as well have been a porcupine quill in an elephant's leg, but it was well placed. The giant stumbled and went to one knee.

The mantis creatures on their beetles had held back, to let the giants have their way, but now, seeing one dead, and one with his knee down, they rushed forward with a squealing and clicking kind of war cry.

One of my new comrade's arrows knocked a mantis from its mount. I jerked his sword from its stuck position in the tree, and sprang forward, landing on the head of one of the beetles, and driving the sword through the chitinous chest of its rider. It was a deathblow, and the mantis tumbled off in a crash that sounded like dry bones rolling over rocks.

I fell off the beetle and saw it scuttle away, but decided I could catch it with my newfound muscles. Springing forward, I landed on its back and caught the long, vine reins and pulled at them, discovered the beetle worked very much like a horse. I wheeled it and saw that the man had finally broken and ran, which was, of course, the only sensible thing to do.

I charged after him, whipping the sword above my head. One of the mantises and its beetle were closing in on him, and as I came up behind the monstrosity, it turned its head and pulled from its belt a sword, tried to wheel its insect steed about to face me.

He was too slow. I was on him. I whipped an arc with my blade and clove his head from his shoulders with a single strike. I plunged the beetle forward, into the thickening foliage, came upon my new companion, darting for cover. I called out to him. Certainly he couldn't understand my words, but he understood my intent. He wheeled about and took my extended hand as I, with effortless ease, swung him up behind me on the beetle.

Behind us the giants and the remaining mantis and its beetle plunged toward us.

The man I had rescued swung around on the backside of the beetle, so that he was facing the rear, and let loose with a volley of arrows. I glanced back once, just in time to see the mantis catch a shaft and fall from its mount into a thick wad of greenery. Then we gained ground, leaving the remaining giants and their poor captives behind.

When we finally stopped, I tied the beetle to a limb with the reins, not knowing what else to do. My companion pulled some leaves and grass here and there, gave it to the beetle. It squatted down with its many legs beneath it, and ate.

The man looked at me and smiled. His face was V-shaped, almost elfin. His hair was very red. I had never seen hair that red. He was all muscles, but the muscles, though similar in construct to mine, seemed somehow overlong and less pronounced, as if they had been drawn taught like a bow string.

He reached out cautiously for his sword, which I still held. I gave it up with minor reluctance. Then he gently touched my shoulder with the palm of his hand, and dipped his chin quickly. I assumed this was this world's equivalent of a handshake.

I did the same in return. He moved away from me immediately, toward a clutch of strange plants that were blue in color, rose up high and were sharp tipped. As I followed, I realized these plants looked just like the blue sword I had been wielding, only longer. The sword, sharp as it was, was in fact a natural creation, and was some form of vegetation. It grew straight up in a large natural crop, and some of the growth was blue, some of it was red. The red blades drooped slightly, and I immediately had the impression that the red ones were a younger growth of the same plant.

My new partner bent down close to the tree into which the sharp plants grew, and got hold of it there. There was no blade there, just a kind of root. He pulled at it, and it came free from the great limb on which we stood; when it popped free, it did so loudly. He had picked one of the shorter growths, about six feet in length, and I saw that at least two feet of it was of the root. The root made a natural handle, except for a mass of fibrous vines that grew out of that portion. Bending down, he placed the fresh-pulled shaft on the tree trunk, and began shaving off the vines, or perhaps a more accurate description is smaller roots, until the larger root from which they grew was smooth. He chopped off part of that, left about seven inches of the haft remaining, the rest sword.

He handed it to me. I took it carefully. There was no guard, as such, but the root flared naturally close to where the blade part of the plant began, proving a kind of protection from your hand sliding up on the sharp edge. It was amazing that such a plant made a fine weapon. It was lighter than most swords of that size I had handled, by quite a bit, and its blade was of extraordinary sharpness and rivaled cold steel. I tapped it a few times on the base of the limb on which we stood, looked up and grinned at him.

He smiled. He took his sword and smashed up the root he had cut off of the sword, the part that was more like wood, and broke it open. He pushed it under my nose. It smelled sweet, kind of like a cross between the honey of a bee and a honey suckle plant. He tasted it, made a universal yum noise to let me know it tasted good.

Handing it to me, I took it, and ripped into it with gusto. I was suddenly starving. And though it was sweet, there was a texture to it that was akin to meat, and after only a few bites, I was feeling strong again.

We moved on by beetle back until the great sun's light thinned through the trees and the sounds of wild animals, and what I assumed were birds, filled the air in recognition of the coming of the night. We stopped just before dark and my companion found a long green plant that sprouted out from the side of a tall tree, the base of which was of phenomenal diameter, and could not have been reached around by the entire East Texas town from which I came if they all linked hands. It went on for what appeared to be miles.

The green shaft of the plant was hollow, and my sword, with a bit of cutting, fit right into it. He handed me my natural sword and sheath, and then went about cutting vines. He took the sword and sheath back, fastened these to it so that I soon had a harness where I could sling the sword over my shoulder.

I thanked him, and though he didn't understand the words, again, the meaning was clear.

He took over control of the beetle, and I rode on the back, as the insect climbed up the side of the tree. There was a saddle for the rider, and an extension on which I could sit, and the back of the saddle had a kind of lift that supported me above my buttocks and kept me from falling. I also quickly learned to lean forward as the amazing bug climbed up into thicker foliage. There were also straps that I could use to harness myself in, and they were easily unstrapped; they were made of some kind of vegetation that worked much like Velcro.

I noticed there were great gaps in the larger limbs, like caverns. My companion soon picked one of these, which was perhaps ten feet high and twenty feet long, and guided our mount into it. Once there, he used some of the vines he had kept to hobble our bug, and went out and got more greenery for it to eat while I stood at the mouth of our cavern and looked out at the dying light.

It was as if the night was a curtain, and it dropped down slow and certain, and soon it was dead dark. Or at least for a moment, but then my eyes adjusted, and up through the limbs of the trees I could see a patch of night sky, and a huge star, pulsating red and blue.

When my partner returned he had some fruits for us to eat, and more food for the bug. He built a fire by using some kind of growth that lit up when touched with a blue root of some sort. I didn't understand it exactly, but it was a little like sticking a nine-volt battery against steel wool. It blazed.

When the fire was going, he pulled some large limbs around it and laid huge leaves over those to block out the direct light of the fire. It struck me that for anyone to see us up within this wood cavern, amidst this great clutch of foliage, deep in this wild and strange jungle, would have been a great feat, and more likely an accident, but I trusted my companion's judgment on this matter far more than mine.

After awhile, I went back to the edge of our immediate home and looked up again at the star. He joined me, stood and looked too.

"Badway," he said.

I looked at him.

He pointed up.

"Badway de moola," he said.

This meant nothing to me. I pointed at the star. "Badway?"

He nodded. "Badway. Badway de moola."

Whatever this meant, we were in agreement.

Back inside he gave me some heavy and very moldable large leaves. We lay on one and wrapped the other one around us. The leaves, like some kind of cocoon, enveloped us and held us loosely in its warmth.

We slept.

Chapter Five
The Horrors

In the night the rain came. It woke me with terrific lightning blasts and rolls of thunder like bowling balls being tumbled about inside a great steel drum. I sat up and saw that my partner sat up too. He lifted a hand, in a kind of wave, and lay back down. For him, I assumed, this was not uncommon. Soon I could hear his breathing, as he went back to sleep.

I got up and stood at the mouth of the tree cavern and watched great waves of rain splash through the jungle, caught up on a cool wind. It became so ferocious I had to back into my wooden cave, pressing my body near the rear. The rain smacked all the way inside of our cubby, and soon the air smelled wet and strange, the aromas fostered by stimulated plants. The smells were mostly unknown to me, but a few had some faint familiarity to boiled coffee and rich vanilla, a twist of lemon, a stinging sensation in the nostrils like sea salt. The rest were beyond my olfactory experience. The smells came in waves. And so did the rain.

I watched it for awhile. I found myself practicing the meditation that Jack had taught me. I didn't levitate, but I did manage to sleep well after I finished and turned back in between my sleeping leaves.

By morning, the water had seeped in, and I was damp. But I noticed a curious thing. The tree wood was sucking up the water. On earth, in this kind of environment, everything would have remained wet for a long time, and rot would have been a problem, but here, the water was absorbed deep into the tree in a short time, so the damp didn't stick around long enough to rot anything.

Physically, I had never felt better. As I said before, my muscles seemed imbued with strength and stamina. It was as if the very air I breathed had filled my veins with energy. I was contemplating all this, when I realized my new companion was up. He looked at me in my wet clothes and grinned. He, wearing only a loincloth, had fewer garments to contend with, and no shoes, and therefore was not as encumbered by water.

Our beetle was waiting patiently for a wad of breakfast greenery that we gave it. It ate contentedly, its sad eyes more like a deer's than an insect's, watching us while we ate stringy vegetation from a broken gourd. The beetle crunched its morning meal contentedly, and something about our sad-eyed mount made me feel affection for it. I decided to call it Butch, at least to myself.

Although I had no idea where we were going or why, or even if we were on a mission other than continued flight from what might be chasing us, I fell in line like a soldier. Pretty soon we were mounted on Butch, heading into the twisting depths of the jungle that grew up from the massive boughs of the trees. It was a jungle contained on one massive tree that covered miles. Other trees with their own jungles could be accessed by our beetle. It was unique, to say the least. Jungles growing on massive trees that intersected with other trees and jungles. It was a world of jungle, populated by little jungles. I had never imagined the possibility of such a thing.

By midday the jungle had turned warm, but not hot. The rain water had been sucked into the plants, and as we went, many of the leaves and branches reached out to touch us like curious children, and then jerked away as if frightened.

From my companion's manner, I was certain he was watching out behind us, to see if we still had pursuers. My thought was it would hardly be worth the trouble for that great band of giants, beetles and insect riders, to pursue a mere two men when they had so many already captured. Why they had been captured I was uncertain, but my guess was slavery.

It took me awhile, but on our second day out, I was able to ascertain that my new friend's name was Booloo. He taught me this by touching his chest and repeating the word until I understood. I taught him my name, or a derivative of it. Brax.

It took me yet another day to ascertain from the position of the sun that we were in fact not fleeing our pursuers, but circling back toward them; this seemed like a less than intelligent procedure, but I was uncertain how to pass this thought along to Booloo, nor was I positive that if I could, it would matter. I might be better off abandoning Booloo if he was going to go back into the jaws of his former captors, but I felt being alone in this world of strange plants and animals without a mount or knowledge of how to survive might be worse. I made the decision to stick with him. For what it was worth, he was now my only friend.

One afternoon as the sun began to dip, and a greenish glow slipped through the jungle, Booloo directed Butch high up into the trees (and I refer to the trees of the little jungle, not the tree that supported it). Our insect scuttled acrobatically over limbs and tangled vines and the tops of trees, with an up-and-down motion that I had finally gotten used to; it was like gaining your sea legs on a ship. It was a great way to observe the dipping sun, and I began to realize that the greenish glow that often persisted was most likely due to floating pollen. With my sinus problems, I was surprised I was not bothered, but I began to think it was the pollen from the trees that was in fact giving me my feelings of strength and stamina.

We came to a plunge in the forest, and Booloo guided Butch down into a grove of great trees, just as the wind picked up and came twisting through the forest like a wraith. The trees we were among were tall and white and had clumps of vegetation at their tops, but were otherwise limbless, smooth, and not that big around. When the wind blew the trees rattled together at their summits and the sound of their striking one another was like the clacking of thousands of hoofbeats.

We rode Butch between the trees, and just before the sun died down behind the world, we saw what looked like a great sheet of gray gauze stretched and wound about a dozen trunks. It twisted up to a height of thirty feet. As soon as we observed it, it was no longer there.

Booloo halted Butch and swung off, dropping the reins. Butch remained in his spot as I climbed down and moved with Booloo toward what had been there only moments ago, but was now nothing more than night. But as we grew closer, Booloo drew his sword, extended it, and slashed. There was a ripping sound, and then what had seemed like growing darkness split apart and dangled down, looking now like the gray gauze it had at first resembled. Whatever it was, it was a natural camouflage. Booloo seemed excited to have discovered it, and he knelt down with his sword and cut off two large swathes. He touched it with his sword, and the sword stuck. He tugged the sword free, and waited. The stickiness, which was white as puss, began to fade. Booloo reached down and picked it up. It was obvious it was no longer sticky. Once cut from its source, that aspect of it appeared to dissolve.

When Booloo saw my confusion, he smiled. It was a glorious smile. He stuck his sword into the ground, or the tree that served as our ground, and flicked the patch around his shoulders and let it fall over the front of his body. He clutched it tight, and a moment later, he seemed to be nothing more than a floating head. He had naturally been camouflaged.

The look on my face made him laugh. He whipped off the cloak, for that's how I now thought of it, and handed it to me. He picked up the other for himself. He bent down and proceeded to roll it up. I held my cloak in front of me. On one side was the part that served as camouflage, but the other side was transparent. I lifted it over my head, saw that I could see through it almost as clearly as if it were not there.

Booloo began to talk, and his words were like a stream. They wouldn't cease. He was telling me about the material he had just cut into patches, of that I was certain, and it seemed to excite him to no end. My guess is that he was trying to explain the rarity of it, and the good fortune of finding it.

It was during his explanation that behind him, on the greater expansion of the gauze, I saw something that made me realize the source of the material Booloo had just cut was not of its own making. A creature that looked very much like an earthly spider was crawling down from on high. It had twelve

legs and large black eyes and dripping chelicerae; it scuttled rapidly on its hairy legs, and my immediate thought was that it was not hurrying down to give us an enthusiastic greeting. Booloo had just cut a portion of its web, and the beast resented the invasion.

I pulled my sword just as Booloo noticed its approach and pulled his, and then the thing leaped. I jumped out of its way, and was amazed to find that the leap was effortless and carried me a great distance. When I wheeled to look back, Booloo was under the spider, and its snapping "jaws" were trying to drive its fangs into him. He was managing to keep it at bay by pushing his sword crossways between the set of fangs, but the power of the creature was weakening his grip and his resolve.

With one step and a leap, I was on the creature's back. I drove my sword down hard into its head. It then bucked, like a horse, and threw me back into the hanging patch of gauze, which I knew now to be a web. I stuck there immediately, but my sword arm was free, and as the monster rushed at me, I stabbed out at it and planted my sword directly into one of its eyes, which exploded a kind of black goo that splattered on me and the web.

As the spider snapped its fangs in the air, I saw Booloo scrambling up over the top of the spider, clutching at it with one hand, while driving his sword deep into its broad back.

I pushed out as far as I could, and tried to cut backwards with my sword. Pinned as I was to the web, I found this difficult, but by slashing over my shoulder, I was able to cut loose enough of my restraint to fall forward and out of the web. Still, it clung to me. I stood and found myself twisted up in it. I cut at it viciously with the sword arm until it came free. A moment later, the web relaxed and fell away from me and onto the tree beneath my feet. The spider may have made it, but it seemed to be a living thing, and any section of it cut down and separated from the rest, lost its life and its stickiness, if not its camouflage.

I turned my attention to Booloo and the spider, saw that it was scuttling up one of the many branches that served as a tree on our giant base tree. Booloo was hanging to it like a parasite with one hand, and with the other, slashing at it with his sword.

I glanced around for Butch, planning to use him as a method of pursuit, and though he was normally content to stand by until we were ready to mount, he, or perhaps she, had scampered out of sight for fear of the spider, or perhaps he had sniffed out something to eat.

I stuck the light sword in my teeth and started to climb, and found that my newly acquired muscles had come with tremendous agility. I was able to scurry up the tree as effortlessly as a squirrel, my only impediment being my shoes, the soles of which slipped as I climbed.

Within instants, I had reached the spider, but had dropped my sword from my mouth. It had struck a limb as I climbed, cutting into the side of my mouth. It seemed the better part of valor was to let it fall than to have it inadvertently slice my head in half. Climbing onto the spider from the rear, dragging myself across its back by holding onto its thick hairs, which sprouted all over its body,

I arrived at the spot where Booloo clung. He too had lost his sword, and was hanging for dear life as the spider navigated rapidly through the branches, trying to drag us off.

Finally, as if on cue, we both abandoned our mount, and nested ourselves onto a tree limb. We looked at each other. Booloo laughed. We looked up at the spider, still climbing, and then it stopped. It turned and we ceased to laugh.

It was coming back.

The spider-thing rushed down the tree, darting between limbs and leaves, set for the attack. Booloo and I moved off to the left and along a narrow limb. The limb parted, like a fork. I set out toward the thinner section of it, while Booloo veered right, climbing upwards and across to another tree. He called to me, repeating my name over and over, realizing we had gone in opposite directions. I ignored him. I had bigger problems. One of those big problems was a spider about the size of a delivery truck. I snatched a large yellow, oblong-shaped nut from one of tree's leafy boughs, wheeled and hurled it just as the monster was turning to pursue Booloo.

The nut hit the spider hard. There came from it a noise that was neither cry nor bark, but somewhere in between. It made the hairs on the back of my neck stand up.

Angry, it switched its path, darted after me. I went out as far on the limb as I could, then leaped to another, grabbing at a thick ropelike vine, feeling it give slightly, allowing me to swing out and down onto the bough of a tree below. When I looked up, the spider leapt from the limb where I had left it, light as a feather in the wind; it sailed across space and barely clutched its multiple legs into a netting of vines, and scrambled down after me. As it did, I jumped onto a narrow limb that rocked beneath my weight, saw there was another, quite some distance away. If I were on Earth I would have had no chance at all reaching it, but now, with my muscles hot-wired by the atmosphere and its strange pollen, I pivoted to watch the spider coming toward me at a leg-clicking run that was made all the more frightening by its leaking, savaged eye, its snapping jaws dripping green poison.

When it was twenty feet away, panic nearly caused me to retreat and leap. But I held my spot. Ten feet away. My knees coiled, and I half turned. Looking over my shoulder I saw that it was no more than six feet from me. I ran along the length of the limb, and jumped, successfully landed across the way on another limb. It gave beneath me, but sprang back to position, nearly tossing me from it.

I turned to see the spider hurtling toward me in midair, its legs flailing. I think both the beast and I knew simultaneously it wasn't going to make it. When it was three feet from my limb, it began to wag its legs and twist its head, and then it dipped and fell, splattering against limbs and tree trunks. It tangled briefly in vines, the vines snapped, and down it dropped, crashing almost directly in front of its web in a confusion of legs and body explosions.

I turned as I heard Booloo let out with a yip of triumph from a tree across the way. He leaped up and down on a limb like an excited monkey, chattering in his strange language.

Chapter Six
The Woman

We gathered up our cloaks from the web of the spider, and went looking for Butch. After some searching, we found the creature amongst a clutch of strange red and blue plants. Butch was munching them contentedly, having forgotten whatever had frightened it in the first place.

Riding Butch again, we continued on our way until we came to the plants from which Booloo had made my now-lost sword. Here we paused and made one a piece, using my pocket knife to cut the plants near their base where they were less strong, and more like common wood. The sword I now possessed was, frankly, not up to the one I had carried before. It was shorter and not as straight, but this was the condition of the entire plant, and no other plant of the same sort was currently within sight. It wasn't ideal, but under the circumstances it would have to do. The swords were still very serviceable.

Again, I was just going along for the ride because to do otherwise would leave me stranded in this strange land without assistance. I could easily starve surrounded by food, and not even know it. But, as we traveled, I carefully noted the fruits and vegetables Booloo chose, so that if we were ever separated I might at least have a fighting chance.

Two days later, after enduring windstorms and rainstorms, sleeping in tree caves, practicing my meditation, dancing about with my sword to accustom myself to its weight, riding until my butt ached, we came upon the giants and the mantis-things. We saw them from a distance. We were high up in a tree, strapped onto Butch, and when we dipped down slightly, letting the limbs of the tree predict our course, we could see through gaps in the leaves and limbs, a patch of devastated forest. Keep in mind that when I refer to forest, I refer to the trees that grew out of one of the great trees that on Earth would make up a small town. In fact, some of these forests, or jungles, were based on what would be a limb of a tree; though the term limb seems inadequate, considering the size of such a growth. To give you some idea of the size, in the distance, if we were high enough, we could see other great trees, looking like continents across an expanse of mist and blowing leaves.

But this smaller part of the forest to which I refer was hacked down and burnt, except for a few spotty, thin trees stripped of limbs. They were left standing, but their purpose was not an aesthetic one. Dangling from them by ropes were field-dressed bodies of men and women, headless, fastened to long hemp-style ropes; the corpses were split open and dripped blood; the corpses were those of men, women, and children.

It was a revolting sight, made all the more revolting, because as we watched, the giants approached one of the trees, tore down a few of the field-dressed bodies, and carried them toward a crackling fire. The fire was fueled by the trees they had chopped down. The meat was tossed directly onto the blazing pile amidst loud sounds of satisfaction from the giants; the meat hissed and popped in the flames. The mantis things, dismounted, came forward then. They moved erratically, as if balanced on stilts. They squatted down, well outside the circle where the giants gathered.

Besides the corpses, there were living men and women—no children, they had all been disposed of by the giants—fixed firmly by long, yellow ropes that were attached to the tops of the trees. The ropes dangled down with the humans tied at their ends. They also had their arms and legs bound as well.

Seeing this, Booloo started to urge Butch forward, but I clasped his shoulder. He turned and looked at me. I shook my head, hoping the movement meant the same here as it did on Earth. He looked at me for a long moment, then dropped his head and turned back into his position on Butch's back. He trembled with anger.

It felt odd for me, for the first time in a long time, to be the rational one.

I gained his attention again, and by method of making signs with my hands, tried to make him realize that our chances were better if we waited until dark. I touched one of the folded up cloaks he had made from the spider's web. He nodded. We dismounted, and led Butch along the limb on which we were traveling, back into thicker foliage. There we tied Butch in a place where he could graze, and we went up a tall, thin tree, thick with foliage. At the top of it we found positions on limbs and looked out and down.

The giants were pulling smoking, blackened bodies from the fire and feeding themselves. They pushed and shoved one another and tore at the partially cooked flesh with their teeth like wild dogs. The things on the backs of their heads lay still, the tentacles not moving.

The mantises waited in a circle around them. From time to time the giants would toss a chunk of the meat outside the circle, and the mantises would scramble and fight for the scraps. After awhile, great gourds were brought forth. Soon the giants were gulping loudly from them.

It didn't take long to determine that the contents of the gourds consisted of some kind of alcoholic beverage, for soon the giants were pushing and shoving one another, fighting, and then falling down to sleep. As they did, the insectoids rushed in and grabbed at the disgusting remains of the meal, the last dregs in the gourds. It was a horrid spectacle.

As we observed, I noted that tied to one of the trees was a woman that stood out like fire on an ice flow. She was the most beautiful amongst a number of beautiful women. In fact, from what I had seen, a trademark of these people seemed to be their astonishing beauty. If the people of Earth could see them, each and every one of them, though constructed slightly different from Earthly humans, would have been thought models or movie stars. But even among a group of beautiful people, she was outstanding.

She was long and lean and curvaceous, with an almost elfin face framed by great waves of scarlet hair. Even from a distance, unable to see the detail of her features, she was striking. She was nude from the waist up, and her breasts were perfectly shaped and firm. Her only clothing was a kind of sarong of dark material fastened about her waist. She was shoeless. I was so stunned by her appearance, for a moment, I nearly lost my grip on a limb that held me in place.

As I was watching her, Booloo tapped my shoulder and pointed directly at her. He touched his chest. "Choona. Choona," he said.

I was uncertain of what he was actually saying, but the meaning seemed obvious. The beautiful redhead was his woman. It became evident now why we had made a wide circle to catch back up with the giants. He wanted to rescue her, though had he been left to his own devices, charging down amongst them on Butch's back, he would have most certainly been enslaved, killed or eaten.

I nodded to him, looked back at the woman, feeling weak, and even envious of Booloo. But when I turned back to him, I clasped his shoulder and nodded, hopefully letting him know I was a willing assistant in any enterprise to rescue her.

The night came down like a drift of crepe paper and fell onto and twisted between the trees and coated them black. With it came the sounds of night birds and creatures, cries and squeaks and grunts and growls. The fires still raged below, and the light from them flickered across the standing trees that held the prisoners. The beautiful woman was nothing more than a shadow now, but I couldn't take my eyes off of her. When I had first seen her she had been standing, regal as a queen, but now she was sitting on the ground, her head hung. Seeing her that way made me angry and sick to my stomach.

If the giants were to move in her direction, perhaps to prepare her as food, I was certain I would hurry down there and do the best I could to save her. Of course, I felt for the others, but I must be honest and say the sight of her, the one Booloo referred to as Choona, gave me a strength and direction I had not felt in days. Without even knowing her, I knew I would give my life for her. I suppose this is what they call Love At First Sight.

Booloo fastened his bow to the side of Butch, because he had no arrows left, and we donned our cloaks and took our swords, and moved silently down among them on foot.

The cloaks made us dark as the night, but they were not perfect. When I looked at Booloo, I could see from time to time that he was like a patch of darkness coming loose from the gloom. I could see him moving, and could discern his shape, and occasionally, when the cloak slipped from where he gathered it at his head with his hand, I could glimpse his face.

But, if I were not expecting to see him, and if I were some distance away, then the probability of seeing him, or me, was small. Or so I hoped.

We stayed as far away as possible from the fires and the giants who were stretched out on the ground sleeping. The mantis creatures were standing near the trees, watching over the captives, stirring about restlessly with their stilt-like moves.

I slid in between two of them without being detected. I had my sword held close to my side, and when I was near the captives, I moved the cloak to reveal my face, ever so slightly. One man, startled by my presence, let out a gasp. I threw a finger to my lips for silence, but it was too late. I could hear movement behind me. I gathered the cloak around me and moved as quietly as I could to the left, and turned ever so slightly, hoping no more than my eye was revealed by the cloak that went from my head to my feet.

One of the mantis things came over to the man who had gasped, and kicked him. It was for no other reason than sport. I remained still. The mantis kicked the man again, made a noise in his throat like someone rattling dice in a tin cup, then moved away to join his chortling comrades.

I saw across the way that Booloo had already managed to cut a number of captives free, and they were slipping off into the darkness. I went about doing the same thing, cutting all those at the tree nearest me free. They drifted away into the gloom, toward where the trees grew thick. Moving quickly, I made the tree where Booloo's sister was held, and arrived there at the same time he did. We actually collided slightly, not noticing one another, veiled as we were.

I'm proud to say it was my sword that sliced away Choona's bonds. As I did it, I let go of my cloak, allowing my face to be shown. Her eyebrows lifted when she saw me. Perhaps, because of the dark, there was little she could make of my features, and perhaps she was trying to associate me with one of her own tribe. When Booloo touched her arm, she smiled and hugged him beneath the cloak.

It was then that I heard a noise behind me. We had revealed too much of ourselves with our movements, and camouflaged or not, we had been seen. The insect warriors let out a series of snapping noises, drew swords and rushed toward us.

In the next moment, I flicked off my cloak, letting it hang over one shoulder. I rammed my sword through a sticklike body with a technique so smooth it was like pushing a hot knife through warm butter. The thing fell, and then the other mantis things were on me.

By this time all the captives had been freed and were scrambling toward the forest outside the chopped and burned circle. I jetted like a bullet between foes, bobbing, weaving, stabbing, and slashing. Everything I had ever learned from Jack Rimbauld I used, and it was such a part of me, I never had to think about a particular move, or method. I was natural, precise, and deadly. Within moments, the mantises lay around me like stacked sticks.

The noise, however, had alerted the giants, who were up, and drunkenly weaving about, grabbing at their swords, swinging wildly, even managing to chop down a couple of their own. The weird growths, or whatever they were at the backs of their necks, flashed out their feet, or tentacle-like appendages, waved them in the air as if directing traffic from all directions.

I finished up with a mantis by dodging under its thrust and coming up with a backhand swing that took off its head, then I broke and ran, barely maintaining my weapon as I threw the cloak over me and dashed across the devastated ground toward where the forest grew thick again.

Chapter Seven
The Warrior Star

In the forest I was able to climb up a tree and find a broad limb on which to rest. I pulled the cloak tight about me, left it open slightly around my face so that I could see.

Below me, the mantises were scrambling about through the forest, and the torch-wielding giants were hacking at the underbrush and small trees with their great broadswords, felling them like they were nothing more than cardboard tubes. Behind them, I could still see the great fires raging. I could also see that some of the humans we had cut loose had been apprehended, and the monsters, both mantis and giant, were making short work of them, not trying to capture them, but going straight for the kill.

A short time later, the giants were setting fire to the forest. The blaze caught slowly, but finally it caught, and I was forced to abandon my tree, move across to another.

Like a monkey, I fled from one tree to the next, grabbing limbs and vines. I couldn't believe how this planet had changed my muscles and abilities. I finally came to a great dip in the vegetation and finally a deep ravine. I scuttled down the tree that was on the edge of that divide, losing my cloak in the process, but I maintained my sword. I had just touched ground, when I heard a whisper, and a soft voice speaking in the language of Booloo.

It was Booloo himself, and Choona. There were two others with them, two men. I had accidentally come upon my new companions.

Booloo, like me, had lost his cloak, but had held onto his sword. We had little time celebrate our reunion. Looking up, I saw bobbing licks of light, realized it was the torches of the giants. I could see a great blaze behind them. They had been trapped by their own fire, and the fire was driving them toward the deep ravine.

Soon, we could see their heads rising up amongst the trees like trees themselves, their three eyes reflecting the flickering light of their torches, their teeth glistening wetly. It was as if I had been caught inside an old Grimm's fairy tale of giants and monsters, for below them, some on the backs of their beetles, some on foot, were the mantises.

A great flash of torchlight fell over us, and one of the giants let out a bellow, and charged forward. I sprang forward with my sword, leaping so that my foot landed on the bent knee of the closest giant. From there I sprang effortlessly until I landed on his belt, and with another leap, I was even with his neck. While in the air, I slashed at his throat with all my might.

Even as I took the long fall down, his hot blood gushed from his throat like a fountain and splashed down on me. I hit the ground with amazing lightness that even I didn't understand. Then I was bounding up a tree, using my free arm to grab and my feet to climb. I leapt from limb to limb and hurtled myself out of the tree and into the face of another giant, grabbing at a long strand of his hair, clutching my fists into it, and plunging my sword into his middle eye with such savage force I felt it touch the back of his skull. My blade had gone through and pierced the thing that clutched to the back of his head; it fell loose from him with a screech, and splattered below.

The giant still stood. He bellowed and grabbed at me, but I swung the sword and severed one of his fingers, swung around on the strand of hair until I was behind him, dangling down his back. With a quick move, I was up and on his shoulder. I reached around and cut his throat from ear to ear with a whipsaw motion.

As he toppled, I rode him to the ground, like a falling tree.

On my feet again, I wheeled and saw that Booloo was attacking the legs of one of the giants, and his two male companions were grabbing a mantis, jerking him off of his beetle mount. I turned again, looking for the girl. She had snatched up the fallen mantis's sword and was jolting across a clear patch of ground. As I watched, she sprang and hit one of the insects, knocking him off the back of his beetle, coming down on him and driving the purloined sword with all her force through his chest. Then she was up, whipping the sword about, doing battle with two other mantises trying to close in on her from left and right.

Choona moved with incredible dexterity, causing one of the mantis's slashes to swing above her and instead find its mark in the side of his companion. And then Choona was up on the beetle behind the remaining mantis, ramming the sword into his back, the point of it leaping out of his chest like an arrow shot from his innards. She dumped him off the beetle, kicked her heels into the bug, and caught up with the other beetle, grabbed its reins and called out to the others of her kind.

The two others were soon on the mount, riding double. Choona loped over to where Booloo and I had joined together, stuck out a hand and pulled Booloo up behind her. He in turn pulled me up behind him. I barely fit back there. Riding double was all right, but triple?

More giants came through the forest, and more mounted mantises, all of them driven forward by the fire and the chugs of foul-smelling smoke. Choona clicked to our bug and rode him down the side of the deep ravine, with me clutching to Booloo so as not to fall.

I thought of poor Butch, back there tied to a branch, waiting. It was my guess that he would eventually work himself free, perhaps even eat his reins, and find his way in the wild. But at that moment, Butch was the least of my worries. Our adversaries were gaining on us. The giants stopped at the edge of the ravine and yelled insults, jerked up small trees and tossed them at us. We saw our companions on their mounts take a hit and tumble off and fall screaming down into the deep ravine; we could hear their bodies strike the water below.

Debris whistled by us, but none of it hit home. We went into the deeper dark of the ravine, and when I turned and looked up, I saw that the fire had made its way nearly to the edge. The giants were blaring out in pain. Flames had enveloped several, and they collapsed inside the inferno. Several of them leaped over the edge of the ravine, into the dark, and moments later I heard the crash of their bodies below.

The mantises, on the backs of the surefooted beetles, were doing fine, however, and they were gaining on us.

I was about to leap off the beetle to lighten the load for Choona and Booloo, cling to the vines that grew down the side of the ravine, and take my chances with the mantises, when I realized they were close, but not actually pursuing. They had given up on us and were now practicing the art of survival. Perhaps without their giant comrades, their masters, they felt little obligation to continue their pursuit of us. Whatever their intent, they veered off and rode their beetles down the side of the canyon, dipped away into darkness.

When we came to the bottom of the ravine, I was surprised to discover that there was not only a run of water, but crashing rapids. Booloo directed our beetle to the edge of the river, and forced it into the churning water. I thought this the height of insanity, not to mention stupidity, but a moment later the beetle was flowing up and down with the route of the water as if it were a raft. Now and again, the beetles' legs would rise from the water and slash, and our direction would turn slightly. As we proceeded, the flames from the fire on the rise above diminished, and finally there was nothing but blackness and wetness; the water sloshed against us and sometimes rolled over our beetle. I determined that the creature was able to see in the dark, and was also smarter than it looked. It could navigate between rocks and swells quite deftly. This is not to say that I felt we were safe, or that the beetle was fail proof, but I did decide after a few moments of bobbing up and down in the racing river that we were far better off than we had been moments before.

I don't know how long we rafted down the river on our beetle, but eventually the creature, perhaps tiring, made landfall. We were exhausted. No sooner had we dismounted and found a place to tie out our mount so that it might graze than we collapsed on the ground and fell fast asleep.

For the next few days we stayed close to the base limb that amounted to our terra firma. We tried to stay out of the trees that grew up from it. Our beetle, though it had the strength to carry the three of us into the trees, wasn't designed to accommodate comfortably, and securely, more than two for great distances in that manner. No doubt, had we tried to climb with all of us on its back, I would have tumbled off and been squashed into the foliage below.

We didn't come across any of the other escapees as we went, and I hoped that they, like us, had been fortunate. I can't tell you exactly how long we traveled. I know that I meant to count days, and did for some time, but eventually lost tally.

I found that much of my time was spent in observing Choona as we rode on the beetle. Her back was all that was visible to me, and sometimes she was in the front of the beetle with Booloo between us. I couldn't help but stare at her well-shaped shoulders over which her hair tumbled like a waterfall of blood.

When we paused for meals, I observed her as carefully as I could, without seeming to stare. She and Booloo spoke to each other often, but there never seemed to be any overly affectionate moments, which, though they certainly would have had the right to have them, would have pained me as deeply as if a knife were stuck in my ribs. On one hand, I wanted to get away from them because of my feelings, and on the other, I couldn't stand the thought of being away from her luminous presence.

The region we were traveling through, though well wooded, was less thick than where Booloo and I had wandered, and at night there were areas where I could clearly see the sky. One night, after a long day of riding, we stopped to rest and eat. I chewed on a root given to me, and drank juice from a large gourd that I had harvested from one of many trees that held them; the liquid inside was almost pure water, but with a slight taste that I can only equate with lemon. As I ate and drank, I sat and looked up at the alien sky. It was littered with stars, but there was nothing about the constellations that was familiar, and there was a huge moon that floated high up and green as grass. I assumed this was due to the pollen that was a constant in the air here. There were a couple of other moons, smaller, that moved swiftly, zipping by and close together as if in a race. They were a tarnished gold, with a veneer of green about them. These sights were amazing and confusing. But there was also this: the great star that Booloo had shown me, the one he had tried to explain to me, was now very visible, and large to the point of distraction. It glowed red and blue, as if it were an alternating neon light. In clearings, its light, combined with that of the moons, was astonishing. If you looked at the ground (or again, what passed as the ground, the bough of a tremendous tree), you could not only see the fine glow of the moons, but the light from the blue-red star; it lit the place up like a floor show.

As we traveled, I made it a point each night—when the foliage allowed—of locating the star and observing it. I felt as if I acquired strength from it, as well as from the trees, the air, and even the pollen; this world was for me like a personal generator that made me not only strong, but made me agile, swift, and gave me the ability to learn and retain things more quickly than on

Earth. And though the days were exhausting, I found that only a few hours' rest reinvigorated me. Some of this may have been an illusion, but the rest of it was irrefutable. There was another thing. My beard didn't grow. I was as smooth-faced now as I was the day I entered the machine that tossed me through space and time and nestled me here amongst the world of trees.

I came to anticipate the evenings with enthusiasm, not only because it gave me a chance to study those magnificent heavens, but because Booloo and Choona took it upon themselves to begin teaching me their language. I once had someone tell me that most languages have only about eight hundred words that matter as far as conversation goes, that the other words were adornments, and therefore, if you set your mind to it, a language could easily be acquired. Having tried learning Spanish and Italian, I can't say that I found this so. But, on this world, with my mental and physical faculties intensified, or perhaps by my actual need to learn the language, I discovered I was a very apt pupil indeed.

I first learned the basics, asking simple questions, and then I learned the names of certain plants, the gourds we drank from, the roots we ate, the plant that could start fires, and so on. Then I began to learn more conversational language. It was done mostly by show and tell.

What I soon discovered was that this world on which I now lived was called Juna, and that the star I was so infatuated with was called Badway de Moola. This, of course, Booloo had told me before, but I had been uncertain then if he actually meant this as a name, or a description of the star. Turned out it was both. The star was called The Warrior Star.

As they explained this to me, Choona reached out and touched my chest. The touch was like an electric shock, so much did I enjoy it. She spoke a few words. They were words I had learned, but it took me a moment to translate them in my mind, and then I got it. She was saying that I was a Son of The Warrior Star. That, she was a Daughter of The Warrior Star, and Booloo was a Brother of The Warrior Star.

It took a moment for me to wrap my mind around that concept, but then I realized that this was a great compliment, and that this was in fact a part of their belief system; the star was their totem, or perhaps, to them, some kind of god.

A few days out and we received a pleasant surprise. Or at least I did. I can't say that Booloo was as sentimental about the event, and, of course, Choona knew nothing of Butch. But as we rounded a bend in a well-traveled trail, there, on the edge of it, punching a wad of grass, was Butch. His reins dangled and he still had his saddle. I can't say that I would have known for certain it was him, or it, or her, without those accouterments, but I fancied there was a distinct look on the beetle's mug that allowed me to distinguish my bug from others, even without that identifiable riding rig. It also seemed to me that Butch was glad to see me. Butch's presence was certainly a convenience, and gave me a mount of my own, though I was a little bewildered when Choona chose to ride with me.

Chapter Eight
The City in the Trees

Eventually the great limb on which we rode narrowed, and became smaller, more like a spit of earth stuck out over a great chasm. The trees that grew up from the limb thinned and became fewer. Finally there was only the limb, and it was perhaps the width of a dozen football fields. Clouds rolled around us, and above us was the great clear sky, tinted with that faint pollen-green haze. The sun looked like a huge puss-filled blister, but the air was no warmer than before.

Behind us were miles and miles of thick jungle, and rising way above the jungle were the base trees that were the foundation of this world.

Moving toward the tip of the limb on which we rode, we saw a drop of miles. Down below there was green darkness. I was amazed I didn't feel any shortage of breath or any kind of mountain sickness. Instead, I felt better than I had ever felt in my life.

Looking from our limb, into the great distance beyond the drop, were more forests, and between two of the great base trees on the far side, something glittered like a wet diamond necklace, dotted with blots of silver and gold. I couldn't make it out exactly, but Choona explained to me that it was a city, Goshon, and it was their home.

In the next moment, we were moving to our left toward the edge of the limb, and when we got there, I saw a great tangle of vines that hung off the edge of the limb and went down, down, down, until they wadded away into the distance.

That was our route. I made sure I was strapped in tight on Butch's saddle, and down I went, this time riding alone, with Choona seated behind Booloo on their beetle, taking the lead.

We spent the night in the nest of vines. When the wind blew—and that night it blew intensely—the great netting swayed like a massive hammock. It might have been a nice way to sleep, had the rain not come, blasting us like a fire hose. For the first time, I felt truly cold.

As morning came, the water was sucked up by the vines, and the air cleared, and turned pleasant. I found that I was drying out quickly. We descended again, and this time Choona chose to ride with me. She put her arms around me as we went, and I glanced at Booloo once or twice, but he seemed not to notice. Perhaps the idea of a mate was different here than on Earth. Which might not be a bad thing, considering on Earth I had injured a rival with a sword over a woman; it wasn't something I wanted to repeat.

After several days we stopped going down, leveled off, and proceeded across a net of closely interwoven vines that went for miles and was perhaps as wide as five acres. As we rode, the vines swayed precariously, but Butch and the other beetle handled the trail without effort.

Eventually, we came to where we could see the city quite clearly. It took my breath away. What had glistened in the distance had not been diamonds or silver and gold, but the constructs of a wall, and buildings that rose up above it. All of it was made of plants; the assemblies were of twists of cable-like gold- and silver-colored vines, and hardened wood, as bright and shiny as diamonds. We rode on a pathway of flattened gold gourds that served in the same manner as stones. From a distance, Goshon looked not too unlike the fabled city of El Dorado that so many lost souls had searched for back home.

When we were within sight of the city gate, guards from the top of the wall let out a cheer. I was amazed at this reception. The gate lowered and warriors dressed in bright red tunics overlapped with wood-plated armor and helmets poured forth. They went directly toward Choona and Booloo, who had dismounted from the beetles, and dropped to their knees and bowed. Soon the path was full with warriors, and then citizens, dressed in all manner of finery.

Booloo walked among the crowd. Men and women reached out to touch his hand. I was uncertain of what to do, so I slipped off Butch, and to stay within custom, got down on my knees as well, realizing that I had not realized Choona and Booloo were royalty of some kind.

As I dropped to my knee, Booloo grabbed my arm and indicated that I should rise. He yelled out to the people.

"We return. And this man, Brax, saved me, and then Choona. He fought with us to help our people. We are, as far as we know, the only survivors, thanks to him. We owe him our lives. Honor him."

A great cheer was thrown to the sky and I was lifted on the hands and backs of the crowd and carried inside the city of Goshon in a manner of much pomp and circumstance.

I had presumed Booloo and Choona were some kind of King and Queen of Goshon, but I soon learned otherwise. They were in fact, prince and princess, brother and sister. Their parents were King and Queen.

I'm going to pause here to explain something about the people of Goshon, and I presumed it was true of everyone on the world of Juna. There were no old people. There were children, but no one who was elderly.

I was to discover from Choona that her people lived to be thousands of years old. They aged only slightly, and when their time came, unless of course they were felled by violence, or the rare disease, they just ceased to live; died and crumbled into dust.

To put it mildly, I found it strange.

But I had a suspicion that the very air and pollen here that had given me my new muscles, reflexes, shaper senses, may well have made me like my newfound friends, and perhaps more so. And considering that a day here was much longer than those on Earth, and therefore a year was much longer as well, a person's life span could be near immeasurable. It was merely a surmise, but from the way I felt, and having noticed that old scars from my sword training on Earth had disappeared, I suspected I just might be right.

But what was most exciting to me was this simple, and now obvious, fact: Choona was Booloo's brother.

I was given nice private quarters in a large building, that was, I presume the equivalent of a palace. It was a several stories up. It wasn't the highest spot in the place, but it was tall. It was comfortable. There was a large window, minus glass, that overlooked the city. A cool breeze rolled through it and the air tasted like a sweet dessert.

For a bed there was a huge hammock fastened to the ceiling. The furniture, including the hammock, like most things on this world, was constructed of plants.

After I was shown my room, food was brought. I sat and ate, felt considerably better and refreshed. I was finishing up a large gourd of that liquid that reminded me of milk, but which I found far more refreshing, when three young women came in. They were beautiful, as they all were. They wore only loincloths, and they spoke to me in their musical language. Many of their words were foreign to me, but I was beginning to understand more and more.

It turned out they were there to bathe me. They pulled back a curtain from an area I hadn't bothered yet to investigate, and behind it was a deep tub. They pulled one of two long ropes and water began to gush from a spout and fill it. It was hot water, and as it flowed into the tub it steamed and hissed. A moment later they pulled the other rope, and from a spout on the opposite side cooler water gushed.

The women immediately set about trying to determine how to remove my clothes. I resisted. Slightly. And then showing them how buttons and zipper worked, I let them undress me, remove my shoes, and help me into the tub. Once I was seated there—the water feeling wonderful on my skin—they removed their loincloths and climbed in with me, took vegetable sponges from the sides of the tub, and went about scrubbing me. The sponges not only felt good, but they provided a light soap. They washed my hair, and much to my embarrassment, and simultaneous delight, they scrubbed every inch of my body. They seemed fascinated with the hair on my chest, and elsewhere. When they finished they wanted me to return the favor, and being within their hospitality, I felt I couldn't deny them, and didn't want to. I went about making sure they were very clean.

When we finished bathing, they climbed out of the tub laughing like babies at bath time, and produced from a nook in the wall a huge towel, handed it to me, then grabbed others for themselves.

I was being dried off by one of the women, while a second stood behind me and dried my hair. I was just about to pass into a heavenly realm, when Choona entered the room and smiled at me.

"Was your bath satisfactory?" she asked.

I felt an embarrassment that she didn't share. I think I flushed a little. "Yes . . ." I said. "It was quite refreshing."

"Good," she clapped her hands, and the women, like crows startled on a fence, moved away from me and folded the towels and departed, left me in all my naked glory.

Choona appraised whatever physical assets I might have with a bold examination that made me feel more than little uncomfortable. I did my best not to show it, realizing their customs were nowhere as prudish as those from where I came.

As for Choona, she was dressed quite differently. Her long hair was well brushed and cascaded over her shoulders like a mountain fire running down hill. She wore a white cloth over her breasts, tied behind her back, exposing her stomach. Her navel was circled by a painting of blue and yellow stars. She wore a gold sarong. On her feet were fine sandals that looked to be made of leather, but from my experience on this world, I determined were most likely made of some vegetable material.

"Come," she said.

Being nude, I eyed the folded towels, but finally gave in, and boldly followed her, resisting the desire to cover certain parts of my anatomy with my hands. She led me to a large closet, opened it, and took out a white cloth. She brought it to me, and proceeded without comment to wrap it between my legs and around my thighs. It was a loincloth. I just stood there stunned.

Finished with this project, she went back to the wardrobe and threw the doors wide so that I might see what was hanging on a rod—a series of colorful robes. She paused, picked out a long, hot pink one, turned with it and held it before me.

I might be nearly nude, but I wasn't going to wear that garish thing. I shook my head. She grinned and hung the robe back in place, and finally settled on a dark blue one. She came over with it, and standing behind me, held it so that I might slip my arms through the sleeves. Then she came around front and pulled it across me and fastened the belt. It fit very comfortably. She then returned to the wardrobe and picked up a pair of sandals from the floor. They looked too small, but she came over and dropped down on one knee and measured them against my foot. They were, in fact, too small. She grabbed them at tip and heel, tugged gently. They stretched like chewing gum. I slipped into them. They were soft and the bottoms of them were warm; they were like living tissue. They wrapped comfortably around my feet. It was easy to figure they were not only designed for comfort, they were constructed in such a way that climbing and leaping from limb to limb could be accomplished without slippage. My tennis shoes had served me, but these were even better designed to move about amongst the trees and vines of this world.

She took my hand and led me to a chair, and had me sit. In front of me was a mirror. It lacked the reflective quality of those on Earth, but it was a mirror nonetheless, crude as a sheet of shiny metal, though I doubted it was metal at all. She picked up a short, sharp stick—the only way I can describe it—and used it to part my hair. There was also a brush there, and though it was a little rough on my scalp, it served the purpose of putting my hair into a kind of do. Considering my hair had not been that long, but was now quite long, I had some idea of how long I had been here. But, my beard had still not grown, though I could see there was a faint outline of it. I decided that it had not ceased growing at all, but for some odd reason facial hair didn't grow that well here. I couldn't make the sense of it.

I also had learned from my bath with the ladies that body hair was not that prevalent on women, and I decided it was most likely the same for the men, and this was why they had such an interest in my chest hair, and that which grew otherwise.

The way Choona had combed my hair made me look a little too much like a rooster, so I borrowed the brush and whipped it into something that resembled my simple, parted, and otherwise left alone, style at home.

I could see Choona in the mirror, studying me. She turned her head, pursed her lips, nodded.

"I like it," she said.

"Thank you," I said.

"You are to be formally introduced to the King and Queen, my mother and father, and honored for saving us."

"I would love to meet them, but no honor is necessary."

"For us, it is a necessity."

My ability to absorb the language seemed to increase by the hour. I was glad of that when I went before the King and Queen.

I said that people don't age here, but they do age in the sense that people reach adulthood, and once there, they begin to age slowly until they might look as if they are forty or so, but a very healthy forty. In fact, I didn't see one overweight or infirm person amongst them. I attributed that to their diet, which was mostly, and perhaps exclusively, made up of plants and plant derivatives, many of which appeared to be high in protein.

So, when I came before the King and Queen, they were among those who had grown to that appearance, fortyish. The King was dressed in great finery, gold and silver robes with strands of pink threaded throughout it, and the Queen, who looked very much like Choona, though her hair was longer, almost to her waist, was dressed in equal finery.

I was led to them with great procession, a blowing of horns and a thumbing of two stringed instruments that made a sound that I was uncertain I could ever comfortably accustom myself to.

Choona and Booloo escorted me, she on my right, he on my left. I went before them, and copying Choona and Booloo, I knelt and dipped my head, then rose up and stood before them.

I won't bother with all they said that day, but it was flattering and pleasing, and I was given full citizenship in Goshon, and then there was a ceremony of some sort, the particulars I was uncertain of, followed by music and dancing. I was given an excellent meal, and then it was over and I was led back to my room. I followed these events with a short nap.

When I was awakened by Choona, she was dressed in a short, loose tunic with a thick, yellow sash, thrown across her shoulder that supported a sheathed sword at her hip. She tossed a dark tunic on the bed, along with a harness similar to hers, and told me it was time to go to work.

Though I had been honored before the King and Queen in a hall filled with hundreds of people, most of them royalty, I was now being drafted into the service of their military. It too was an honor, according to Choona. It suited me fine. I was a fighting man, and on my world I had been like a tiger in a cage. Here, I could follow my true course, as instructor of the sword and hand-to-hand combat.

Chapter Nine
A Cultural Problem

When I was before the warriors, they eyed me with what I can only call suspicion. I didn't blame them. It was the way of the fighting man and woman, for their warriors were of both sexes, to doubt the skills of an outsider that had been placed in a role of authority without having earned it in front of them.

Their former general, for lack of a better word, was a man named Tallo. He came forward and looked at me in a manner that I didn't mistake for friendly.

"I know you are something special to the princess. I respect that. But, you are nothing to us, and you are nothing to me. Yet."

I grinned at him. "Shall we work out a bit," I said. "Just you and I."

He smiled. "Why not."

A circle of warriors formed around us, and many of them moved back to where there were arena seats and seated themselves there. Tallo drew his sword and I drew mine.

"Shall we?" I said.

"First blood," he said.

Tallo moved. And let me tell you, he was quick. Very quick. He was the fastest swordsman I had seen, with the exception of my instructor, Jack Rimbauld. But speed isn't always the answer. It is an important part of the equation, but distance is also important. He was the first to attack, and his speed, as I said, was impressive, but he had to cover six feet to touch me with the sword. I had but to move a few inches to parry, and as soon as I did, I glided over the ground like a bullet, lifted the pommel of my sword under his chin and knocked him down. And out.

There was a murmur from the crowd of warriors. I sheathed my sword and lifted him to a sitting position, and placed my knee in the small of his back, and reached over and pushed my hands up and down on his chest to revive him. It was actually a technique to revive an unconscious person from being choked out, but I had found that it was also good for bringing a knocked out person around; it let their bodies know they should be awake.

When Tallo revived, shook his head, he tried to stand, and I helped him. On his feet, he reached out with one hand and clasped my shoulder and dipped his head. He said, "I am your servant."

Moments later, I began their training.

Day in and day out, I showed them the art of the sword. Don't misunderstand me. They were warriors. They were willing and they were serviceable with their weapons, and they had a number of methods, techniques I had not seen before. But they were lacking in discipline. Here in Goshon, training was regular, but somewhat lax.

Tallo became my right-hand man. I used him to show my approach. The Goshon warriors fought not as a unit, but as individuals. In battle, they chose whoever they wanted to fight, and fought on a personal basis. They had a good initial attack, but from that moment on, they were defensive. It's a good way to be, but there are times when the other is appropriate, and in war, more so. I taught them there was more than just a quick initial lunge, like Tallo had tried on me.

The Goshon sword is not a short sword, nor is it a long sword. It is, frankly, any length the user chooses. I changed that. Soon I had them all bearing three-foot swords. I taught them patterns akin to that of the Romans; it was methodology Jack Rimbauld had made me study. I taught them to hold their ground by pressing together behind a shield. Before I started training them, some had shields, some did not. Now, I insisted everyone bear a shield. I also taught them that when they were no longer on flat "ground," or Father Tree, as they called what was beneath them, they should resort to a more free style of fighting, but with an awareness of teamwork and the concept of staying as close together as possible.

I went at this work with great and joyful deliberation, discovering as I went better and better methods for them to be warriors, better methods for fighting the Juloon, which was their name for the giants, and the Norwat, the mantis-like creatures. One of these methods was the use of the long spear, or pike. I taught them that in the case of the giants, it was better strategy to cut them down from below instead of trying to reach their vital organs with spears and swords. Instead, the cutting of muscles behind the ankle and calf, and thrusts to the arteries inside the legs, were essential methods of bringing the giants down to size, causing them to fall and end up on their faces, or at the least, on their knees where new opportunities were available. The lungs, liver, heart, throat, eyes. All the vital points. For that matter, a good thrust to the artery inside the leg, especially close to the groin, could end a fight immediately, as your victim would bleed out in seconds.

At the end of each day of training I ate with the men and women in the mess, for there was no segregation of sex, but when they returned to their barracks,

I returned to the quarters Choona had arranged for me. I felt somewhat guilty about this, but no doubt the softness of my bed, and the fact that each night Choona joined me there, made it a lure I could not resist. We had fallen into this pattern quite naturally, as if we had known each other all our lives.

Each night, before bed, I would strip down nude, and Choona would watch as I meditated, the way Rimbauld had shown me. After a time, she too would strip down and join me. We always chose the middle of the room, in line with the window through which a sweet breeze came and cooled, and invigorated us. I did my best to explain to her what it was I was doing, and how I was doing it. She was a quick study. Unfortunately for her, I didn't feel I had that much to teach her.

It was a nice life, but I knew it would not stay nice forever. The reason for this was simple. War was coming. The Juloon and the Norwat were constantly waging war against the city of Goshon, taking slaves for food, and far worse reasons. It would soon happen again. The reason for this was Dargat, which loosely translates as The Masters. These were the plant-squid-like things I had seen on the backs of their necks and skulls. They were the ones who directed things. The giants were dangerous enough, but on their own they were not particularly organized. Some years back, The Masters and the Juloon had made a sort of unspoken pact. The Masters supplied the brains and the will, and the Juloon the muscle. The Norwat were the scavengers, the low among the low.

"The Juloon and the Norwat, they are the yuloo for the Dargat," Choona explained to me.

"The what for the what?" I said.

It took a bit of explaining, but apparently, yuloo is a word for a kind of worm that eats its own excrement, makes houses of it, and births its young in piles of the same. It's a large creature, and smells, and isn't edible, which was something I ascertained well before Choona finished explaining them to me.

After this insult, she explained The Masters to me in greater detail, and finally, The One. To put it in as small a nutshell as I possible can, way out where the woods grew the thickest, where the woods were chopped and burned and used without worry, because they grew back so incredibly fast, there was a group of plant beings. I know no other way to describe them. Large, plump, white plants with vines, thick as octopus tentacles, with suckers on their tips; I've described them before, clinging to the backs of the giants' necks. The creatures on the backs of the giants' necks were a kind of hive mind, and they were in turn ruled by a creature that Choona called The One. The One was of their sort, but like a Queen Bee, a creature that lived off Goshon slaves by fastening to them with its tentacles and sucker mouths. It sucked their blood, and brains, bone marrow, and energy; it took from their very core of being until they were withered shells, dead and useless. Some of the humans were kept to breed with each other, to keep a supply of food when The Master's lackeys were not raiding Goshon. Simply put, they farmed the humans for The Masters and The One, and the giants got a portion of the stock, and the mantises got the scraps.

This had gone on for years, the giants and mantises attacking and raiding Goshon, and the warriors of Goshon protecting themselves enough to keep their population and way of life alive. Still the giants and mantises came, and the population of Goshon shrunk while the population of their enemies grew.

I quizzed Choona some more, and it was, to say the least, a baffling discussion.

"So how do you fight them?" I asked.

"When they come, we fight," Choona said.

"You say there are many more of them than there are of you?"

"Yes," she said.

"So they come, and breach the walls, and you fight them, and they take slaves and retreat?"

"That is correct."

"And then you go after them, to rescue the captives?"

I had an idea what the answer to this would be, as I had learned some of their culture's thinking in the time I had been training the warriors, but I wanted to know for sure.

Choona considered this. "It is thought to be pointless to go after them."

"You were rescued."

She nodded. "Booloo escaped. You helped him. He came back for me, and you were with him."

"So, why don't your people do that, come for the captured ones I mean?"

"Because it is pointless."

"You are home, and so is Booloo."

"Once the giants have us, that does not happen."

"But it did."

"Thanks to you."

"Thanks to Booloo, he went back for you, and I was with him. He chose to do things different."

This confused Choona's way of thinking. I realized it wasn't lack of intelligence, it was culture. Their culture was accustomed to fending for itself in the city, but outside the city, if something happened to one of their people, they were on their own, unless one or two warriors chose, by their own choice, to do something out of the ordinary. It was a thing that happened, but according to Choona, not often.

I found this way of thinking frustrating. "But why don't you just go after the captives?"

"It is not done," she said.

"Except when it is."

"Yes. But that is the choice of the individual. Not the King or Queen. Not the city."

Our discussion was becoming circuitous, but I tried to stay with it.

"Why?" I asked. "Why is it only done now and again. Why is it not always done?"

"Because it is not done."

I knew I was repeating myself, but I couldn't help but think if I phrased the question simply, and correctly, I would receive what I thought of as a more common-sense answer.

"No one goes after the captives?" I asked.

"Sometimes. But not far. This is our home. We live on the forest around us, and we live in Goshon. We do not go into the lands of the giants, and we certainly do not go into the lands of the Dargats."

"You should."

"But why? Once captives are taken, they rarely come back."

"But sometimes they do."

"Sometimes they escape," she said.

"Or they are rescued."

"Yes."

"But no one goes after them as a force, as an army?"

She walked to the window and pointed. Where she was pointing was the forest on the other side of the bridge. "We go there, and a ways beyond that. No more."

"That doesn't make sense," I said.

"It is how we do it."

"Change it."

She gave me a perplexed look.

"Why?"

I took her hands and led her to what served as a couch. When we were seated, I continued to hold her hands. I said, "If we go after them, we turn the tables. Instead of waiting for them to attack, we can attack them. If a few warriors now and then are rescued, than why not many by a larger force?"

She thought about it.

"No one has ever done that," she said.

I tried not to sigh too audibly.

"Did you make me the leader of your warriors?"

"Yes."

"Why?"

"You have great skill."

"Do you trust my judgment?"

"Of course."

"Then, what you have to do is discard cultural barriers that have kept you in the position you are in now with your enemies. This way of thinking may even have been beneficial in the past, may have become a way of doing things because at one point it worked well, or well enough. It's not working now. Gradually, you, and all of your people, will be enslaved or destroyed. Bravery, and even skill with weapons, is not enough against enemies like this. "

She nodded slowly. "We have considered this."

"But you haven't changed. If you do something and it isn't working, and you keep doing it, you get the same results. You know that, right?"

"We still exist."

"Yes, but you are being slowly whittled down, like cutting chunks from a large tree. No matter how big the tree, if you keep cutting, it will fall down."

"And then grow back."

I realized that on this world my analogy was not a good one. The growth rate was so tremendous you couldn't get ahead of it.

"Let me put it like this. The cultural reason you do not leave the city is buried in memory. You do not even know why it is that way anymore, do you?"

She wrinkled her pretty brow.

"Because it has always been that way. The gods made us that way, and left us that way, and we follow the law of the gods."

"But you are warriors. You worship The Warrior Star."

She let go of my hands. "We are warriors."

"No doubt. But you have to be proactive warriors."

I had spoken in her language, but not knowing any other word for proactive, that was the word I had used. I tried to explain it to her in her language, but found it difficult.

"We shall take the fight to them first," I said.

"But it has never been done that way."

I was becoming frustrated.

"Then, Choona, my dear one, we will change things, you and I, and Booloo, and the warriors of Goshon."

Chapter Ten
Meditation and the Arts of War

Before the King and Queen, I presented my ideas.

The Queen said, "But we have never done it that way before."

"It would go against custom," said the King.

Choona was with me, and so was Booloo.

Booloo, an immediate convert to the idea, said, "Brax saved us from our enemies. His training of our warriors has improved them dramatically. He has discarded many old methods, and his new methods are making our warriors superior. Perhaps it is time we change some of our views."

"But those views are what make us . . . us," the King said.

"Yes," Booloo said, "but Father, there are a whole lot less of us now. Once we fought a certain way against a certain enemy. But the Dargats, the Juloons, and the Norwats are a different kind of enemy. They have killed many other clans all across our great forests. To the best of my knowledge, we are the last of our kind."

The Queen said, "We protect our walls. We stay in our place."

"Commendable," I said. "No one should want war or start war or war against those who are not threatening them. But these creatures have come to you and taken your people for food, for slaves. It is time to take the fight to them."

I was amazed at how complicated this was for them. It seemed obvious to me. But to those of the city of Goshon it was not. What would have been a silly discussion at home was dead serious here.

"Father," Booloo said. "All things change. It is the way of the jungle. It grows. It dies. It rebirths. But there must be something left of it, a seed, a root, a stalk, the breath of the plant (he was referring to the pollen) to bring it back. When we are gone our bones will not rebirth our flesh. Our stalks will be dried and rotted."

"They will become one with all others," said the King.

"Yes," Booloo said, nodding. "But it will not be our people. Our people's remains will be no different from the remains of all things."

"That is the way of all death," the King said.

"Yes, Father," Choona said. "But it is not the way of all life. It is change. It is different. But I see Brax's way. His way is our way now. He is the trainer of our warriors. His is the greatest sword we have ever seen. He is Goshon now."

The King and Queen sat silent for a long time. The King looked at the Queen. Something passed between them that only passes between those who have lived with one another so long words are not always necessary.

"Very well," said the King. "It is strange, but if this is what Brax believes, we will take the fight to them."

Each night after training the warriors, I went about my ritual, and before bed, I meditated as Jack Rimbauld had taught me. Choona still meditated with me. She wanted to learn the ways of meditation because I told her it was part of what Jack Rimbauld had taught me, and that it made me a better warrior.

I was mostly speaking in a rote way, because, except for a certain calm that meditation gave me, I had yet to glean the real merits of the art. And then, one night, while I was meditating, and was in a deep state, Choona said, "Brax."

I opened my eyes. I was looking down on her.

"You . . ." she said. "You . . . you are floating."

And so I was. I was a good six feet off the ground, hovering in the air, legs crossed, nothing to support me. The moment I realized it, I crashed painfully to the floor.

"I was not sure I believed you," she said. "When you told me your master trainer could float in the air, and make many of himself. But, you, Brax. You were floating."

I gathered myself together and sat on the couch, stunned. "I was," I said. "I was indeed. And I was not sure I believed it when I told you either."

She laughed.

"I am more than a little glad that I did not turn out to be liar," I said.

We soon went to bed, chattering excitedly about what had happened. It took awhile, but finally we ceased talking, and Choona drifted off to sleep. I could not sleep. I arose, went to a spot beneath the window, and sat cross-legged, and concentrated, and this time, immediately I rose up from the floor. I went up and down at will for some time, practicing. I begin to think about all that Jack had taught me. If I could do this, why not astral projection, all manner of skills he had possessed.

I was so excited I couldn't sleep that night.

Despite this lack of visitation from Morpheus, I was energized the next day. I fenced with warrior after warrior, finding that I was moving with greater ease and skill than ever before. I couldn't decide if years of practice had finally paid off, or if it was that along with a combination of the environment that accelerated my skills. The only thing that mattered now was that I was different, and better.

The next night, while Choona slept, I sat before the open window in my cross-legged position, tried to send my thoughts out across the city, over the walls and the web bridge, back the way we had come, back to where I had first seen the giants.

Nothing happened.

I thought about it longer and harder, and then, in my mind, my naked body was moving through the forest, or rather the forest was moving through me. I was still sitting cross-legged, but it was as if I were a ghost. I opened my eyes. It was not all in my head. I was in the air and I was traveling swiftly, right through tree trunks and boughs and vines and all manner of growth; traveling through them without so much as rustling a leaf.

I was a spirit, an astral body flowing across this world of great vegetation with the swiftness of thought. My mind sought out my target. I came to a monumental tree. It was the size of a continent, and on it lived the giants, the mantises, and most importantly, the Dargots, and among the Dargots, more importantly, The One. I could sense him the way animals sense oncoming rain.

I can't explain how I went there, as it was a place I didn't know. But my thoughts were pulled across that vast expanse toward The One, as if it were calling me to it as diligently as I was trying to find it.

It touched me, probed with its mind. It was as if The One was a boulder and I was a river, and I flowed around it. Images flashed in my mind; they came from all directions, so fast I couldn't organize them: I saw the Dargots, The Masters, on the necks and backs of the giants. I saw the mantises, lurking about on the fringes, clothed in shadow, and then . . . once again, I felt before I saw . . . The One.

I saw a great pile of human skulls and broken bones and desiccated corpses, living humans who thrashed and withered and appeared little more than mummies, the naked bodies of hundreds, the bones of thousands, and on top of them, writhing and twisting, was something I could recognize as a Dargot, but different, larger. It was The One. A thing that was like them, and not. Monstrous, dark as the night, oily as the slick on-water remains of a sunken tanker. Forty feet high. Its long, dark tentacles waved at the air and the suckers that lay beneath them drew at the air as if they could pull it completely out of being, suck the atmosphere, and the world, and the very moon and stars, and the blackness of space into it. Roots near its base coiled and uncoiled, dripped the gooey remains of the humans below them.

Closer and closer I came, traveling across the gap between space and time, hurtling toward The One. Those tentacles reached out and touched me, the roots caressed me, a dry tongue flicked out of what served as its face, and tasted me. I felt as if my brain were being shocked with an electric current. Foul sensations, like the rotting innards of the dead licked about in my brain. I could momentarily feel what it felt, a kind of dark superiority, a brilliance of mind that was directed toward the simplicity of one single purpose—survival.

There was a sensation of falling down a long, cold, dark tunnel, followed by exhaustion; it was as if my brain cells struck an invisible wall and exploded in all directions.

And then—

—nothing.

When I awoke, Choona was wiping my brow with a wet towel.

"Brax, are you sick?"

"No," I said. "I am far worse than sick. The Dargots and their lackeys. And The One. They are coming. We must go forward. As soon as possible."

In the morning I set about pushing the Goshon warriors hard. We worked the pikes, we worked the swords. We drilled as a wall of men and weapons, learned to break apart and attack, and come together and attack.

As the night came and The Warrior Star rode high in the sky, I led the warriors off the training field and out into the city plaza. There were perhaps no more than three thousand, but we filled the plaza.

In the camp of the Dargots I had sensed many more. Counting the giants, the mantises, and The Masters, and The One, they were perhaps ten thousand. They were formidable, but there wasn't any true organization about them, just a hive mind that directed them in a general manner; there was no individuality of thought.

I climbed up on a prominent stone wall that surrounded a fountain spewing water. I pointed up at The Warrior Star. Criers throughout the group carried my words across the mass of humanity as I spoke.

"Tomorrow, we will go after our enemies. We will go after them before they come to us. You are the warriors of that star. You are trained, and you have the hearts of true warriors. I pledge by that star that I will lead you into battle. I will say, come after me, warriors, follow me, not go after them and I will wait here for you. I will be there with you. All of us, together, as one."

Tallo came forward. He stepped up on the rim around the fountain and touched my shoulder.

"I have known this man, Brax, for only a short time. But he is a great warrior. He is a great teacher of the arts of war. You know that. You have seen. I will follow him anywhere. That is my word, and that is all of my word."

Then the commanders in the army, the men and women who directed groups of our soldiers, came forward, and each in his turn promised me their support, and vowed to die in my service. They bowed before me, and I went to each of them, took hold of them and helped them to a standing position. I walked back to my place on the fountain, and I called those leaders up, men and women. I had them stand on the fountain wall with me.

"No warrior here bows before another warrior," I said. "It is a new time. It is a new war. And we are the new warriors. We are one."

Choona came forward. She was dressed only in a white sarong. The light of the moon and The Warrior Star made it luminous. Her dark body and red hair were like a beautiful sculpture.

She said, "As of this moment, I, Choona, and my brother, Booloo, we are warriors, like you. We are not the Prince and Princess. We are warriors, and we too will follow Brax into battle, and we will fight to the bloody end."

A wild cheer went up.

As we used to say in grade school: It was on.

Chapter Eleven
Preparations

The next morning the warriors of Goshon—with the exception of a well-trained skeleton force left to protect the city—were riding their beetles or marching outside of the walls, heading toward the enemy. Individual warriors had done this sort of thing, guerrilla tactics, but never as a group, never as a war party. For them, this was an amazing event, and it was going against all they had been taught as part of their survival.

By now, however, they were convinced. Or convinced enough to follow me. We were ready, and we were at war.

I had been reunited with Butch, and though it may well have been my imagination, I felt certain that the beast recognized me, and was glad to see me. I know I was glad to see him . . . or she . . . or it. I made a mental note to ask Choona at some point what Butch's sex actually was.

There were a number of our warriors who bore cloaks made from the web of the spider. Since these spiders were not the approachable sort, and lived deep within the forests, only those who had ventured out in search of food, or singular adventure—which was far more prized here than accomplishments in packs—ever came across them and their webs. So there was very little of this material available. But there were at least a hundred of these cloaks, and Choona, Booloo, and myself each possessed one. It would have been better, of course, if everyone in my army had one, for it goes without saying that being invisible is a great boon in battle. But this was not an option.

Although I had taught the warriors how to work as a unit, I began to realize there was a reason these kinds of tactics had not been used before. On this world, to travel, one must move up and down and all around. A path for one was not always a path fit for two, let alone thousands. It occurred to me then why the idea of individuality, except as part of the city, was so important. On this world it was difficult to work as a unit; the world worked against you.

The environment dictated our route. We were a unit, but a unit not always in sight or position of one another. The plan, of course, was to fight on a solid limb, some broad space surrounded by jungle. A cavalry charge followed by foot soldiers. Before that, I planned to use the invisible one hundred to wreak havoc on the enemy, to have them in a state of flux before the main attack occurred.

If we failed, our city and its small clutch of defenders would be at the mercy of their enemies. It was an all-out assault, and it was up to us to hit our foes hard and finish it.

In my head it was simple, but I realized, though I had studied strategy from Jack Rimbauld, read and reread *The Art of War*, and *The Book of Five Rings*, Caesar's memoirs, reading strategy and experiencing war first hand were two different things.

There's no point in telling you about all the problems we ran up against, but suffice it to say there were numerous encounters with wild creatures, great gaps to traverse by natural vine webbings, as well as a number of warriors lost to accident. But we persisted. At night we would camp, and I would meditate. I could see the place where our enemy was gathered by astral travel, and in the morning, as if by instinct, I could lead us in that direction.

Each time I drifted out of my body in my astral state, I could sense and feel the power of the Dargats, and most specifically the power of The One.

"Are we close?" Choona asked from time to time.

"Closer," I would say.

"We will defeat them," she would say.

"Yes," I would say.

And each night we would repeat this, like a mantra. It was akin to boxers working themselves up before a fight.

When we were within a day's march, and could arrive there by midday, I halted our party, had them camp. My plan was to come at them on the fringe of the morrow. Sleep during the day, then move the last bit of distance to where they waited, and just before morning, come at them like the flames of hell.

I slept uncomfortably. I did not try to meditate. I knew where we were. I knew how close we were, and the path to arrive at our destination. But The One reached out for me. It was probing my mind. I could sense it, and I didn't want to give anything away. I built brick walls in my brain, and I would see its tentacles grab at them and move them aside. I would rebuild. It would probe again, cracking through.

I sat up and shook Choona awake.

"What is it, Brax?"

"Talk to me," I said.

"What?"

"About anything."

She saw the look on my face, nodded. She began to talk. She talked for an hour, telling me all manner of information about her world, her city, her parents and brother, and herself. She talked until I felt The One's mental tentacles retreat in defeat from my thoughts. When it was over, I explained to Choona what had happened.

"Does that mean they know we are coming?"

"It means he knows that I have been prying at its thoughts. It has known that from the first time I touched its mind. As for the other, I cannot say. I hope not."

"Should we pull back?"

I shook my head. "No. We have come this far, and even if they know we are coming, they still have to defeat us. If we go home, then all we are doing is waiting for them to come to us, same as before."

"To the death," she said.

"Let us hope things are not that severe, though I fear that tomorrow many warriors will fall."

"They know their duty," she said.

"Yes," I said. "Soldiers always do. But the leaders, they are a little less certain."

I said this knowing I had put fuel to their pride, and that I was pushing them toward battle. On Earth I had seen it many times. Wars fought for political gain. Wars fought for pride. I hoped my war, the one I had created, my self-defense war, was worth it, and that in the end, Goshon would have peace.

W e, The Invisible One Hundred, left our mounts among the main body of the army. Wearing our cloaks of invisibility, I led our under-cover band of warriors into position for an advance attack. Among the one hundred were, of course, Booloo and Choona, and Tallo.

Choona is a warrior, but the idea of having the woman you love exposed to danger is a hard concept to swallow. Choona, however, did not give me a choice.

We crept through the woods where water gathered around the roots. Though we blended in quite well in our cloaks, showing our heads so that we could stay in contact with one another, we had to be careful not to make too much noise; our feet sloshing in the water would give us away in an instant. Therefore, our progress was slow and tedious.

Along the way, I left some of the warriors behind to form a kind of relay. When it was time for the beetle-backed cavalry to ride forward, they would be informed by one of our cloaked runners. The cavalry would ride down the middle, where it was clear. This would happen after our advance attack, where we would hit our targets clandestinely, hidden behind our cloaks of invisibility. We would dent them, the cavalry would tear them, and our foot soldiers would come from all sides and break them completely apart.

As the open field became visible through the trees, I halted our group, handed my cloak to Choona, and climbed up a thin tree, nimble as a monkey, if I say so myself, and I do. I positioned myself on a high limb, peeled back the leaves and took a look.

There were great fires all over the field, and the field was many acres wide and many acres deep. I could see the giants squatting by the fires, and as before, many were partaking of horrible meals made of humans. I could see the strange, treelike growths clutched to the backs of their heads, tentacles, thrashing at the air as if in enjoyment of the meals the giants ate. As before, the mantises lurked outside the circle, just within firelight, hoping for scraps. Nearby, in a kind of makeshift corral of vines and sticks, were the beetles that made up the mantis cavalry. There were thousands of the beasts.

I closed my eyes briefly, tried to remember what I had seen when I had traveled in my astral body. I knew that at the far end of the field, in the shadows, The One waited. I could sense it, and I could visualize it, but not in a complete way. It was akin to reaching down in dark water and clutching at something loathsome, something you could not quite describe in shape or size, but something that squirmed and touched a place in the soul that made you weak and afraid.

I made it a point to make The One my mission. Maybe I could even attack and destroy it before our enemy knew we were among them. I had a feeling that with The One gone, it might not end the battle, but it would certainly cause problems for the enemy. For without The One, I knew from my astral sensations that the tree creatures and their hosts, as well as the scavenger mantises, would be less willful. The One was the master of the hive, and they were the drones.

When I was on the ground, Choona returned my cloak.

I gathered my band around me. I said, "We will go silently among them. We will leave a trail of warriors here, so we can carry our messages to the others. But the bulk of us, we will split up in threes, and we will go in and do our damage under the cover of the cloaks. Once they know to look for us, though they will have some trouble seeing us, it won't be the same as when we're not expected. We cannot use the swords without revealing ourselves to some degree. So mind your attacks. Make them quick. Make them simple."

"It will be done," Tallo said.

"Good," I said. "Tallo, you are with me."

"And so am I," Booloo said.

"No," said Choona, "he is my man, and it is right that I should go with him."

I didn't say it, but I was glad of this. The idea of Choona being out of my sight was a terrible thought, especially during battle. Yet, it was not a suggestion I would have made. Now that it was made by her, I accepted it gladly.

"Booloo," I said. "You will break the others into groups. Do it now. We must be ready to move forward in moments."

"It is done," he said, and moved away, the cloak wrapped around his shoulders, only his head visible, floating among the trees and undergrowth.

Chapter Twelve
The Great Battle

We wrapped our cloaks around our bodies and our heads, tied them close around our faces with straps so that only our eyes were visible. Our swords were inside our cloaks, our hands near their hilts.

Under the light of The Warrior Star, we moved to the outskirts of the fires, toward the mantises, and moving like apparitions, we attacked the creatures with their backs to us. We came upon them slowly and with great precision. A half-dozen were dead before any of the others realized something was wrong.

All along the outer circle, the mantises fell dead. One after another, swords seemingly reaching out from another dimension brought them down. By the time they realized something was amiss—and I must state that these creatures are not the sharpest knives in the drawer—a good fifty or so were dead.

I revealed my face to Choona and Tallo, beckoned with my head for them to follow me. I pulled the cloak tight around my face again, charged toward where the beetles were kept in a corral.

As we approached, one of the guards, a blue giant, retched his meal, his stomach most likely soured by some sort of crude alcoholic drink. He paused, shook his head, and looked in our direction. I knew what he saw. The light of the moons and The Warrior Star were revealing our footprints in the soft bed of needles and rotting leaves.

By the time he realized what was going on, it was too late.

The giant bellowed and drew his sword. I raced toward him, but not as fast as Tallo, who flung back his cloak and revealed himself, causing the giant to lurch after him. The giant's huge sword came crashing down with a tremendous chop. Tallo deftly sidestepped and stuck the giant's hand with his own sword, causing the colossus to bellow loud enough to cause the other giants by the fires to stir.

Tallo dodged a swing of the giant's sword, darted between his legs, jabbed up with the sword, finding a most delicate target. The giant slashed down between his own legs, trying to nail Tallo, but in his haste, he managed to cut off a portion of his own foot.

By this time, Choona and I had arrived to Tallo's aid. He didn't need us. The giant had dropped to one knee, and grasped his ruined foot. With a deft leap, Tallo thrust his blade deep within the giant's liver.

The giant wobbled and fell.

I grabbed up Tallo's cloak and shoved it at him. "Your bravery is appreciated. But your survival is even more needed."

Grinning, he slung the cloak over his shoulders. When I looked up, the corral gate was opening, and I could hear the invisible Choona yelling inside. She was stampeding the beetles. The startled creatures thundered out of the enclosure, filling the open gap until they were pushing against the railings, knocking the whole thing down.

Mantises and giants were surging toward the corral. Our invisible guerrilla team was engaging them, and for the moment, the battle was one-sided in our favor.

I pulled from my belt pack a bit of the igniting plant, got it to flame to life. I waved it above my head. I knew that from the protection of the woods our relay team could only see a bit of fire moving back and forth in the dark, and I hoped they were alert enough to notice. If they saw my warning, the relay was already being carried, and soon our cavalry would appear, riding down the middle of the plain, hitting our adversaries while they were engaged with invisible fighters and escaping beetles.

Since we could not see one another without revealing ourselves, I made no effort to let Choona or Tallo know what I was doing next. We, the invisible, were all on our own. Our job was to harass and confuse the enemy until the real action started. I ran as fast as I could across the field, engaging panicked mantises along the way, cutting them down with what seemed to them a disembodied sword.

I glanced back to see the giants slashing at the night, trying to score on my invisible warriors. I saw at least two of my soldiers cut from their cloaks by great broadswords, sent to the ground and pinned there by blades.

It was all I could do not to turn back and engage the giants, but I knew I had a bigger goal, and I could not be deterred from it. As I moved away from the lights of the fire, the darkness enveloped me. I went more by instinct than design.

And then I felt it.

The One. It was like being hit by a lightning bolt. I dropped to my knees, losing my sword, grabbing my head.

The One had caught me off guard.

It had sensed me.

It was nearby, and being this near, its power was strong.

Inside my skull the thing moved and twisted and sought the core of my being. I fought back. I built walls, but the walls were torn down. I put up a forest, swamp water around the trunks. But that was not enough. The water was sucked away, as if by a vacuum, and the trees were felled by an invisible axe.

Before, I had been able to hold it at bay. My powers were stronger at a distance. But mind against mind I could feel that The One was superior. I was growing weaker. Roots broke up from a dark surface and wound themselves around me. Vines drooped down and enveloped my head. I felt as if I were being crushed. My lungs were shutting down.

It's all in your mind, I told myself.

But that was cold comfort. In my head or not, The One was slowly killing me.

I imagined the light at daybreak, pushing away the darkness like an anxious child tossing off covers.

I imagined Choona, in our bedroom, back in the city of Goshon. I could see her smile. I could hear her voice and her musical laugh. Her naked body was a delight. Vines wrapped around me, dark and seeking, pushing into my imaginings, turning the day slowly black. The air filled with a stench. I could smell it as surely as if I had been dropped into a sewage pit. My head was a dark cloud. It was becoming harder and harder to breathe. I tried to concentrate on where I really was. Lying on the ground, battling The One with my mind.

But it was useless.

All I could see was that cloud, and all I could feel were those tentacles, the life slowly being crushed out of me, the deepest recesses of my thoughts being touched by something awful and polluted.

And I hadn't so much as seen my enemy.

In the background, I heard a great clash of warriors, tremendous shouts. I concentrated on those noises, and they brought me back a little. The cloud receded slightly. I put my thoughts back on the beautiful Choona, our most intimate moments. The cloud pulled back, the tentacles recoiled. The positive thoughts in my brain had repulsed it.

Now I was breathing again, rising, taking up my sword, moving in the direction from which I felt the power.

It tried to stop me with another mental push.

I threw up a wall of light, not bricks, and I felt the tentacles recoil and retreat at a savage pace. I began to run.

Still, it wasn't easy. There were moments when I felt I was trying to swim through an ocean of peanut butter. Each step made me grunt with exertion. Each breath made my lungs burn as if they were stuffed with hot coals. The One's foul smell stuffed up my head and made me pause to throw up. It projected heat, like something that had been set on fire and smoldered down to coals and ash and wafts of fetid smoke. But that was alright. I followed the stink, the heat.

Into the shadows I went, and then the shadows began to move, and they were not shadows at all. They were The One. Sight of it almost made me drop my sword. It was shrouded in darkness, but, wearing my cloak, so was I. But neither mattered. The One's darkness or my invisibility. We could, in our way, see each other clearly.

It writhed and coiled on top of the great mound of flesh and bones that I had seen in my astral journey. There were bare skulls mounded up around living beings who could barely move, fluttering arms, kicking legs. Wriggling down from that thing at the top of the pile were thousands of vibrating roots; the tips of the roots were in the eyes and noses and mouths and ears of the living. When the little moons passed quickly across the sky, I could see their desperate thrashings clearly. Some of them were little more than mummified flesh.

I dropped the cloak from my shoulders for greater mobility. I climbed onto the mound, onto the skulls and bones and dying flesh, and went upwards.

Behind me the war was in full swing. I could hear the cries of warriors, both Goshon warriors and giants. The screeching and clicking of the mantises. The clashing of swords and shields and the thumping of flesh and bone. But that was not my mission. My mission was The One.

Tentacles slashed at me and knocked me back, sent me rattling down the pile of meat and bones. I got my feet under me and put my new abilities to work, leaping and bounding, until I was even with the creature, perching at the top of the mound. I stuck my sword in its body. It was like sticking a toothpick through gelatin. It did about as much damage as vile remarks.

A stinging sensation made my face go numb. A root from The One had popped up from below and struck my face; it was like being hit by an angry jellyfish.

Leaping upwards, my feet landed on the middle of the thing. I grabbed at one of its tentacles to steady myself, and then I thrust forward with my sword. The tentacle burned my arm where it held me, and my sword thrust was useless. I hacked at the tentacles that popped at me like whips, managing to cut a few of them apart. Tentacles and roots snatched at me and picked me up and tore my feet free of The One's base. The great beast tossed me like I was nothing more than a worrisome flea.

I smashed into the bones and flesh of the dead the dying, and then I was up again, scrambling to the peak of that pile, toward The One.

And when those fast moons sailed across the sky again, I saw its one hard, yellow eye peeking out from under a hood of flesh that protected it, and below that I saw spittle sparkle on its beak, which was huge, like that of the largest parrot you could imagine.

But more importantly, I saw coming up behind it, leaping like a grasshopper, her cloak falling away from her like a snake shedding skin, Choona, my lovely warrior.

During its preoccupation with me, she had come from the rear, and now she was bringing her sword down violently on its head. There was a noise like a gunshot, followed by the cracking of Choona's sword, and then the thing's tentacles and roots grabbed her.

I gave it all I had, leaping, and gliding, using the abilities Jack had taught me, abilities I didn't know I possessed until that moment. I went up, and along with me went multiple projections of myself, three to be exact. Three and me. I was as much the core of a hive mind as The One now. My multiple selves charged up with me. Straight up we went. When we were even with that hard, yellow, boiled egg eye, we threw our swords, all of them solid, made with the power of my mind; we threw them with all our strength. We were greeted with a happy sight. Our swords buried to the hilt in that eye, down deep in that powerful and repulsive brain. The tentacles and roots went loose, letting go of Choona, causing her to tumble down the mound.

I had lost my footing as well. I was weak from the mental exertion. The multiple Braxs faded. My legs were like rubber, and then they folded under me.

I bounced and bumped until I hit the ground. When I looked up, The One's tentacles were tearing my sword out of its skull; the other swords, though they had been real enough on contact, had gone the route of my astral selves.

I grabbed up a human skull from the mound, cocked back and threw it like a football. It was a good throw. It hit the injured, wobbling beast and knocked it off its pedestal. It went tumbling backwards from the mound.

I rushed around the mound after it. Choona was on her feet and heading in the same direction. When we came to The One, it was no longer moving.

I took a deep breath, let my thoughts loose. They reached out and touched—

—nothing.

The One was finished.

T he war had gone well. It was a riot. And with the death of The One, the Dargat lost their grips on the blue giants; their hive minds died, and they dropped off of their hosts like bloated dog ticks. The giants were now about their own devices. They and the mantises retreated, or were captured, and I must admit, killed without mercy. It would not have been my will, but before I could stop it, all of them were slain. This was not a world of great consideration for the enemy.

There was much celebration that daybreak, and all through the day, and night. The following morning, before we moved out, we set fire to The One's corpse. The flames turned it to black cinders in instants. Those humans who were alive in the mound were so far gone they were put to death as a form of mercy. They were no longer human. They weren't really living. They were existing. They were shells that writhed, their brain matter turned to mush.

W e were a day out from our victory when it happened.

Booloo, Choona, and myself drifted off from the others to a spot where the great limb we were on ended, at least on that far side. We dismounted and stood on the edge and looked out over the great world of trees. Below we could see mountains and clouds and little thin lines of water that had to be raging rivers.

We were enjoying the sights, though I was feeling kind of woozy. I thought perhaps it was due to my battle with The One. I wasn't exactly sick, but I felt a little disoriented.

Then there was an eruption of arms and legs from a growth of foliage nearby, and one of the mantises, wounded, crazed, charged out of it with a sword.

I wheeled.

I was in direct line with it.

I drew my sword and sidestepped and planted it so that it went straight though the mantis's chitin chest. But, as fate would have it, my disorientation slowed me down, didn't allow me to dodge fully out of the way. The thing collided with me in a whiplash motion, knocking the both of us off the edge of the limb, out into the void of what might as well have been a bottomless world.

Chapter Thirteen
Back to the Beginning

I glanced up as I fell. I saw Choona and Booloo, on their knees, looking over the edge, their eyes wide, and just to the side and above me, the lighter body of the mantis drifted like chaff.

And then something even more unexpected happened. I had become so much a part of their world, I had forgotten mine.

I had temporarily forgotten the ball and that at some point it would call me back. That had been the source of the disorientation I had felt. It was happening. I was being pulled back.

I saw my hands and arms turn to light, and then there was brief sensation of being back in the ball, and the next moment I was striking the wall of the laboratory so hard the ball burst apart, shattering all over the floor and dropping me like a ton of bricks.

When I gathered myself enough to sit up, I saw that I was in the room from where I had departed. The place had been ravaged. And across the way, the glass that had been between this room and the room that held the universe was knocked out, leaving only pieces of jagged glass.

The universe was gone.

I searched the place from one end to the other. It was wrecked. Computers were smashed; all of the equipment was destroyed. Rooms were emptied out and there was no one present. I walked around confused and dazed. What had happened here?

The kitchen was still pretty much intact, though everything in the refrigerator was spoiled. I found candles for light. As the night fell, I sat in the kitchen at the counter where the cooks had worked, and ate potted meat from a can by the light of those candles.

That night, I slept in my old room.

I had no idea what I was going to do. Everything that meant anything to me was in that universe, on that world, in the eyes of that woman, Choona. Now it was all lost to me, including, it appeared, the entire universe. Had that been why I had been sucked back? The universe had been destroyed?

I couldn't wrap my mind around it.

And then I heard movement down the hall. I had a flashlight I had found, and I carried it with me, but didn't turn it on. I had it for a weapon. I didn't need its light. Even in the dead dark I knew my way along that hall. I had traversed it often when I was healing up from the plane crash.

I saw light shining through a crack in the kitchen door, peaked through and saw a bearded man sitting there. His hair was stringy, his clothes looked ragged. He had a large battery-powered lantern light sitting on the counter. He was eating from a can with a spoon.

It was Dr. Wright.

I pushed the door open.

I said, "Hello, Dr. Wright."

My God," he said, "you're alive."

"Yes."

"It brought you back?"

"Not what I wanted. How long have I been gone?"

"I don't know. I've lost count. Six months maybe. I've been hiding here. I've no place to go. I have perhaps three or four months worth of food left. They destroyed most things, but there are a lot of canned goods all over the place."

"What happened here?"

"They shut us down."

"The government?"

He nodded. "The special ops. We were . . . eliminated. The workers were killed, the place was trashed . . . All gone."

"But you?"

"I had a hiding place for just that sort of situation," he said. "They probably have no idea I wasn't killed. You see . . . It was such a mess. Terrible weapons. People blown apart."

"You're the only survivor?" I moved to the counter and stood near him.

"Yes," he said. "You really went? You went into the universe we created?"

Using English again felt strange. "I didn't want to come back. I liked it there. But the ball brought me back, and now it's destroyed. Of course, it doesn't matter, so is the universe and the world, The Warrior Star, Choona."

"What? Who?"

I told him briefly of my adventures. When I finished, he said, "Not all is lost."

"What do you mean?" I asked.

"The universe. I stored it the week before they came."

"Stored it?"

"You'll like this. In a bottle."

"A bottle?"

"You sound like a parrot," he said.

I grabbed his arm. "Explain yourself, now."

"You're hurting me."

"And I'll hurt you worse if you don't tell me about the universe . . . In a bottle."

"Superman comics. The old ones. He put the city of Kandor in a big bottle. I realized that with a bit of mathematical formulae, a lot of instrumentation, I could do the same. I had a feeling that we were soon to be put out of operation. I thought I had more time. I was going to make it portable, take it with me. Now, I have no place to go."

"Show it to me," I said.

The doctor's office was trashed, but he touched something close to the baseboards, a hidden button, and the wall slid back. It smelled like sweat and old food in there. It was large enough to house a desk and a chair. There were empty shelves and a few books.

He sat the battery lantern on his desk. It lit up the room a little. In the corner was a large jar, and inside it were the cosmic swirls of a universe. I bent down and looked inside. The contents seemed to go on forever, and in the center of one of millions of solar systems was a little dot. That was the sun of Juna, and there was a large star that I decided must be The Warrior Star. It was all speculation on my part. From my point of view they were nothing more than dots in the foreground. The bottle had a wooden cork jammed into its mouth. That made me smile.

"How does it exist here?"

"It takes care of itself, just like our universe, our solar system. Once it was put into play, as long as it's contained, it exists."

"Then I can go back?"

"No. The machinery, the device and the equipment that allowed that . . . All destroyed."

"Then you can rebuild it?"

"No. No, I can't. It would take billions of dollars and a lot of help. It can't be done."

That night I slept in my old room and thought about things, and in the middle of the night I got up and went to Dr. Wright's hideaway. He had left it open; the wall still slid back.

I awoke him. I said, "I can go back."

He stirred, half awake. "I'm sorry, Brax. You can't."

"I can," I said, and I explained to him about the meditation, my ability to travel by astral projection. He looked at me like I was crazy.

I sat on the floor, legs crossed, and within seconds, effortlessly floated.

"My God," he said.

He reached out to touch me. But there was nothing there. I tapped him on the shoulder from behind.

"Heavens," he said. "You can really do it. I thought it was impossible."

"So did I," I said. "But now I think I can go back to Juna, just by using my mind."

"It's an amazing idea, but . . ."

"Listen," I said. "If I do, what will become of the bottle? What will become of you?"

"I don't know. I've thought about that a lot."

"You believe they think you're dead?" I said.

"I do."

"Then walk out and take the bottle with you. Protect it. It's your greatest work. There is a world inside of that bottle, inside that universe, and I know now that it's my home. No telling how many other worlds are there, inside that silly corked bottle."

So now I sit here writing all that has happened to me. I don't know if anyone will ever read it. When I finish writing it, the doctor will take it with him. He knows a writer named Joe Lansdale that he believes might be able to do something with it, though he assumes, and perhaps correctly, that no one will believe it's a true story, just something from his imagination. Of course, he has to get out of here and make his way down to the southern United States where Lansdale lives. That's a tall order right now.

As for this being believed, it doesn't matter. I have recorded this for my own satisfaction.

But tonight, before I sat down to finish this, I finished something else. Dr. Wright and I have been planning for several days now. We have put together enough supplies, found enough clothes and necessary items for him to in fact walk out. The weather is at its best. It's summer here. I gave him a map. I know this area enough to at least set him off in the right direction. We even found a rifle and ammunition so that he can protect himself if the need should arise.

I know of a cabin where he can stay. A place my old boss owns. He seldom uses it. It will most likely be empty. It's a chance worth taking. It's a place to pause before he moves on. And if he's lucky, he will make his way to some place more permanent, someplace safe. There he will protect the universe he has created; I depend on his ego for that.

When I finish this, I am going to say goodbye to Dr. Wright. And then, if I am fortunate, if what Jack Rimbauld taught me is well learned, I will try to imagine the world of Juna, the city of Goshon, and my sweet Choona.

If my abilities allow, I will concentrate, meditate, and I will send my astral self across time and space to my new home. I will separate that self from my body here. If I do it right, my former true self will die, and my new self will become solid and permanent on Juna.

If not, then I will go blindly into the jar and lose my way and cease to exist.

For me, the chance of being with Choona again is worth it.

So I go now to sit cross-legged on the floor in front of the jar. I will close my eyes and imagine the world of Juna and myself being there.

If Lady Luck is with me, I will leave this worthless husk behind, and I will return to Choona, my one true love, and live the life that is truly meant for me.

If you read this, I hope you have wished me luck.

ABOUT THE AUTHORS

MICHAEL MOORCOCK (1939–) has been recognized since the 1960s as one of the most important speculative fiction writers alive. Born in London, Moorcock began editing the magazine *Tarzan Adventures* at the age of 15, and quickly gained notoriety for his character Elric of Melniboné, an antihero written as a deliberate reversal of recurring themes he saw in the writings of authors like J. R. R. Tolkien and Robert E. Howard. Many of his works, including the Elric books, the Sojan tales, and stories of his popular androgynous secret agent Jerry Cornelius, are tied together around the concept of the Eternal Champion, a warrior whose many incarnations battle to maintain the balance between Law and Chaos in the multiverse, a term popularized by Moorcock referring to many overlapping dimensions. In addition, Moorcock has also been recognized for his non-genre literary work, and his influence today extends into music, film, and popular culture. His writing has won numerous critical accolades, including the Nebula Award, the World Fantasy Award, the British Fantasy Award, and the Bram Stoker Lifetime Achievement Award. In 2002 he was inducted into the Science Fiction Hall of Fame.

Well known and loved for his Texas Mojo storytelling style, JOE R. LANSDALE (1951–) is the author of more than twenty novels and two hundred short works, including *Act of Love*, *The Nightrunners*, *Cold in July*, *Savage Season*, *The Bottoms*, and the "Hap and Leonard" and "Drive-In" series of novels, as well as scripts for both comics and film. Two of his stories, the cult classic "Bubba Ho-Tep" and "Incident On and Off a Mountain Road," have been adapted for film. He has had the honor of being chosen to complete an unfinished Tarzan novel by Edgar Rice Burroughs, one of the founding authors of the sword and planet genre, published in 1995 as *Tarzan: The Lost Adventure*. Lansdale has also been a student of the martial arts for more than thirty years—learning how to take a punch being a self-admitted ingredient of good Mojo storytelling—and he is a two-time inductee into the International Martial Arts Hall of Fame. He has won the Edgar Award, the British Fantasy Award, the American Mystery Award, the Grinzani Prize for Literature, the International Horror Guild Award, and six Bram Stoker Awards, and in 2007 he was named a Grand Master of Horror.

Collect all of these exciting Planet Stories adventures!

THE WALRUS AND THE WARWOLF
BY HUGH COOK
INTRODUCTION BY CHINA MIÉVILLE

Sixteen-year-old Drake Duoay loves nothing more than wine, women, and getting into trouble. But when he's abducted by pirates and pursued by a new religion bent solely on his destruction, only the love of a red-skinned priestess will see him through the insectile terror of the Swarms.

ISBN: 978-1-60125-214-2

WHO FEARS THE DEVIL?
BY MANLY WADE WELLMAN
INTRODUCTION BY MIKE RESNICK

In the back woods of Appalachia, folk-singer and monster-hunter Silver John comes face to face with the ghosts and demons of rural Americana in this classic collection of eerie stories from Pulitzer Prize-nominee Manly Wade Wellman.

ISBN: 978-1-60125-188-6

THE SECRET OF SINHARAT
BY LEIGH BRACKETT
INTRODUCTION BY MICHAEL MOORCOCK

In the Martian Drylands, a criminal conspiracy leads wild man Eric John Stark to a secret that could shake the Red Planet to its core. In a bonus novel, *People of the Talisman*, Stark ventures to the polar ice cap of Mars to return a stolen talisman to an oppressed people.

ISBN: 978-1-60125-047-6

THE GINGER STAR
BY LEIGH BRACKETT
INTRODUCTION BY BEN BOVA

Eric John Stark journeys to the dying world of Skaith in search of his kidnapped foster father, only to find himself the subject of a revolutionary prophecy. In completing his mission, will he be forced to fulfill the prophecy as well?

ISBN: 978-1-60125-084-1

THE HOUNDS OF SKAITH
BY LEIGH BRACKETT
INTRODUCTION BY F. PAUL WILSON

Eric John Stark has destroyed the Citadel of the Lords Protector, but the war for Skaith's freedom is just beginning. Together with his foster father Simon Ashton, Stark will have to unite some of the strangest and most bloodthirsty peoples the galaxy has ever seen if he ever wants to return home.

ISBN: 978-1-60125-135-0

THE REAVERS OF SKAITH
BY LEIGH BRACKETT
INTRODUCTION BY GEORGE LUCAS

Betrayed and left to die on a savage planet, Eric John Stark and his foster-father Simon Ashton must ally with cannibals and feral warriors to topple an empire and bring an enslaved civilization to the stars. But in fulfilling the prophecy, will Stark sacrifice that which he values most?

ISBN: 978-1-60125-084-1

CITY OF THE BEAST
BY MICHAEL MOORCOCK
INTRODUCTION BY KIM MOHAN

Moorcock's Eternal Champion returns as Michael Kane, an American physicist and expert duelist whose strange experiments catapult him through space and time to a Mars of the distant past—and into the arms of the gorgeous princess Shizala. But can he defeat the Blue Giants of the Argzoon in time to win her hand?

ISBN: 978-1-60125-044-5

LORD OF THE SPIDERS
BY MICHAEL MOORCOCK
INTRODUCTION BY ROY THOMAS

Michael Kane returns to the Red Planet, only to find himself far from his destination and caught in the midst of a civil war between giants! Will his wits and sword keep him alive long enough to find his true love once more?

ISBN: 978-1-60125-082-7

MASTERS OF THE PIT
BY MICHAEL MOORCOCK
INTRODUCTION BY SAMUEL R. DELANY

A new peril threatens physicist Michael Kane's adopted Martian homeland—a plague spread by zealots more machine than human. Now Kane will need to cross oceans, battle hideous mutants and barbarians, and perhaps even sacrifice his adopted kingdom in his attempt to prevail against an enemy that cannot be killed!

ISBN: 978-1-60125-104-6

NORTHWEST OF EARTH
BY C. L. MOORE
INTRODUCTION BY C. J. CHERRYH

Ray gun blasting, Earth-born mercenary and adventurer Northwest Smith dodges and weaves his way through the solar system, cutting shady deals with aliens and magicians alike, always one step ahead of the law.

ISBN: 978-1-60125-081-0

BLACK GOD'S KISS
BY C. L. MOORE
INTRODUCTION BY SUZY MCKEE CHARNAS

The first female sword and sorcery protagonist takes up her greatsword and challenges gods and monsters in the groundbreaking stories that inspired a generation of female authors. Of particular interest to fans of Robert E. Howard and H. P. Lovecraft.

ISBN: 978-1-60125-045-2

THE ANUBIS MURDERS
BY GARY GYGAX
INTRODUCTION BY ERIK MONA

Someone is murdering the world's most powerful sorcerers, and the trail of blood leads straight to Anubis, the solemn god known as the Master of Jackals. Can Magister Setne Inhetep, personal philosopher-wizard to the Pharaoh, reach the distant kingdom of Avillonia and put an end to the Anubis Murders, or will he be claimed as the latest victim?

ISBN: 978-1-60125-042-1

Collect all of these exciting Planet Stories adventures!

THE SWORD OF RHIANNON
BY LEIGH BRACKETT
INTRODUCTION BY NICOLA GRIFFITH

Captured by the cruel and beautiful princess of a degenerate empire, Martian archaeologist-turned-looter Matthew Carse must ally with the Red Planet's rebellious Sea Kings and their strange psychic allies to defeat the tyrannical people of the Serpent.

ISBN: 978-1-60125-152-7

INFERNAL SORCERESS
BY GARY GYGAX
INTRODUCTION BY ERIK MONA

When the shadowy Ferret and the broad-shouldered mercenary Raker are framed for the one crime they didn't commit, the scoundrels are faced with a choice: bring the true culprits to justice, or dance a gallows jig. Can even this canny, ruthless duo prevail against the beautiful witch that plots their downfall?

ISBN: 978-1-60125-117-6

STEPPE
BY PIERS ANTHONY
INTRODUCTION BY CHRIS ROBERSON

After facing a brutal death at the hands of enemy tribesmen upon the Eurasian steppe, the 9th-century warrior-chieftain Alp awakes fifteen hundred years in the future only to find himself a pawn in a ruthless game that spans the stars.

ISBN: 978-1-60125-182-4

WORLDS OF THEIR OWN
EDITED BY JAMES LOWDER

From R. A. Salvatore and Ed Greenwood to Michael A. Stackpole and Elaine Cunningham, shared world books have launched the careers of some of science fiction and fantasy's biggest names. Yet what happens when these authors break out and write tales in worlds entirely of their own devising, in which they have absolute control over every word? Contains 18 creator-owned stories by the genre's most prominent authors.

ISBN: 978-1-60125-118-3

ALMURIC
BY ROBERT E. HOWARD
INTRODUCTION BY JOE R. LANSDALE

From the creator of Conan, Almuric is a savage planet of crumbling stone ruins and debased, near-human inhabitants. Into this world comes Esau Cairn—Earthman, swordsman, murderer. Can one man overthrow the terrible devils that enslave Almuric?

ISBN: 978-1-60125-043-8

SOS THE ROPE
BY PIERS ANTHONY
INTRODUCTION BY ROBERT E. VARDEMAN

In a post apocalyptic future where duels to the death are everyday occurrences, the exiled warrior Sos sets out to rebuild civilization—or destroy it.

ISBN: 978-1-60125-194-7

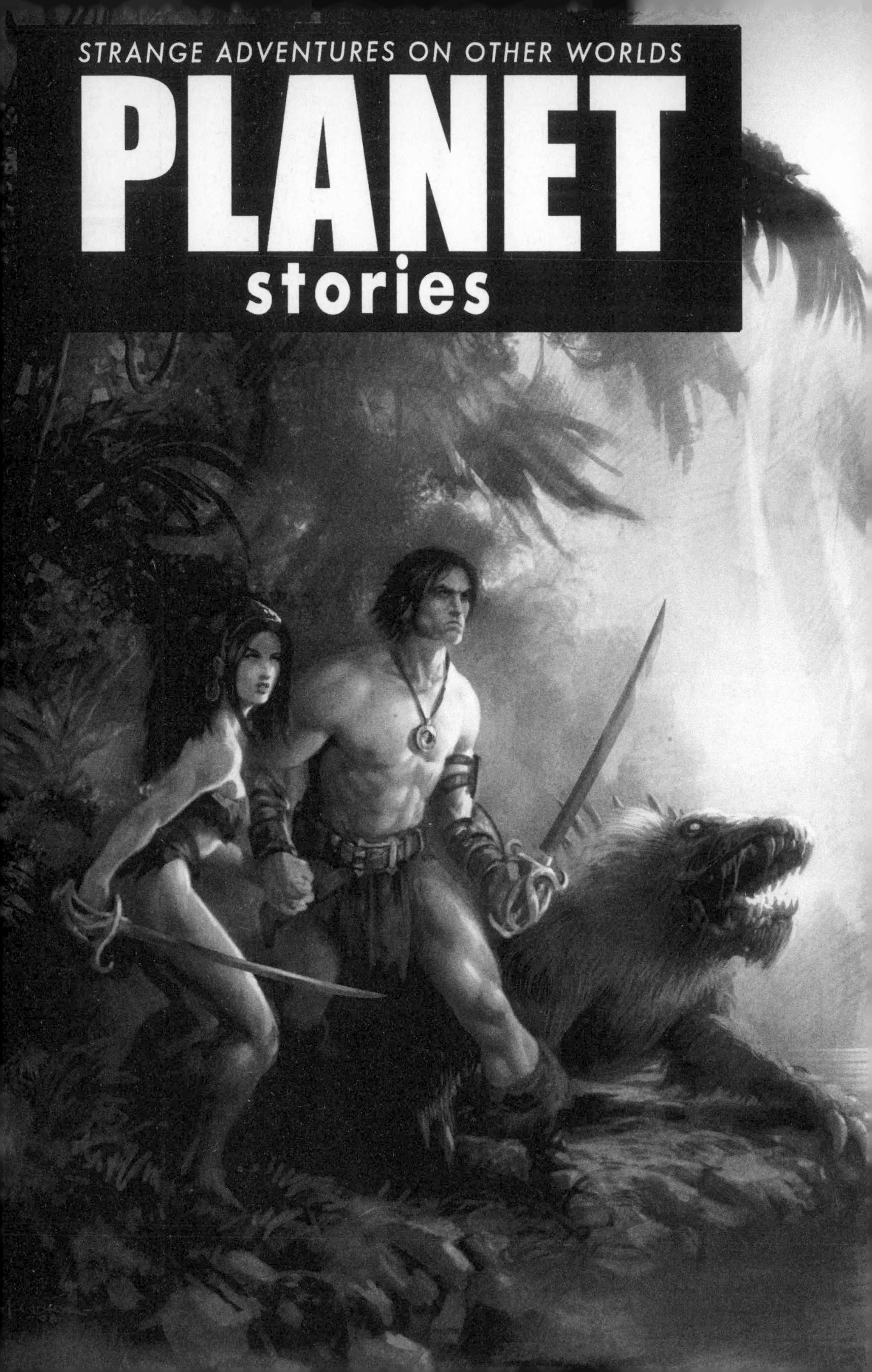
STRANGE ADVENTURES ON OTHER WORLDS
PLANET
stories

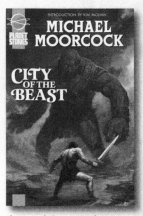
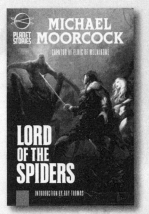
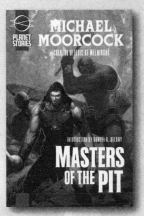
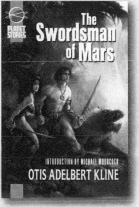
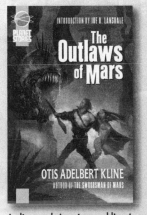

STRANGE ADVENTURES ON OTHER WORLDS

PLANET
stories

QUEEN OF THE PULPS!

William Faulkner's co-writer on *The Big Sleep* and the author of the original screenplay for *The Empire Strikes Back*, Leigh Brackett is one of the most important authors in the history of science fiction and fantasy—now read her most classics works!

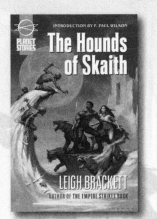

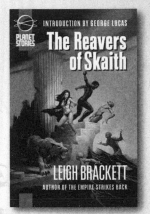

Eric John Stark finds himself at the center of a mysterious prophecy on the dying world of Skaith.
ISBN 978-1-60125-084-1
$12.99

Stark seeks the help of a band of motley revolutionaries to confront the Wandsmen of Skaith.
ISBN 978-1-60125-135-0
$12.99

The revolution Stark has longed for is here, but what will he have to sacrifice for it to succeed?
ISBN 978-1-60125-138-1
$12.99

Stark holds a dark secret that could shake the Red Planet to its core! Collected with the bonus novel *People of the Talisman*.
ISBN 978-1-60125-047-6
$12.99

Martian archaeologist-turned-looter Matthew Carse hurtles back in time to battle the super-science of a lost race.
ISBN 978-1-60125-152-7
$12.99

"Fiction at its most exciting, in the hands of a master storyteller."

George Lucas

"Brackett combines the best of A. Merritt and Edgar Rice Burroughs with much that is uniquely her own!"

F. Paul Wilson

Available now at quality bookstores and **pazio.com/planetstories**

HIDDEN WORLDS AND ANCIENT MYSTERIES

PLANET
stories

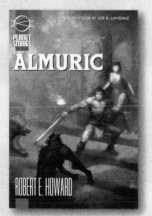

EXPLORE THE WORLDS OF HENRY KUTTNER!

From brutal worlds of flashing swords and primal magic to futures portraying binge-drinking scientists and uncooperative robot assistants, Henry Kuttner's creations rank as some of the most influential in the entirety of the speculative fiction genre.

....

"A neglected master . . . a man who shaped science fiction and fantasy in its most important years."

Ray Bradbury

"I consider the work of Henry Kuttner to be the finest science-fantasy ever written."

Marion Zimmer Bradley

"The most imaginative, technically skilled and literarily adroit of science-fantasy authors."

The New York Herald Tribune

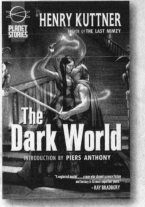

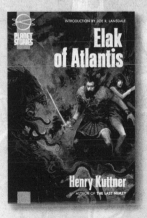

A scientist wakes from each drunken bender having created an amazing new invention—now if he could only remember how it worked!
ISBN 978-1-60125-153-4
$12.99

Edward Bond falls through a portal into an alternate dimension only to find himself trapped in the body of the evil wizard Ganelon.
ISBN 978-1-60125-136-7
$12.99

A dashing swordsman with a mysterious past battles his way through warriors and warlocks in the land of doomed Atlantis.
ISBN 978-1-60125-046-9
$12.99

Available now at quality bookstores and **pazio.com/planetstories**

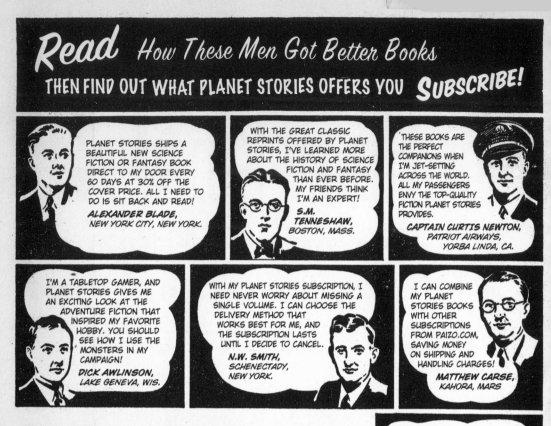